Herein you will discover,

presented for your amusement and edification, a varied and unique assortment of tales to awaken the senses and tantalize the imagination. In your very hands, or perhaps within your pocket analytical engine, you hold twelve tales of desire and adventure, the contents of which include but are not limited to desire outside matrimonial bounds, the miracles of modern medicine, theatrical pursuits both on and off the stage, and forbidden love across lines of class and propriety!

Within the pages of this volume are heroes and villains, lovers both requited and not, all seeking their satisfaction amid the smoke and mysteries and miraculous automata of the age of Passion and Steam!

Also recommended...

You may also enjoy these other ForbiddenFiction works:

Liquid Longing by Annabeth Leong

From Annabeth Leong's penetrating view of the sensual, the sacred, and the profane comes an anthology of erotic tales of wonder. Passion flows, mercurial, through these eleven tales of sex, death, and rebirth. Curiosity mingles with shame, anger revels in worship, exploring desire of all types. Here are dead gods, undead starlets, and immortal creatures hungry for connection—a collection of love letters to human nature, with no easy answers among them.

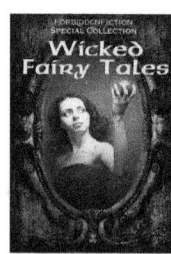

Wicked Fairy Tales

An anthology of bedtime stories for adults!

Just what kind of happy goes into "happily ever after?" As children, it was enough that Pinocchio got to be a real boy and that Red wasn't eaten by the wolf. As adults, we have a slightly different perspective. Being a real boy means having boy parts, and being eaten by someone big and bad doesn't mean quite the same thing it once did.

Of Passion and Steam

Affairs of a Curious and Sordid Nature

ForbiddenFiction
www.forbiddenfiction.com

an imprint of

Fantastic Fiction Publishing
www.fantasticfictionpublishing.com

OF PASSION AND STEAM

A ForbiddenFiction book

Fantastic Fiction Publishing
Hayward, California

© D. M. Atkins, 2017

CREDITS
Editor: Lon Sarver, Kel Draves, Rylan Hunter, and James L. Wolf
Cover Design: Siolnatine
Cover Art: Siolnatine with images from katalinks at Shutterstock.com, Viktor Pravdica at Dreamstime.com, and OpenClipart-Vectors and Gic at Pixabay.com
Internal cover art: Cover art by Siolnatine with images from historical and public domain sources including "Godey's Lady's Book" 1873, the Donaldson Litho. Co., Lord Frederick Leighton, J.M. Adams (John Manley) and Woolstone Bros, and stock photography by drizzd at Pixmac, Les3photo8, Studioimagen, Viki2win, and Frenk and Danielle Kaufmann at Dreamstime.com
Internal cover design: Siolnatine, and D.M. Atkins
Production Editor: Kaye O'Malley
Proofreading: Aislinn, Derrick N. Davidson, Erika L Firanc, JhP323, Todd Michaels, and Kailin Morgan
Font: Wellrock Slab, by Manfred Klein

SKU: SPC-1.100013-01 FFP
ISBN: 978-1-62234-312-6

Published in the United States of America

DISCLAIMER

This book is a work of fiction which contains explicit erotic content; it is intended for mature readers. Do not read this if it's not legal for you.

All the characters, locations and events herein are fictional. While elements of existing locations or historical characters or events may be used fictitiously, any resemblance to actual people, places or events is coincidental.

This story is not intended to be used as an instruction manual. It may contain descriptions of erotic acts that are immoral, illegal, or unsafe. Do not take the events in this story as proof of the plausibility or safety of any particular practice.

Contents

> *In which a young woman's desire proves more than a match for science.*

> *In which a frustrated housewife seeks relief at the fair.*

> *In which an antiquarian uncovers a most penetrating mystery.*

> *In which a creative lady teaches a valuable lesson to a callous nobleman.*

> *In which the true drama of the play is hidden from the audience.*

> *In which a loyal guard faces a choice between passion and duty.*

> *In which a clash of religious principles is resolved in an intimate manner.*

Heart of Brass

Chapter 1:
The Chastarium of Jameson Dashiell:
or, The Locomotive

"My goodness!" said the first appointment of the morning. "What manner of Chastity Machine is *that*?"

Dr. Jameson H. Dashiell followed his patient's gaze to the Machine that loomed, oiled and glimmering, over the foot of the treatment-room bed. "I call it 'The Inverted Velocipede'," said the doctor. "The patient lies on her back and sets her feet atop the pedals above her. The pedal power is what drives the therapeutic end."

Ms. Jennings approached the apparatus. Her hand drifted to said therapeutic end, her eyes glittering as brightly as the polished gears. She stroked the smooth rubber. "This one's under my own power? So, I can make it go as fast as I wish?"

Dashiell stepped in closer, his own therapeutic end twitching in eager sympathy. "Indeed. After your treatment session on 'The Pogostick' last week, you did remark that it was powerful enough, but too uninteresting."

Ms. Jennings withdrew her hand from the rubber and curled her fingers into her skirts. She pulled upward, in a hesitant tease, baring the first hint of her ivory legs. "May I...?"

Dashiell held out a hand.

He helped Ms. Jennings onto the bed. He wanted to also place his palms against those exposed ivory ankles and push upward, plowing her skirts aside and baring her secret valley to his own attentions, but Dashiell was no Chastity Machine. He was, one could say, anything but. Best to let Ms. Jennings arrange herself and tease her skirts upward at her leisure. Best for Dashiell to content himself with watching, as she wriggled back and revealed herself, and set her glistening fur against that ever-hungry rubber. And raised her legs to the pedals, spreading herself open like a blossoming flower, ready to be plucked. "Like this...?"

"Yes," Dashiell said, his eyes locked upon her blossom. "Now—"

The call bell clanged.

"Oh," said Ms. Jennings. "I suppose you're being summoned."

"Never mind it," said Dashiell. "I'm sure it's just the pipes clanging in one of the steam-powered Machines."

The call bell clanged again. "Perhaps not," said Ms. Jennings. "That's all right. Don't worry about me, Doctor. I think I can manage by myself this week."

She wriggled down a bit further, her pinkened folds nudging the rubber, like a kiss.

Dashiell tore his eyes away and excused himself.

He left the basement and mounted the steps to the first-floor offices, ready to be curt with the first boy he ran across, but none of the assistants would stand still long enough to acknowledge him. Instead, everyone hurried from room to room in a frenzy of unnecessary tidying, eyes wide and lips squeezed together.

Dashiell finally caught someone by the arm. "All right, Hammersmith—what is all this?"

The boy gulped. "Lady Gallantine!"

The doctor tightened his grip. "What?"

"Lady Gallantine, sir! The Duke's daughter. She's in the parlor!"

"Lady Gallantine? In our *parlor*?"

The boy squirmed. Dashiell let him go, and stood in the hallway for a moment in stupefied shock. What on earth would a member of the Lavenlock nobility want with a Chastarium? They had each other. In fact, if rumors of their phenomenal, debauched interludes could be believed, then goodness, did they ever have each other.

The call bell clanged again, and Hammersmith's voice piped, "Doctor!"

Dashiell collected himself and proceeded to the pair of French doors that led to the parlor. No less than four boys were crowding around the colored panes, gaping at the visitor who waited beyond.

When Dashiell entered her company, he understood why.

Lady Gallantine awaited him on the settee, her legs pressed together and ankles crossed, her bone-china hands clenched nervously in her lap. Her eyes were wide and frightened. The light from the window behind her haloed her sweet, perfect face, and for a moment, Dashiell was stunned by her impossible beauty.

When he finally dropped his eyes to take in the rest of her, he nearly forgot to breathe.

The brocade of Lady Gallantine's dress ran from neck to ankle, but not even noble modesty could hide what luscious abundance Heaven had given her. Her face and neck had no hard lines, and that softness only plunged and widened beneath the brocade. Those gentle shoulders. Those heavy, beckoning breasts. That narrow waist above those ripe and womanly hips. Lady Gallantine shifted in anxious discomfort, and Dashiell imagined her warm thighs sliding across each other beneath all those skirts.

She brushed a jet curl away from her face. "Doctor?"

Dashiell bowed. His face and ears grew mortifyingly hot; the front of his trousers, suddenly and disastrously ill-fitting. "My Lady. You honor my establishment with your visit."

"Thank you." She bit her lower lip, gently. Delicate color flushed through her cheeks. "I beg your pardon. I'm a little nervous."

Dashiell hastily seated himself to hide his problem, crossing his own legs and folding his hands. Lady Gallantine inhaled, her shapely chest straining against the brocade, and Dashiell's desire throbbed. "You see, I... my father doesn't know that I have come."

Dashiell nodded.

"He thinks I am with Cousin Tristi. He'd be beside himself if he knew where I really was. You won't tell, will you?"

"Madam," said Dashiell. "I am a doctor. My livelihood depends upon my discretion. I shall not tell a soul."

"Good," Lady Gallantine burst out. "Because Father will hate me forever if he hears of it!"

She began to cry. Dashiell leapt to her side, produced a handkerchief, and dared lay a hand upon her warm, quivering back. "Hush now. You're perfectly safe here. Come—let's go to my office, where we can converse a bit more privately."

Sniffling, Lady Gallantine took his arm, and Dashiell led her toward the back and into his office. "There you are. Please, have a seat. May I get you anything? A glass of water, perhaps?"

Heart of Brass

Lady Gallantine dabbed her eyes. "No, thank you. I'm so sorry."

"Please, think nothing of it." Dashiell took the chair that faced her. "Now. Speak as freely as you wish. I am concerned for absolutely nothing but your health."

Lady Gallantine dabbed her eyes again. "I'm sorry. I'm just so frightened. I asked Mother, and she said that I was coming of age. Doctor, I have these... feelings." She lowered her eyes. "When I look at men. My body is on fire, like I'm ill with fever, and I yearn to be touched all over. And all the men at home smile at me so, the servants and the stable-hands and visiting Lords, and they stroke my shoulders and whisper in my ear, and I—oh! I've heard what people do, Doctor, and I am dying to have a try!"

Dashiell's breath quickened. "Go on."

Her color rose again. "I told Father before I told Mother, and he grew very agitated. He said I must stay away from men, and that I may take after Mother in 'certain respects', but he would not tell me what. And he says I must bathe in cold water now, and wear full pajamas to bed, and wash my private places quickly, and—he's even hired a governess! A governess, Doctor, though I am 19 years, to watch me at night and ensure my purity!"

Dashiell gaped at her. Had the Duke really insisted upon keeping her so innocent?

Lady Gallantine was ripe, all right. Ripe to bursting.

"He says I mustn't lose my chastity. And I heard—that is, I heard —"

"Yes?"

Lady Gallantine dropped her voice. "That you can safely treat and tame lascivious desire. Is it true?"

Dashiell stared. He imagined drawing up her skirts, her exposed desire perfuming the room, and how wet and ready she'd be; her nervous fear as he laid her down and whispered, "Just relax, now, and you'll feel better soon;" the furnace in the sub-basement below beginning to blaze, the heat mounting, pipes clanging, steam hissing through valves, as the Machine awoke and began its first inexorable thrust—

Dashiell swallowed. "Different patients have different reasons for wanting the treatment," he said. "But it all achieves the same effect.

"In any case—Lady Gallantine, treating you will be my greatest pleasure."

4

She sniffed. "Thank you. I suppose I must make a formal appointment?"

Dashiell cleared his throat. "You could, but since you're already here, and since it seems that you have such difficulty getting away, we could try a treatment now."

Lady Gallantine leapt up. "Could we? Oh, please, Doctor!"

Dashiell gestured for her to exit the room. As soon as she turned away from him, Dashiell stood and snatched a notebook from his desk to hold in front of himself, to shield his embarrassment. "Certainly. Let us adjourn to the basement."

Once promised so ripe a fruit, Dashiell was aching to get on with it, but for the Lady's sake, he allowed her to descend the basement staircase slowly and stand at its foot in hesitant wonder. The Long Hall stood before her: an oak-paneled passage flanked by doors upon doors, turning to the right at the far end.

The wave of familiar heat rose to meet them.

"Why is it so hot down here?" she whispered.

In a distant corner of The Chastarium, pipes began to clang. Lady Gallantine cocked her head. Answering clangs arose from within a few of the rooms, ringing a prelude to release.

"The fires in the sub-basement beneath us," said Dashiell. "Most of my treatments are steam-powered."

"Steam-powered?"

Dashiell moved past her, their thighs just barely brushing. In his hand, the notebook he held grew sweaty, and not thanks to the heat of the fires. "Don't be afraid. Come."

She stepped beside him, her hand wandering to his arm. From within a room to their left came an animal moan, low and near-delirious. The Lady opened her mouth to ask, and a distant steam valve whistled in emergency release. Somewhere unseen, a boy shouted instructions: "Stoke up 3. And ease up on 8, you lot, or the 10:00'll get split wide open. Jus' keep 'er purrin'."

Lady Gallantine pressed herself against Dashiell's side.

They reached the bend and kept going. The hallway now went past a bank of street-level windows on the left, covered in black cloth. Dashiell stopped beside a door on their right and took a ring of keys from his belt.

"What shall happen to me?" asked the Lady, timidly.

Dashiell smiled.

He unlocked the door. Within the treatment room, crouching with the menace of a great mechanical panther, sat The Chastarium's primary claim to fame and infamy. The Machine was a thing of darkness and raw strength, made of durable iron and steel, indestructible as a canon. Pipes pierced its belly and back, tethering it to the room below and a complex network of pipes above. A mat lay on the floor before it, like a low altar, and above the mat stretched a long steel rod, tipped with the key to her release.

Gauges waited at zero, and the pipes around it hissed in readiness.

"Madam," said Dashiell. "May I present The Locomotive."

Lady Gallantine exhaled. She entered the room in awe. "Why... it's so curious."

"Can you guess how it works?"

She shook her head.

Dashiell swallowed. He entered after her, the room's heat rolling over him, coaxing sweat from his brow and neck. "Lie on the mat on your back, with your feet toward the Machine. Arrange yourself such that the therapeutic end—this piece here—is just touching the doorway to your places."

"My places?"

Dashiell inhaled. "Yes. Your entrance."

Lady Gallantine frowned at him in incomprehension.

Dashiell closed his eyes. The heat was rising quickly in here. He knelt by the mat, removing his jacket and pushing up his shirtsleeves. "I'll show you. Sit down and lift up your skirts."

She obeyed.

A drop of sweat rolled down Dashiell's temple. The sight of such luscious, virgin thighs near so ruthless a Machine was enough to make a man insensible. Dashiell coughed; he could barely speak. "You have an entrance within your folds. Did you know that?"

"Yes," she said shyly. "But I don't know where, exactly. Oh—is this supposed to go *inside* of me?"

"It is. Move forward, please. I shall guide..." Dashiell nearly lost his composure, as the Lady obeyed and parted her thighs to receive.

Her garden was exquisite, symmetrical and sweetly perfumed, pink as the smooth interior of a seashell. "I shall guide the therapeutic end where it needs to be."

"Can that really fit inside of me?"

Dashiell swallowed again. The heat had boiled his mouth bone-dry. "It can."

"Will it hurt?"

Dashiell guided it into place, the gears at the base of The Locomotive's rod turning in oiled, well-practiced silence. "Perhaps at first."

The Lady nodded solemnly.

Dashiell adjusted the height of the rod, then stood and placed himself next to the pipes, his hands on the valves and one eye on the gauges. The other eye he kept on her.

He turned a stopcock.

The Locomotive hissed. Slowly, almost imperceptibly, the rod surged forward.

Should he watch her face? The way her eyes widened in sudden knowledge, as her nostrils flared and her mouth opened in shock? Or should he watch his masterful Machine pierce and conquer her, even as her hungry entrance helped pull it in?

Dashiell's gasps became commingled with hers.

"More," she whispered.

Dashiell stroked the valves. The Locomotive stroked her. She and the Machine fell into a slow, gentle rhythm, hissing and moaning in concert. Sweat glimmered in her hair. Her eyes drifted closed, and Dashiell's right hand drifted down to caress himself though the front of his trousers. He whimpered and leaned into his touch, even as Lady Gallantine whimpered and arched her back.

"More," she said.

Dashiell obeyed. Steam puffed through the Machine in rhythmic bursts, and gears clicked and flashed. The rod's strokes grew long and deep, strong and sure. Lady Gallantine's breaths grew deeper, in a trance of ecstasy. Her body moved in swells, now rocking in need with the thrust, now melting in bliss with the retreat. The smell of her rose with the steam. Dashiell was intoxicated; he couldn't stop touching himself, couldn't stop staring at the way she seamlessly merged divinity and Eros in the simple act of her first pleasure.

7

And even though she hadn't said "More," he opened the valves further.

The Locomotive answered. The rod leaned harder, faster. Lady Gallantine cried out, her throat bobbing with the strokes, the beads of sweat in her hair thickening. Her hands left her skirts, clawing blindly at the mat. She spread her legs wider, in welcome and demand, a river of wet trickling to the floor, glimmering over the length of the end. Her chest pumped like a bellows. Her back was nearly frozen in an arch now, begging the unheeding Machine with her body.

She didn't have to say it aloud. Dashiell opened the valves all the way.

The Locomotive pounded. Lady Gallantine screamed, the high thin wail of a cat in heat, as the Machine rode her body to the end. Dashiell's own body lunged for the brink, and he yelled at himself in scorn beneath her triumphant cry, snatching his hands away and biting his fingers. But maybe he would lose control just from watching her, because without Dashiell's hands on the valves to order it otherwise, The Locomotive kept pounding, but Lady Gallantine kept coming.

Dashiell squeezed his eyes shut. She did not stop. Still she wailed, a siren song of raw joy; when she finally ceased, Dashiell dared to open his eyes and lower his hands, but still another wave embraced her. Lady Gallantine squealed and rocked, her hips urging for more.

And the tireless Machine obliged.

"Doctor," she cried out. "O God in Heaven! Doctor, don't stop!"

A pressure gauge swung abruptly to the left. Dashiell fiddled with the valves, compensating, somewhere between bursting and numb. He had seen a few patients like this. Those who just kept going. For them, pleasure was not a peak—it was a high plateau, and it sprawled for miles.

When would hers end?

She cried out again. Dashiell's need throbbed in agony. He clenched his hands over the stopcocks, breathing so fast his throat felt raw, and told himself that damn it all, he was a *doctor*, not some naïve school boy who couldn't control himself.

She writhed on the mat, toes clenching and relaxing, while The Locomotive pounded.

Another pressure gauge swung. Dashiell fumbled. A puddle grew beneath Lady Gallantine, and patches of moisture grew upon her dress. *I should have made you take it off*, thought Dashiell stupidly, and the image of her unclothed body rocking beneath The Locomotive, her breasts swaying and thighs clenching, was enough to break him.

Dashiell arrived. A match struck the length of his spine, sparking his need to a blaze, and in seconds, he was immolated in pleasure where he stood, releasing a torrent inside his clothing. He grappled for purchase on something; valves spun beneath his desperate fingers, steam hissed, and metal squealed. The Locomotive groaned and sputtered to a halt.

"Oh!" cried Lady Gallantine, still rocking. "Oh— Doctor, is that all?"

Dashiell knelt on the floor, shaking.

Lady Gallantine paused. "Doctor?"

"I'm fine," Dashiell whispered. Sweat dripped from his face. "I— forgive me. The heat."

The Lady nodded and lay back. She sighed in satisfaction and longing, then, the therapeutic end still buried within her folds, now winking with her most recent release. "Oh, Doctor," she murmured. "Oh, that was—I have no words. I feel *ever* so much better."

Dashiell nodded. He closed his eyes in mortification. Where had he placed that shielding notebook?

"But yet... but yet not entirely." Lady Gallantine glanced shyly at The Locomotive. "Can you... start it up again? For just a bit more, perhaps?"

"I'm afraid I've damaged a valve or two," Dashiell mumbled. "My clumsiness. No fault of yours."

"That's all right." The Lady inched herself backward. The Locomotive's end eased out, and her folds reluctantly gathered in its wake. But not quite all the way. She'd never be as tight again.

Well, that was fine—by the sound of things, Lady Gallantine was eager for more.

Dashiell closed his eyes. "I think we are through for the day."

"May I come back again? I don't think you've quite treated all of my desire."

Oh, God— I shall have to keep a spare pair of trousers here, Dashiell thought, but aloud he said, "Please do. And next time, we may try a Machine that could be more suitable."

"When should I come back?"

Forgetting about her agitated father, Dashiell said, "Tomorrow."

Chapter 2:
An Unwelcome Interruption:
or, The Ouroboros

Dashiell did not know how Lady Gallantine covered her tracks in regards to her unvisited cousin, or how precisely a woman of her standing could slip away from her household so wholly unnoticed. He only knew that his night was filled with fervid, lascivious dreams, and that little in the way of clerical work got done the next morning before the Lady arrived at 9 o'clock sharp.

When the doorbell rang, Dashiell was more than ready.

Hammersmith knocked upon his office door to announce her, but Dashiell swept out and past him before the boy could utter a word. He stepped into the parlor. "My Lady."

To the untrained eye, her manner was much the same as it was yesterday, but Dashiell's eye was not untrained. To be sure, she sat with legs together and hands clenched in her lap, but today, it was not frustration that gripped her, but anticipation.

"Good morning, Doctor," she said shyly, and smiled.

Dashiell inclined his head. Lady Gallantine wriggled her hips and scooted to the edge of the settee, her blue velvet skirts pushing up about her, baring the faintest hint of her sleek ankles. Lady Gallantine glanced down, realizing her faux pas. "Oh my." She smoothed down her skirts and blushed. "Forgive me, Doctor. Perhaps I'm a little overeager."

"Yes. We must begin at once."

"I came early today, so that we may have plenty of time."

"I think that's best."

"My Father believes I'm at the spa. Do you think that's convincing?"

"My Lady," said Dashiell, facing toward the back and offering his elbow, "we haven't the time to fritter away discussing such trivialities. You are in urgent need of medical attention. Come, and let's finish addressing yesterday's business."

The Lady smiled. She stood and took his arm, oh so gently, her fingertips just fluttering against his sleeve. "You are a saint, sir, with a heart of gold."

"Well," said Dashiell, as he led her toward the basement. "I might not say that. But I do my best."

The heat of The Chastarium proper rose to meet them. Lady Gallantine inhaled, as if sampling the wild scents of a forest on the currents of warmth, and Dashiell found himself following suit: iron, sweat, and animal need; metal and rubber and wood; heat and wood smoke and leather.

In Dashiell's opinion, it was a good deal better than a forest.

Lady Gallantine practically tugged on his arm in her urgency. "It was this way, yes?"

Dashiell let her drag him, past open doors revealing Machine-cleaning boys, past closed doors concealing the gasps of the anonymous and the clicks of a hundred cogs. "Very good," murmured another doctor, from behind a closed door. "Keep breathing."

Lady Gallantine took him around the bend, to the door opposite the cloth-covered windows. "Here? Yes?"

Dashiell smiled. "Today, my dear, we try something a little more powerful."

The Lady squeezed his arm.

Dashiell guided them once more, to the end of the windowed hall, and then around another bend to the right. Oak doors once again flanked them on either side, but these were all closed and all silent.

"What is here?" The Lady whispered.

"Machines too powerful for most." Dashiell stopped at the far right door, Lady Gallantine still squeezing. He once again withdrew his keys. "The Horse. The Golden Box. The Giant's Playpen. The Woodcutter. And of course—"

Dashiell swung open the door.

The Machine awaited them in the silence. A great wheel of wood and metal, edged in leather and shaped like a monstrous discus, sat in a deep groove along the length of the floor. The heart of the discus, fat with gears and pipes, hissed softly to itself in readiness.

"May I present The Ouroboros."

Lady Gallantine was speechless.

Dashiell drew her in. He closed the door and turned up the gas, and the lamplight glimmered over the intricacies of polished metal and oiled leather. "The patient is strapped along the padded rim of the wheel, which you will notice is actually two wheels quite close together. This allows the central engine, which is set upon gimbals, to always remain upright as the Machine is rolled along the track, and for the intake pipe extending downward to move neatly along the track in the floor. If you peer closely, you can see the sub-basement below.

"The Machine has several therapeutic ends, which can extend outward from the engine, and which are fully adjustable. This permits treatment of more than one entrance."

The Lady's eyes grew wide. "I have more than one?"

Another man might have laughed at her innocence still, but Dashiell only felt the heat from the crack below grow stronger. "I mean to say, the other entrance and exit upon your person that you already utilize for other purposes."

Her eyes grew wider still. "I may feel such pleasure with these?"

In the sub-basement beneath their feet, an assistant barked orders, and Dashiell caught a glimmer of orange and the sound of wood striking wood. The smell of wood smoke rose. "Not... not the same. But also... desirable. Complementary, with some."

"Complementary," she echoed, in fascination.

Dashiell felt dizzy. The smoke, perhaps. "Please remove your dress."

"All right..." She hesitated. "My buttons—do you mind?"

Dashiell moved behind her. His sweaty fingers fumbled with her buttons, and the dark velvet parted, slowly, revealing her smooth flesh, so glowing and alive. Beneath them, the fires rose. The naked expanse of her back grew; her soft shoulders emerged, her inviting breasts. Her milky arms. Her skin was flawless and smooth, like glass, smoother than the velvet that pooled at her feet.

"Thank you," she whispered.

Dashiell laid his hands upon her hips and pulled down, fingers curling into her skirts. Her underbelly emerged, softer than down; her round hips swelled to life. And where they met her perfect thighs, her still-wild garden grew, hungering and waiting.

Dashiell sighed, and nearly brushed his lips against her knee.

Nearly.

He looked at up her. She was staring at him with parted lips, riveted, her fine hands curled into quivering fists, as Dashiell slid the last of her skirts past her tender calves.

But he was a doctor.

Dashiell leaned back, letting the dress drop to the floor. "Step to the wheel, please," he said, through a suddenly rusty throat.

Lady Gallantine obeyed.

She moved to the Machine, feet on either side on the chasm, firelight from below making her nether hair sparkle. She leaned into the wheel's great curve, sighing against the padded leather, stretching her arms delicately over its slope, though Dashiell had not told her to. He moved behind her. The heat from the chasm was nigh unbearable already. But this close, it was she who burned hotter than a forge.

With the aid of leather thongs on the spokes, Dashiell tied her down where she straddled.

"Doctor?" She was breathless. "Will I fall, otherwise?"

In answer, Dashiell stepped to the central engine to make some adjustments, and The Ouroboros rolled.

The Lady gave a cry as the wheel turned in its track, raising her inexorably to its apex, trussed and splayed in place like a swan for the roasting.

And what was a roast, without the spit?

Dashiell played the stopcocks like a pianist at his keys. From within the depths of the cloven Machine, twin therapeutic ends arose, one to meet the Lady's own cleft place, and the other to meet her mouth. She uttered another cry, and with a spin of a dial, Dashiell silenced it beneath a length of hard, polished rubber.

Its twin joined her body from behind. She squealed, then, a muffled thing of horror and delight. She gasped as they left her; they returned in a sudden burst, and she squealed again. Again and again, they caught her unawares, leaving her uncertain of when to

14

yield or buck, forcing her to lay still and accommodate a will that would never tire.

The squeals transmogrified into moans.

Dashiell's fingers trembled. He eased open the rear stopcock, and from within The Ouroboros, valves hissed and whined. "Stoke 'er up," someone called from below, and within the creaking wood and gleaming metal, machinery clicked faster. The Lady moaned around the rubber, straining backward into her bonds, trying in vain to aid The Ouroboros in its unending quest to perfectly skewer.

Pipes below began to clang. Needles climbed in pressure gauges, and blurred in Dashiell's vision. He wiped sweat from his eyes with a trembling arm and set his unsteady fingers back upon the valves. The heat was merciless, blurring everything into quivering lines, but even so, clear enough was the way her body writhed on the wheel. Moisture beaded on her flanks, and dribbled down her chin, from the mouth that had gone from crying out to sucking in uncertain, restless hunger; from between her parted legs, whenever the Machine withdrew, nectar dripped. Beneath her, the padded leather grew slick.

Dashiell could not see the gauges. Sweat rained into his eyes. But he knew the song The Ouroboros sang, and his knowing hands opened the valves further.

His Machine obeyed. And under its demanding rhythm, Lady Gallantine only grew hotter. Her breath came harder, and her back grew tighter. Color bloomed over her face. Her fists clenched. She pulled against her bonds, and the soft sides of her breasts spilled further out. Her eyes rolled back and closed. She began her climb.

Dashiell's hands shook harder, but he remembered yesterday, and did his damnedest to steady his touch. His desire was sheer torment. *You must not do it again*, he thought, through the hot and delirious heat. *You are a doctor. You are a doctor!*

And Heaven, how I'm wishing it were not so!

His hand jerked. The stopcock leapt open, and The Ouroboros leapt faster.

Lady Gallantine arrived, squealing in joy. She shook like a thundercloud, raining sweat and nectar and tears, and the wood beneath her chirped in protest beneath the louder wails of steam.

Beneath the cacophony, Dashiell moaned. How long would she go today? How long must he watch? Surely, a brief touch couldn't hurt— Dashiell took his hand from the valves, and when he settled it upon himself, it was sweet relief—

Another sound reached his ears.

Dashiell froze. Lady Gallantine rode on, wailing, leather thongs squealing at the force of her unending release. And again, beneath the noise of her abandon, the call bell clanged.

Dashiell could have screamed. He twisted the stopcocks back, and The Ouroboros immediately slowed. "No!" The Lady cried. "No, please! Please, Doctor! I beg you!"

"I have to go upstairs," Dashiell said. "The call bell. I—"

"Leave it on!"

"But my Lady! You could—"

"Doctor!" she sobbed. "Doctor, *please!*"

Dashiell flushed. *What are you doing?* he demanded himself, as he opened the stopcocks once more. *My God, what are you doing? You can't leave a patient alone in a Machine!*

The Ouroboros awakened again, its rhythm quickening. Lady Gallantine moaned in relief.

And Dashiell left her there.

He ran through the basement, breathless before he even took the first step. His arousal preceded him, endeavoring to pierce his trousers the way the Machine pierced her, alone and bound. O God! What had he done?

But how she'd moaned. How she'd begged.

Dashiell ran up to the first floor. No need to grab an assistant for an inquiry—the answer to Dashiell's breathless disorientation came bellowing down the hall like the flames from a dragon.

"So help me, if any one of you has so much as laid your eyes upon my daughter's face, I will have you strung up by your heels on a meat hook and gutted like a sow!"

Dashiell burst into the parlor. "Your Grace!"

Standing by the picture-widow, in front of the very settee his daughter so favored, stood Duke Gallantine. His massive hands clenched in an effort to contain a roiling panic, and the emotion that twisted over his dramatic features was enough to make Dashiell's desire shrivel on the spot.

The Duke's gaze ran over the doctor, once down and once up, and his anxiety soured into suspicion.

Dashiell drew a breath. He straightened and smoothed himself over, speaking as though his heart were calm and steady, and his face, not slimed with sweat. "Your Grace," he repeated.

"And you are?"

Dashiell withdrew a handkerchief and deftly wiped his brow. "Doctor Jameson H. Dashiell, Senior Physician and proprietor of The Chastarium. You must pardon my appearance. You have interrupted my appointment with a patient, sir, and The Chastarium proper is quite hot."

The Duke stared at him, hands relaxing and clenching, like a tiger uncertain of whether to tense its hindquarters for the pounce. "You had better mind your tone with me, Doctor," he said uneasily. "Do you know who stands before you?"

"I do," replied Dashiell. He forced himself to avert his gaze, as if at ease, and passed the handkerchief several times about his face and neck. "And I mean no disrespect. I only take my work very seriously."

"I see." The Duke folded his arms across his powerful chest, hands still in anxious fists beneath the ropey muscles. "And who were you working with, Doctor?"

"I beg your pardon. I cannot say."

"You cannot *say*?"

"My patients' reputations hinge upon my silence. As does the viability of my practice. But come, I am sure you did not arrive in such a haste to exchange such rumors and gossip. How may I help you today?"

The Duke's eyes narrowed.

Dashiell regarded him calmly. Beneath their feet, the tireless Ouroboros steamed on, a Lady still lashed in place astride it, doomed to be at its mercy for—? Dashiell thought of her, leather lashed around her ankles and elbows and knees, black hair spilling over black leather, raining sweat and nectar. What ecstasy was she crying out, now, on her way across that long plateau? To Dashiell's horror, his arousal began to warm and rise again.

"I am missing a daughter," said the Duke, his tone dangerously soft. "A daughter who is curious and willful. And in need of strict controlling."

Dashiell imagined himself at her side, hand pressed upon the small of her back, just above where her hips flared, urging her down onto the leather and into the thrust of his Machine. His arousal sharpened. His mortification rose with it. Dashiell turned and faced a looking-glass on the wall, tidying his hair and moustache, fiercely willing his problem to go away. "And you suspect she'd come here?"

"If not someplace even worse."

"I see."

"You haven't seen her?"

"I cannot say."

The reflection of the Duke narrowed its eyes even further, and a sound came from his throat, like a hiss of steam. "You are treading on thin ice, Doctor, and it grows thinner with every step."

"So be it." Under reasonable control once more, Dashiell turned back to face him. "I can confirm or deny nothing."

"Try denying me entry again, Doctor," said the Duke, turning to the door, "if I hear for certain that you are harboring my daughter."

The Duke shut the door with unnecessary briskness on the way out.

The windows rattled in their panes. Beyond them, the burly Duke stomped into a waiting carriage, which shuddered with the force of his entry.

Dashiell turned around. The parlor doors were still open, and terrified faces peeped from around corners, silently.

"Attention, Commitment, and Always Discretion," said Dashiell, repeating The Chastarium's motto.

The faces exchanged dubious glances.

Dashiell returned to the staircase leading below, sure to hold himself with grace as he did so. He followed the turns in the Long Hall with the same carriage, determined to keep his desire in check.

Even though he heard her ecstasy before he turned the first corner.

Dashiell clenched his jaw. Lady Gallantine's cries rose in volume and pitch as he approached, melding into the whistles of steam and squeal of wood. *You mustn't think about this,* he counseled himself. He opened the door without hesitation, ignoring the wave of raw heat, and went straight to the controls.

"Ah... Doctor..."

"I'm sorry," said Dashiell firmly. The stopcocks eased shut beneath his masterful touch. "I'm afraid this will be all for the day."

"Oh..." Lady Gallantine slumped within her bonds, laying her cheek on the sweat-slick leather. Between the Machine's halves, the therapeutic ends withdrew and stilled, shining with her moisture. "Oh, Doctor..."

Dashiell looked away from this. He concentrated on rolling The Ouroboros backward, until Lady Gallantine's feet were once again within reach of the floor. "How long have I been down here?" she murmured.

"Long enough." Dashiell undid her bonds without looking at her, willing his touch to remain deft and impersonal. "I would have it be longer, but I'm afraid your whereabouts are being questioned, and it is probably in the interest of prudence that you be on your way and concoct another excuse for your absence."

"My whereabouts?" Lady Gallantine stepped down to the floor, her knees quaking. "Questioned?"

Dashiell turned away and withdrew a towel from a cabinet. "I have just received the Duke of Gallantine."

The Lady reached out a hand to the Machine, her trembling fingers gripping the leather. "What did you say?" she whispered.

Dashiell handed her the towel. She took it timorously, unfolding it and shrinking into its cover, and Dashiell hated such a man who could instill such shame and fear in his begotten. "Don't worry," said Dashiell. "I told him nothing."

Lady Gallantine shyly met his eyes.

Dashiell cleared his throat. "It's no business of his," he said brusquely. "As I have said, my livelihood depends upon my discretion."

She nodded.

Dashiell looked away again as she rubbed herself dry and began to dress. "How was your treatment?" he asked.

"I enjoyed it very much, thank you." Dashiell listened to the rustle of her skirts. "I again feel greatly improved. Only—"

"Yes?"

"There's something... I know not what. *Something* is still missing. Perhaps I am only imagining it. Doctor? My buttons?"

Dashiell turned. He buttoned Lady Gallantine's gown as quickly as he dared, focusing on the fabric and not on the warm, supple skin. Once she was clothed, she turned and smiled, radiating the sweet, gentle languor of the recently treated. How could even such an innocent thing as this arouse him again, and turn his insides into water?

"What shall we do about my father?" the Lady asked.

Dashiell raised his eyes to the ceiling above them, as if the Duke were overhead, listening.

"Doctor?"

Dashiell admitted, "I don't know."

Lady Gallantine cast her eyes down, fussing with her skirts.

"Now that he suspects, will you be able to get away?"

"I cannot say."

Silence descended between them. Elsewhere in The Chastarium, a single valve gave a lonely, distant whistle.

"If you *can* come back," said Dashiell, his insides aching, "I will be here."

The Lady touched his hand in thanks. Dashiell nodded coolly, though all he could think of was grasping her fine fingers in his, and raising them to his lips.

Chapter 3:
The End of the Hall:
or, Jameson's Cage

One day passed without the Lady Gallantine calling. And another. And several, several more.

Each night, as The Chastarium settled into sleep around him, Dashiell's spirits ebbed a little further. The evening routine remained unchanged: the assistants took their satchels and exited, chatting in pairs; the doctors retreated into their offices for a final hour of clerical work; the Machinists came up from below, grimy and solemn, wiping foreheads and exchanging supper plans in their working-class argot. Each night, Dashiell watched them all go, his heart growing heavier as the offices grew emptier. She would not come today, then.

One evening, instead of sitting alone in his office, Dashiell moved to the picture-window in the front parlor and placed his weary forehead against the glass. *You may be a doctor*, he thought, *but you are also a fool.* Lady Gallantine would not come again. And why should it matter anyhow?

Soon enough, the other doctors left, and Dashiell was alone. He lit a lamp and lay down on the settee, to stare at the shadows on the ceiling and pine like a lovesick simpleton. He was a fool, all right.

Someone paused outside his picture-window.

Dashiell turned his head. A pale, feminine hand rose to knock against the glass, but before the knuckles had even descended, Dashiell was up and throwing open the door.

"My Lady!"

Lady Gallantine, dressed in black beneath a veiled hat, raised a finger to her soft lips.

"Go inside!" Dashiell hissed. "Get!"

Lady Gallantine picked up her skirts and skittered through a bed of primrose toward him. Dashiell stepped back from the door, but not quickly enough, and the Lady's body brushed against his like a warm breeze, the smell of gardenias trailing in her wake.

Dashiell inhaled, already half-insensible.

"Doctor!"

He darted into the room and snuffed the lamp, "Forgive me— quickly, then, to the basement, if that's why you're here!"

She offered no protest. Dashiell took her elbow and urged her down the dark hall, the smell of gardenias fanning out behind them, threatening to weaken his knees. Had he even shut the front door properly? Her nearness, her very existence suffused everything with giddy heat, and Dashiell could not remember. They descended into the basement. Had he not shut the door at the top of the steps either?

"Doctor! Wait— I cannot see a thing—"

He halted her at the bottom of the steps and lit a candle on a small table. "All right?"

Lady Gallantine nodded. She removed her hat and fanned her face with it, reddened from effort and fright. "I am so very sorry! Doctor, I beg you, forgive me for coming here like this— I tried to come hours ago, you see, but I just couldn't get away, and now it's likely past 7 at least, and I'm sure you haven't had supper, and—"

Dashiell placed his hands on her arms. To silence her, or as an excuse to touch? "Hush now. My Lady, this arrangement is absolutely fine. You are in a unique position, after all, and if this is the only time in which you may see me, then I will be happy to arrange the appointment."

"But Doctor..." Lady Gallantine lowered her hat and peered down the Long Hall, deserted and silent. "If everyone else has gone home for the evening, who will tend the fires in the sub-basement?"

"Not all my Machines are powered from there."

"Oh?"

Dashiell gazed at her, her fair skin glowing in the light of the candle flame, her inviting breasts rising and falling with her recovering breath. He burned to take her to the first door on the left this instant, where The Inverted Velocipede awaited; or perhaps one more down, so they could mount the Built For Two.

But this was not the time. There was total silence from below. The Chastarium was empty, and now offered a privacy beyond price.

"My Lady," said Dashiell, offering his arm. "Let us walk to the end."

Lady Gallantine took the candle and his arm. "Yes," she said, clearly mystified. "Let's."

He led her down the Long Hall, turning ever inward like the path of a nautilus shell, each subsequent leg shorter than the last. One right turn, and past the door to The Locomotive; another right turn, and past The Ouroboros; one final turn, to face a hallway that held no doors at all—save for one, on the right, at the end.

Dashiell pulled the ring of keys from his belt. Lady Gallantine's face peered over the candle, still so innocent, so sweet. "My Lady," Dashiell said, unlocking the door. "May I present Jameson's Cage."

The door opened inward—not upon iron and concrete, but surprising elegance. They stepped across a polished, hardwood floor, complemented by matching wainscoting and trim. The walls were finished, and painted a mellow cream, with several mirrors hung to make the space seem larger. "Why, it's a drawing room—" the Lady began to say, but then she noticed the centerpiece.

Dashiell moved to the dais. He laid a hand upon the Machine's cool, polished brass, his heart pounding harder than The Locomotive, unable to believe that he was bringing her here—that he was bringing *anyone* here. This room was supposed to be for fantasies only, not patients.

Then again, which had she become?

"Jameson's Cage is the Machine of all Machines. The framework does not look impressive, I am sure, but the modularity of its design is the key to its power. The knots of machinery that you see attached to the brass frame can accommodate a near infinite variety of attachments, which can be used for treatment in any entrance, suspension or immobilization of the patient, and accompanying treatment across other areas of the body. Please—have a look."

Lady Gallantine approached in fascinated wonder, entirely forgetting to shut the door. "How do I interact with it?" she asked.

He imagined her inside, on her hands and knees, canvas slung under her belly and hips, supporting her exhausted body while the

Machine dealt with her from below and above and in front, loosening all of her sweet pink holes, preparing her inexorably for more. It was suddenly difficult to speak. "You... simply crawl inside."

She laid a hand upon her breast, at the black beadwork that glimmered at the throat of her dress. "Should I... disrobe?"

Mutely, Dashiell nodded.

Lady Gallantine set the candle upon a shelf and reached behind her. She grasped the end of a fine velvet cord and pulled, unraveling a knot and loosening the strings that laced up her back. The gown slipped to the floor. Her beauty emerged, like a moonrise over dark waters, and when she raised her head and smiled at him, Dashiell could not speak at all.

"Doctor?"

Mesmerized, Dashiell took a step toward her. And another. Her face turned opened and surprised. He was close enough now to feel the heat from her skin, to smell the echo of gardenias, to see the glow from the warm flame highlighting the soft curve of her shoulder, like sunrise beckoning beyond the horizon. His hand rose and moved of its own accord, and her eyes tracked it, startled.

He forced it to move past her.

Lady Gallantine opened her mouth. Dashiell's hand set upon a hidden drawer in the wainscoting, and he removed from it a tri-armed chain, the magnum opus of some anonymous silversmith.

A tiny clamp lay at the end of each arm.

"Doctor—"

Hand trembling, Dashiell cupped her breast.

Lady's Gallantine's eyelids flickered. She leaned into him, inhaling, pressing her bountiful softness against his fingers, overflowing his grasp. Dashiell's desire leaned toward her in aching, delirious answer, but instead of closing the final distance between them, he opened a clamp with his other hand and set it upon her breast's rosy bud.

Her eyelids flew open. "Oh!"

"Augments the treatment," Dashiell whispered.

Lady Gallantine blushed. She took an arm of the chain and clamped it upon her other bud. "Like so?" she murmured.

Dashiell nodded.

"And the third clamp...?"

Dashiell sunk to his knees, hands trembling harder, and raised his fingers to her secret place. Her dew had already fallen. She was panting lightly, staring down at him from beyond the little length of maddening chain, the buds of her breasts beginning to darken and swell.

He parted her folds, so soft and smooth, and set the final clamp upon the tender heart of her pleasure.

Lady Gallantine gasped. A tremor ran through her flesh.

Dashiell rose. "Now," he whispered, "you may crawl inside."

She took a tremulous step. Dashiell stood aside, his breath coming hot and quick, staring as she tried to move under the torment. He must yet gather fuel from the bins in the walls, build a fire within the dais to power the Cage, turn on the water for the steam, select the perfect attachments... but first, he would finish watching her...

Dashiell readied the Cage. The Lady removed her shoes and crawled inside. "And now?"

Dashiell stood by the bank of valves, staring at her as her hands fluttered wantonly over her skin, seeking an outlet and not knowing where to look. Around them, the light in the room rose, as the mirrors reflected the dazzle of brass and mounting flame. "Get on your hands and knees."

She rolled over to obey. By now, her buds were large and tender, and she cried out as they brushed the dais. The chain jingled as she positioned herself.

Dashiell eased open the first valve.

Lady Gallantine nearly swooned as the jointed arm came down and plunged the rubber into her secret. The end eased out; she drew breath for a cry. The end plunged home again, and she bucked into it, her heavy breasts swaying beneath her and against the tight lines of the chain. She moaned a wordless plea. Dashiell opened more valves in answer.

A second arm swung down from the front, filling her mouth and silencing her. But he knew it would take more than rubber over her tongue to satiate her hunger. Dashiell pumped a rubber bulb placed among the valves, and her bucking hips shuddered. The therapeutic end she rode began to inflate.

Color rushed across Lady Gallantine's skin. She squirmed against the attachment, unable to decide between pain and unbearable pleasure. The Machine kept up its relentless thrust, indifferent to her dilemma, fighting her until she yielded. And when she finally submitted to the rhythm, Dashiell pumped the bulb again.

"Oh—"

Dashiell withdrew a small pair of weights from his pocket and ignored her.

The end thrust home. The Lady groaned and writhed around its girth, helplessly overfilled, helplessly compelled to endure it to reach that final plane of ecstasy. As the Machine drew out again, Dashiell drew in, and before Lady Gallantine could understand his design, he clipped the weights to the short arms of the chain.

Dashiell pulled back. The thickened end plunged, and as Lady Gallantine thrust to meet it, the weights tugged coyly down.

Her arrival was explosive. She squealed in shock, every tremor of her body jarring the weights and sending new bolts of pleasure into all three of her clamped and swollen buds. Dashiell opened a valve further, to keep pace with her bucking hips, and realized that his other hand was upon himself again. Surely, a brief touch, in front of his fantasy Machine—

No.

Even here, he was a doctor.

Dashiell gritted his teeth. Lady Gallantine quaked in ecstasy inside the brass, like an exotic dove trembling inside a gilded cage, but no matter how rare and beautiful she was or how alone they were in The Chastarium's heart, or how clever and magnificent a Machine Dashiell concocted, it was all the same in the end.

His Machine was touching her. And he was not.

Dashiell's head bent to his breast. Lady Gallantine kept thrusting, chain and weights jingling, moisture spattering down, as she rode across her glorious plateau. He could leave the Machine alone, now, and she'd still be in Paradise. She didn't in fact need him at all. What was the point?

"Doctor," she cried, between the thrusts into her mouth. "It's still —I want—is there—?"

"There's more," said Dashiell softly.

He manually readied the end of the final appendage, unable to even look at her, tortured by the echo of her joy from every gleaming mirror. Dashiell stepped back and eased open a valve to the third arm, and a surrounding score of Lady Gallantines gasped at the sudden pressure against their exits. Unable to stop climaxing, they could only ride on as the Machine rode a new way in.

"*Oh!*"

Dashiell tweaked the stopcocks. The Cage thrust in a syncopated rhythm, always fulfilling part of her, but never fulfilling all.

"I still—oh please—"

He played with the valves, switching rhythms and intensities. His miserable desire rose into a half-mad frenzy. Dashiell pumped the bulbs for every therapeutic end, pushing her to the edge of what pleasure could withstand, and while she knelt there half-sobbing, he stoked up the Cage's fire. Pressure mounted within the Cage's pipes, within Dashiell's own system, until the pain of it grew heavy and throbbing. If he did not find release soon—

"It's not enough," Lady Gallantine sobbed, between thrusts. "I don't know—something's missing—it's still not enough!"

Dashiell spun all the stopcocks closed.

The Cage froze, emergency release valves squealing from the pressure. Lady Gallantine wailed in despair, unfulfilled save for the therapeutic end that speared and spread her garden, leaving her conquered where she knelt. "No! *No!*"

"If it's not enough," cried Dashiell, "then to Hell with Machines!"

Lady Gallantine opened her mouth to speak, but Dashiell never heard it. In a trice he was inside the Cage and upon her, pushing her forward and away from the unfeeling apparatus, hands running over her warm and slippery skin. He flipped her over, her chain jingling and her buds still dark and swollen, and as her back hit the dais, her fevered gaze cleared and sharpened.

Dashiell ripped open his fly.

His arousal sprang out, thickened and more than ready. But he was no Machine, inflated or otherwise, and Dashiell felt suddenly self-conscious.

My God. What are you doing?

Lady Gallantine's curious gaze settled upon him. "Oh my," she whispered. The bright fever returned to her eyes. "Is that what it looks like?"

"I'm so sorry," Dashiell whispered, moving to withdraw. "Forgive me."

"Where are you going?"

Dashiell froze.

Lady Gallantine's voice turned breathy and thick. "Where are you going, Doctor?"

"I—"

She sat up and pulled him down.

Lady Gallantine was sweeter than Dashiell had ever conceived. She was yielding but resilient, and tireless in her compelling, hypnotic rhythm. Dashiell buried his face in her hair, inhaling the scent of gardenias commingled with the scent of her hot desire. He clasped his fingers with hers, leaning into her full breasts, the clamps hard against his ribs. She lifted her legs and wrapped them round his back, gripping him with her silky thighs, urging him deeper with her heels.

"Yes," she whispered. "Yes."

He moved his face to her neck, to caress her there with lips and tongue. She sighed and rolled her head, exposing her throat to him, arching her back to urge her breasts to his mouth. He moved to them and undid the clamps with his teeth. Two arms of the chain fell away, and with the aid of his hand, the third arm; she half-sobbed in relief as her untethered breasts swung free. He placed his lips where the clamps had been. The sounds she made were exquisite.

"That's it," she whispered.

Dashiell wrapped his arms around her, beneath her, pressing the length of his body to hers. She slid her fine hands around his back, plucking at his shirt; he pulled away from her to remove it, to remove everything. He left his clothes hanging on the bars of the Cage. When he returned to her, his bare skin felt it all.

She sighed in relief.

Dashiell began his climb. Lady Gallantine moved beneath him in gentle obedience, utterly languid, utterly pliable, like a living toy who only breathed to please him, and derived her deepest happiness from the act. Indeed, as Dashiell's pleasure heightened, she watched him with a dreamy smile, already satisfied and content.

If Lady Gallantine's arrival had been explosive, Dashiell's was apocalyptic.

He rammed into her with a blind and desperate violence. But Lady Gallantine only purred, rocking her hips with his, naturally accepting all he had to give, even melting beneath the onslaught. On and on Dashiell rammed, ridden by the waves of his release, and still, she moaned in docile delight.

One final thrust, long frozen at its apex, and he collapsed atop her.

Her hands ran over the bare skin of his back, at once soothing and profoundly grateful. "Ahhh, Doctor," she whispered. "That's it. That's what was missing."

"What?"

"You." She laughed softly into the hollow of his shoulder. "Your own touch and pleasure. Oh—it is all too wonderful for words."

A new voice whispered, "Is it?"

The blood in Dashiell's veins turned to ice. His head turned to face the open door, and to his horror, he recognized the white-knuckled man that stood there.

The man's eyes flicked, once, to his prone and conquered daughter.

The Lady gasped.

Dashiell scrambled away from her, snatching his clothing from the Machine. Lady Gallantine's arms flew to her breasts as she sat upright, legs together and face burning. "Your Grace," Dashiell stammered.

"Father, what are you *doing* here?" the Lady cried. "Can't you leave me alone for a single hour!"

"Your Grace, please believe me, this was never my intent!"

"What did you do to come here?" Lady Gallantine demanded. "Did you break into the building?"

"The door—my Lady, we left the door open in our haste—"

"Then you were *following* me?"

All the while, Duke Gallantine remained in the doorway, hands clenched and trembling, saying nothing. His breath was slow and measured; his gaze, averted from both his daughter and the mirrors. He would not answer her.

Half-clothed, Dashiell crawled from the Cage and retrieved the Lady's dress.

"Here you are," he said to her kindly. Lady Gallantine emerged from the Cage, still blushing furiously. Dashiell shielded her with his body as she covered herself, though a score of mirrors mocked his chivalrous gesture. Dashiell also assisted in lacing her up. Only when she was presentable did the doctor turn to face the Duke.

"Your Grace," he said, struggling to mimic the Duke's eerie poise. "I believe we must have a conversation."

The Duke said nothing.

"Shall we go upstairs?"

Duke Gallantine looked back and forth between his daughter and the doctor. "No," he said calmly. "We shall not."

Dashiell raised his eyebrows, though his heart began to pound.

"My daughter and I shall go home," said the Duke. "And you and I shall have our conversation later."

"Your Grace—"

"Come here, Melinda."

Lady Gallantine shrank into herself, but she obeyed.

"Your Grace—" Dashiell insisted. The further she stepped from him, the larger the sudden ache in his soul. "Please—"

"No," said the Duke softly. "Doctor."

Dashiell fell into miserable silence. Lady Gallantine, her head bowed, shivered as the Duke placed a commanding hand upon her shoulder and steered her from the room.

They left him alone. He listened to their footfalls recede down the Long Hall, and when they had vanished, he listened to the fire popping beneath the dais, and the hissing of overwhelmed valves fighting to contain pressure that had nowhere to go.

Chapter 4:
The Proposal

The next morning, after a night of thin and broken sleep, Dashiell returned to The Chastarium with a heavy knot of fear around his heart.

The building was still standing and open for business, though this did nothing to quiet Dashiell's state of mind. Duke Gallantine could be waiting to make a public gesture with police at midday. Or perhaps the Duke's acknowledgment would come much later, in the form of a court notice ordering the entire Chastarium to be shut down.

Instead, however, the Duke was waiting for Dashiell inside.

"Your Grace," said Dashiell, stopping short in the foyer. In the parlor, the Duke sat in an armchair on the opposite wall, meaty hands gripping the armrests and head pressed back against the antimacassar in a pastiche of relaxation.

"Doctor," said the Duke.

A stammering explanation rose to Dashiell's lips, but he clamped his mouth shut around it. He, if not his entire business and staff, was already done for. Best to face the facts with grace and courage. "Your Grace," said Dashiell courteously, instead. "Welcome. Shall we adjourn to my office?"

The Duke glanced at the French doors out of Dashiell's line of sight, as if conferring with a pair of discreetly positioned officers on the other side, and gave Dashiell a tight nod.

Dashiell indicated the way, and the Duke rose and walked ahead. Once inside the office, Dashiell shut the door behind him (never again would he make that mistake…) and hung his hat upon the hat rack. "Please. Have a seat."

"Thank you." The Duke took it. "I was beginning to wonder if you would not show for work today. I'd been waiting more than a quarter of an hour."

"My apologies. Shall I have a boy bring us some tea? Or light refreshment, perhaps?"

The Duke sighed. "Doctor, I have no patience for these frivolous formalities."

Dashiell fought to steady his voice. "Your pardon. We may get to the point if you wish."

"I wish." The Duke shifted in his chair. "She doesn't stop, does she?"

Dashiell stared at him. For a moment, he didn't understand what his guest was saying. "What?"

The Duke stared back, still holding himself stiffly. Dashiell had the sudden impression that the man was not holding back anger—but rather, fear.

"Your Grace?"

"Melinda. She doesn't stop, once she begins." The Duke frowned uncomfortably. "You know what I mean."

"I... Your Grace." Dashiell foundered for words to cover his shock. "I have said. I may not divulge any details about my patients, and I can neither confirm nor deny—"

"Like her mother," said the Duke.

Dashiell fell quiet.

"Her mother is just like that," said the Duke. He leaned forward and gripped his knees, knuckles taut with the tension. "I knew it. I *knew* it. My wife, Doctor—she discovered her desire at 13. Can you imagine? Having to endure so young an unending hunger like that, that no partner can satisfy? She was forever unhappy in love, and convinced that something was wrong with her body. When we began our courtship, I will be honest, I was a little overwhelmed, but she was ecstatic that there even existed someone who could keep up.

"She told me she wished she had kept herself pure for me—not out of some misguided sense of morality; please, Doctor, I'm no monster—but because she knew now, after so much heartache, that a natural drive of her magnitude must be treated with the utmost caution and respect, and she should have left it asleep for as long as possible to spare herself the frustration. And it would have given her own mother, who bore the same curse, time to examine the available men and procure for her a happy match.

"Do you see what I am saying, Doctor?"

Dashiell kept staring. At some point, the doctor had leaned back onto his desk and gripped the edge to steady himself, but he didn't remember doing so. "...Do I?"

"I'm saying that you nearly wrecked everything," said the Duke, "and unleashed a desire that neither she nor her parents were yet prepared to address."

Dashiell didn't know what to say.

"Don't look so abashed," grumbled the Duke. "I said *nearly.* You *nearly* wrecked it, Doctor."

"Oh?"

"Melinda said you actually satisfied her. Didn't she?"

Dashiell felt a blush creep down his ears. "I couldn't say," he mumbled. "I cannot share details about our patients."

"Damn you, Doctor," said the Duke, rising from his chair. "I'm saying that I don't care what you've done, because you and she are a match. Understand? You're below her in station but you're still a match, and I demand that you start properly courting her, because she will have a Hell of a time finding another."

A silhouette appeared in the crack beneath the door. "Father!" exclaimed a voice beyond. "You said you had no anger!"

"I'm not angry!" shouted the Duke. To Dashiell, he said, "You will come by my house for tea tomorrow at 4, so her mother and I may get to know you."

"I..." fumbled Dashiell. He could hardly see. His vision was drowning in Lady Gallantine, the memory of her sparkling eyes and smooth skin, her wild cries and eager, dissecting glances. He could have her. All of her, and not just her lovely body; all the passion and ecstasy that her flesh radiated in coupling, he could see projected and practiced in the entire world outside. He would get to watch those inquisitive eyes light up at every newness and adventure, great and small, fantastic and mundane, intellectual—and sensual.

It was more than he ever dared conceive.

"At 4," said the Duke, firmly.

"Yes, Your Grace," stuttered Dashiell.

"Very good." The Duke turned and opened the door, revealing his waiting daughter, fidgeting with a lock of her hair. "I shall see you tomorrow, Doctor."

Dashiell managed a bow. The Duke left, but Lady Gallantine remained, smiling and casting her eyes down.

"My Lady," said Dashiell. "After you."

Lady Gallantine laughed. "Don't be silly, Doctor."

"Your pardon?"

"Doctor Dashiell," said Lady Gallantine, imitating the stiff and pompous manner of her father. "I have come to your establishment, as per usual, to seek treatment for my condition. Are you saying that you are going to turn me away unassisted?"

Dashiell drew breath. Down the hall, a pair of assistants whispered and elbowed each other, eyeing Lady Gallantine's considerable assets with longing and disbelief.

Dashiell straightened. A grin spread beneath his moustache, and he offered her his arm. "My Lady," he said, replying in kind. "I am a doctor. I would never turn away a patient in need. Please, step this way at once."

Lady Gallantine took his arm. Her fine touch ignited a foreshadowing warmth that spread through his veins, finer than brass, hotter than flame.

"So you can help me, Doctor?" she asked, as they walked toward the sub-basement.

"For as long as it takes," Dashiell promised.

The Fair, Laudanum and Passion

The Fair, Laudanum and Passion

Gabe pulled her through the crowds past tall, brightly lit booths, each sign at the entrance proclaiming a lurid horror within.

"Abraham the Half-Man," roared one of the moustachioed barkers, his eyes wide with frenzy as he beckoned his customers inside, "the eighth wonder of the world!"

Ettie saw the carnival poster on Blackfriars Road in London. "Wiley's World of Wonders," it screamed, "New Year's Day of 1880, one day only." She hopped up and down despite the weight of her bustle, but one glance at Gabe's arched black eyebrow sank her excitement. A familiar half smile crossed his thin face. He leaned his tall frame over her small one and smoothed the ends of her light brown hair.

"As a new partner at Bradford's, I'm expected to keep up appearances," he chided gently. "As my wife, you will be expected to purchase ball gowns and hold parlour soirees. We simply haven't the time or expense for such frivolity." Ettie followed him meekly, but after a few steps he replied. "Look at your pout; it's as if a child was told she could no longer play with a doll. Perhaps it would do us good to be seen enjoying ourselves. Very well my dear, we shall go. Now, to the boutique for my new waistcoat."

And go they did. Clowns made balloon animals and contortionists stretched on a plinth while the sideshow tents lurked from the borders of the melee. Ettie pursed her lips against the roughness of her husband's grip, smiling forcedly when he shot her a shrewd look; she could almost hear him denounce the funfair's claims of terror. As he said often, he was a travelled man about town while Ettie's parents had been furiously protective after her bout of cholera.

She glanced nervously at signs for two-headed calves and dog-faced boys, the bellows from their terrible wardens and the squeals from the crowds pervading the air.

"You will soon see, my dear, these folk are nothing but liars and thieves," said Gabe. "Stay close to me; this is no place for a woman alone."

Ettie paused to watch fire-breathers in Indian dress spouting flames higher and higher, while others spun figures of eight against the darkening sky with long burning sticks. A small crowd gathered to watch a young girl as she lay on her front on the miniature stage, contorting her legs from behind and placing her feet beside her head. The ladies squealed in delighted outrage when she tipped them a lascivious wink.

"They live for this," said Gabe derisively, "a flash of colour and sulphur in their magnolia tea-room existences. They'll go home and tell their friends how awful it is, over and over as they savour the details." Ettie sighed heavily, wishing they could enjoy themselves for once.

"Come see the world-famous Great Ra-mi, Sword Swallower extraordinaire. You will not believe your own eyes!" boomed the nearest barker. Ettie turned to Gabe, who elaborately checked the time on his gold chain pocket watch. Ettie wanted to scream, to weep with frustration, but she dutifully waited for him to place it neatly back in his frock coat.

"Very well, my dear," he said ponderously, "we shall go inside and see what chicanery awaits us." Ettie breathed in as they were ushered into the tent, filling herself with excitement.

The cheap grease lamps cast everything in a smoky red glow and they were ushered to the back to join a small crowd. A lady in a fussy lilac dress told all who listened about the best flowers to plant in London, her voice a touch too shrill for relaxed chatter.

"Of course, roses look best against one of Charles Frederick Worth's dresses; he truly is a master," she simpered until a movement forced her into silence. The smartly dressed man appearing from the back of the tent was of slender, wiry build, his brown moustache jauntily upturned in the corners. His dark eyes glinted with promises of mischief.

"Ladies and gentlemen, boys and girls," announced the barker, "for you the Great Ra-mi shall perform this act so dangerous, so terrifying, I must ask you to leave if you are at all faint of heart." Despite ripples of concern, everyone stayed put.

"And now, in front of your very eyes, The Great Ra-mi will attempt to swallow this very sword!"

Ettie's lilac-gloved hand flew to her mouth in shock; she heard a dismissive snort from Gabe.

"These people have been rehearsing and performing such acts for many years. The likelihood of his death is rather minimal," he muttered.

The Great Ra-mi pulled an apple from his pocket, offering it to the crowd to touch.

"As you can see," he said with a warm smile, "this is a regular apple." With that he placed it onto the floor and sliced downwards, chopping it in two. The crowd gasped. He raised the sword above his head, sharpened tip pointing downwards. Silence spread through the crowd and even Gabe was transfixed. The Great Ra-mi opened his gullet and allowed the thick steel to slide down into his gullet.

"Oh my," wailed the chattering lady. The crowd was mesmerised. Down and down it went and was removed with a flourish, his eyes barely watering. Ettie applauded with the others, a strange sensation tickling her hardening nipples and the secret crevices between her legs. The oddness of him, the contrast between him and Gabe's staid pompousness intrigued her.

To her dismay The Great Ra-mi didn't pay Ettie any special attention, and as they filed out she tried to ignore the disappointment weighing on her chest.

"Well, that was better than expected," Gabe said. "Now, please can we make our way out of this place?"

"Yes, Gabe," said Ettie.

They wandered towards the exit only to be confronted with a clown selling candy floss, his eyes black crosses and his mouth a humourless grin.

"Right," muttered Gabe, his mouth pinched and eyebrows rigid. Ettie was silent as they tried another way, no street signs visible.

"Why do we not ask somebody?" Ettie suggested gently as they almost knocked into a man thrusting swords into a tiny box.

"I come to London every day. I have no need to ask for directions like some fresh-faced apprentice."

"Yes, I am aware," soothed Ettie, "but it is quite impossible for us to know where we are amongst this mayhem."

"Of course it is difficult," Gabe smiled reassuringly, "my little muffin barely knows what's at the end of the road. Take my arm; we can't have you getting frightened." Ettie reached out as a large family crashed between them. She wandered past them, hoping to reach the end of their group and re-join her husband. When she arrived at the expected spot, however, he wasn't there.

Raising her hand to her throat Ettie tried to quieten her jittering heartbeat. She described Gabe to various people and was met with the same blank look. She crashed through families and chaperoned sweethearts, their voices reaching a furious pitch until she knew she had to hide from the loudness around her. She needed a few minutes to be calm, she told herself, before she found her husband. If Gabe knew she was having one of her hysterical moments he would be furious. She couldn't bear the doctor's disapproving appraisals or his courses of phosphates. The bitter liquid made her feel as though she were in a different room to everyone else.

Patches of sweat soaked her gloves when she reached a wooden, green painted building, almost tripping on a board leaning against the door. She kicked it out of the way and threw herself into the quiet safety inside. She tiptoed up the stairs, her chest tightening again when the steps slanted madly to the left. Gripping tightly onto the rail, she reached a long hallway where rows of mirrors hung from dusty, attic-scented walls. The screams and laughter faded as she wandered down the darkening corridor, the tapping of her shoes echoing loudly.

Her reflection in the mirror beside her stretched upwards to impossible heights, and in the next her body was compressed into a squat troll. Her heart skipped again, but instead of screaming and wailing for help she began to giggle. She placed a hand over her mouth to regain composure but couldn't stop, and when she saw herself with great long legs and a tiny body she cackled like an old maid until her eyes watered.

Shuffling on she noticed a door slightly ajar and pushed it, finding herself standing in a sparse room containing five threadbare armchairs. Seated in one was a woman she'd seen handling snakes. Her flowing blue dress was almost thin enough to be scandalous and barely covered her toothpick legs, and knots made a bird's nest of her thick black hair. Next to her the strongman casually filled a pipe. His eastern outfit sparkled while his muscles and bald head glowed under the flickering light of a candle lantern. In another chair sat the Great Ra-mi, frock coat draped on the seat behind him and white shirt un-tucked. The mischief had gone from his brown eyes; he lightly tugged the end of his moustache in what seemed an action of habit. Ettie realised at once she wasn't supposed to be in there and her corset seemed to tighten.

"Hello?" said the strongman, as all eyes turned to her.

"I am terribly sorry, I must have – well, I shall be off," she said, turning back to the corridor.

"Is anybody with you?" asked The Great Ra-mi sharply.

"N-no," she replied, immediately wishing she had lied.

"Then there is no need for you to go," he said, rising from his seat. "We put a sign outside closing the Funhouse after a lady twisted her ankle, but no harm has been done," he smiled easily.

Dust rose when Ettie sat in the armchair, specks floating in front of her. She felt she ought to speak but had no conversation for the circumstance.

"Did you truly swallow that sword, Great Ra-mi?" asked Ettie eventually, and the snake-girl snorted with laughter.

"His name's Art," she said in a coarse East End voice.

"Pleased to meet you," Art took her hand. Ettie noticed a long metal nail and hammer on a table beside him. "Oh," he gestured vaguely, "I shall be hammering that into my nostril later. It's quite safe," he assured hurriedly, "it merely enters the nasal cavity here," he said, pointing to a spot near the bridge of his nose.

"Oh, I see," said Ettie, at once repelled and fascinated.

"Why not have some brandy with us?" he offered eagerly, seemingly concerned she was frightened.

"Good idea," said the snake-girl, "I've got a bottle of Laudanum in my bag. We should add some." The strongman cheered.

"Heathens," joked Art. "You can just have straight brandy if you would prefer," he said, turning to Ettie.

"No," she replied, drawing a shocked glance. "I shall have some. A small glass," she corrected herself hurriedly. Her words filled her with a delirious freedom, the like of which she had never experienced. It felt like the most outrageous thing anybody had ever done. She reasoned the hours spent lighting the gas-lamps against the dark, waiting for Gabe to shuffle indoors with the reek of bordellos and opium dens oozing from his coat, had earned her the right to taste his world.

"Here you are," said the snake-girl after slopping the contents of a bottle into glasses of amber liquid. "My name's Penny."

The liquid burned, and Ettie's eyes watered for the second time that day. Art shrugged and accepted a glass himself, and for a time they chatted amiably. As the strongman, Gus, explained that the weights were not as heavy as some were led to believe, Ettie noticed the beautiful way the dust floated in the candlelight. A silence followed.

"I have always wanted," said Gus eventually, his voice soft and thoughtful, "to be a voyeur, or to instigate a group situation."

Ettie almost choked, too shocked to speak.

Penny laughed, "This again. You should stop talking about it and just do it."

Ettie glanced at Art, who shifted uncomfortably in his seat.

"Perhaps I will," said Gus petulantly.

"Very well, then do so," replied Penny provokingly.

Gus lowered himself to the ground in front of Penny. Ettie's mouth opened in horror when she realised what he was going to do. She had seen it in the pictures in Gabe's secret books but had never thought of it as something people truly did. Penny giggled self-consciously and opened her legs for him. Ettie realised her own breath was quickening as Gus lifted Penny's skirts to remove her undergarments. She helped him, sighing deeply when his lips made contact with her private ones. The embarrassment seemed to leave her as she opened her legs wider, making soft appreciative noises. She pulled her arms free of her dress, exposing her breasts and hard nipples. Ettie hoped her sharp intake of breath was inaudible, realising she was hot and wet between her legs.

She glanced at Art as Penny bucked against Gus's face, her moaning increasing. Ettie experienced another surge of heat and confusion when she saw the bulge straining against Art's trousers, his knuckles turning white as he gripped the arms of his chair. She knew she should be running from them in horror, shrieking for her husband, but she didn't want to move. Her heart tightened when Penny turned her brown eyes to her, rising from the chair and discarding her dress completely. Her body, though small, was an acre of exposed flesh to Ettie; a vast expanse of nudity glowing white under the candlelight.

"You should join me," she whispered.

Ettie opened her mouth to refuse, to tell them she was leaving, and found herself unbuttoning her blouse. Her hands shook with excitement and she flung the gloves as far as she could throw. Penny slowly untied her corset and Ettie took a great breath in, dizzy with weightlessness. When Penny helped her step free of her skirts and long underwear she saw her thighs were slick with wetness. All three pairs of eyes flicked over her appreciatively.

Ettie was uncertain of her next move, her arms hanging limply at her sides, when Penny leaned in to kiss her, her hair smelling of sandalwood. Ettie thought kissing a girl felt much less insistent than kissing a man, the lips softer and gentler. The quick motion of Gus stroking himself caught her eye and instinctively she placed a hand near her private lips. Penny turned her attentions to Art, kneeling to the floor and pulling at his trousers until he was free. His erection sprang forward and she took the shaft into her mouth, a soft moan escaping his lips.

Ettie had never done such a thing for Gabe, but now Penny was motioning for her to take charge. Nervously, Ettie sank down next to Penny and tried to copy her, the eagerness plain in Art's face. The scent of his soap was laced with sweat, and his blood pulsed as she gently licked around the head. His hand gripped her shoulder as she sucked downwards, taking in as much as she was able. Before rising she flicked her tongue upwards, proud of the satisfaction she was giving him.

As she gently rubbed her hand along his shaft she glimpsed Penny guide Gus to the floor, laying him on his back and lowering herself onto him. Gus gave a great gasp and reached for her hips, pulling her up and down.

Her pupils dilated and cheeks red with pleasure, Penny beckoned to Ettie. When she crawled nearer Penny took her hand and placed it over her breast, which Ettie gripped gently with wonder and tweaked the hard brown nipples. Growing in confidence, she traced her fingertips down to Penny's private lips as they rose and fell over Gus. Wondering if Penny had the same spot between her legs that felt good when rubbed, Ettie tickled her wetness, her question answered when the other girl bit her lip and sighed. As Ettie circled the hardening nodule, Penny's breathing quickened and her hips bucked against her fingertip as Gus gripped her tightly.

"Is that good?" Ettie asked her.

"Yes," Penny sighed.

Art stroked his shaft as Penny cried out, her face reddening and body shuddering. Gus pumped hard inside her and Penny leaned down to him, her hair covering their faces.

Ettie turned back to Art, her own private lips aching for attention. Too shy to speak, she opened her legs as a hint. He kneeled to the ground, his lips apart and pupils large, their eyes catching each other self-consciously. His fingers sought her private lips and she moaned with relief, goose-bumps rising over her skin. She looped her hands behind his neck and wrapped her legs around him, pressing herself against his hot bare skin and sliding onto his erection. "Oh," she moaned, needles of sensation flooding her body. Looking directly into his face she saw his red flush and furrowed brow, his excitement inducing fresh waves of pleasure in her. The sounds of Penny and Gus's moaning enveloped her as Art's length stroked her from inside, and she dug her teeth and nails into his shoulders to keep him there, keep him a part of her.

All shyness gone, Ettie freed herself from him and turned away, meeting the eyes of Penny as she writhed on top of Gus. Ettie leaned forwards, the floorboards hard against her hands and knees, waiting and praying she hadn't gone too far, that she hadn't shocked him. With relief she felt him wrap one arm around her waist as he fumbled to guide himself in, gasping as he pushed himself deep. His tip stroked her innermost point, her furthest hidden reaches. Penny's eyes were on her as Ettie grabbed Art's hand and led it to her private lips, circling the nodule with his finger until he understood. She rocked against him as the heat and the wetness built higher and higher, his shaft growing more and more insistent. She kept her eyes on Penny as Gus's hands slid from her hips to her breasts, and in turn Penny watched them.

Ettie's nipples tightened and the fire spread from her groin upwards, and at the same time Penny's moans deepened. Ettie knew the other girl was reaching her peak and she tried to hold hers, to hang on until they could reach it together. Penny's brow furrowed and Ettie knew she couldn't hold back the release, and soon it spread from her groin throughout her body and flooding her brain as she stiffened and cried out. When she was still, Art pushed against her harder than before, her body more pleasantly sensitive to him, until he moaned his last and loudest.

His seed tickled her inside and she felt him pulse until his body became a heavy weight. They lay down together on the wooden floor, the scent of the old chairs and their sex mixing with the dust. She half expected Art to cast her aside like the women in the cautionary books she had read, but instead he ran his fingers gently over her skin. Already she began to form the words of her farewell letter to Gabe. She felt a small twinge, reminding herself the man she thought she married never truly existed.

The following year, the tents were up by dusk when the first curious locals drifted in. A few performers were changing their clothes and rehearsing as Ettie sighed contentedly by the ticket booths.

"You'd better stay wake if you're to sell those," said Art, his voice making her jump.

"I was lost in my own world," she laughed, embracing him. His skin still smelled of soap.

"The clowns will have a difficult time tonight; Markus' ankle hasn't healed," said Art pensively.

"Oh dear," said Ettie, "tell him to put it in a pail of ice." Art nodded and turned to leave. "Oh," called Ettie, "remind Penny she's to teach me more of the snake-dancing tomorrow." Art nodded.

"Oh, and Art," she called again, a smile forming at the corner of her lips, "tell her we shall see her later." As she watched him tip his hat and saunter away, she hummed a merry tune.

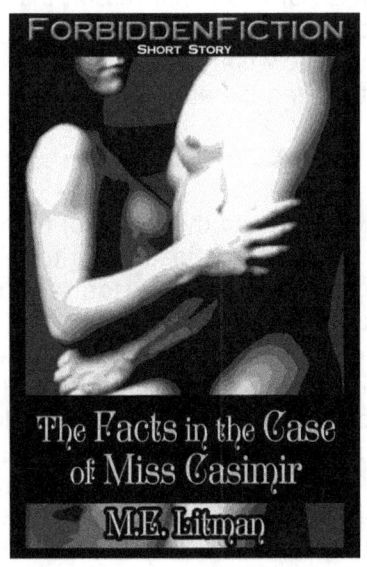

The Facts in the Case of Miss Casimir

The Facts in the Case of Miss Casimir

For the account that follows, I neither expect nor solicit belief. To do so would test the limits of my sanity, which I myself have already come to question. It is partly for that reason that I put pen to paper now — I hope that by laying out the facts, the truth of my strange experience, that I will be able to examine them rationally, tracing from the causes to their terrible effects.

The air was heavy with rain and the rolling of thunder the night I met the writhing horrors that lurk beneath Warriton Hall. I stood on the doorstep, waiting for the late-summer storm and clutching the small statue that had brought me there.

The statue came to me through an antiquities dealer, a stout, balding man who often sold to the university. He claimed to have bought it from an oyster harvester who had dredged it up from the coastal shelf. The sailor had babbled of visions and dark dreams — which the antiques dealer took to be the ravings of a superstitious drunkard, and used to drive down the price. Unable to place it himself, he brought it to the university as a curiosity. But as soon as I set eyes on it, I knew it was something more.

The figurine was no more than two inches in diameter at its widest point, and only a hand and a half in length. It was carved from some kind of blue marble, run through with veins of black and silver. I would have admired the skill and detail in which it was rendered, and the excellent condition despite its immense age, were its form not so unsettling.

An unnatural abstraction rose up from a rounded dais inscribed with untranslatable hieroglyphs. The figure was composed of twisted tentacles and unnatural curves, and upon closer inspection I found that it had something resembling a spine, but with no clear beginning or end, more like the shell of a centipede than human bone. As I examined it, the carved monster stared back at me with dozens of eyes, peering out of the bulges and ridges of its form in no natural pattern.

Looking at it, I felt a strange pulling in my core, and something akin to nausea rose up in me. It pooled in the pit of my stomach. A voice in the back of my mind told me to lock the thing away, or throw it into the sea, or smash it against the cobbles — to be rid of it, never set eyes on it again.

But I dismissed it as superstition unbecoming of an academic like myself. I paid the dealer and took the statue on as my next project.

I immediately began a far-flung body of inquiry, from local history to the statuary of the proto-Sumerians, which I suspected had some connection to my carving. How very wrong I was!

In the course of my research, I happened upon a newspaper dated some fifteen years ago, which bore mention of a strange statue whose description matched my own. The sole survivor of a mining accident, a Mr. Thomas Galding, had been found clutching the statue and babbling about demon cults and unholy rites when he was rescued. This peaked my interest – could my statue be an idol of some barbaric religion? The idea that any sane creature could worship such a thing as it depicted sent chills down my spine. I excavated the newspapers for more information about Mr. Galding or the accident. Indeed, a few weeks later, another article was published, announcing Thomas Galding's death by unknown natural causes. He left no widow, nor family that could be found. The statue was put to auction, but was stolen before it could be delivered to the winner. Auction house records indicated that the highest bidder was an H. Casimir.

I sought out this Mr. Casimir, but the only other mention I could find of the name was in the records of the Kelwich Museum of Natural History, a small but well-funded collection on the outskirts of the city. I uncovered receipts for several exhibits which had been bought from the private collection of an E. Casimir.

But as my research progressed, I was beset by a series of unwholesome dreams, in which I flew over antediluvian landscapes and cities with impossible geometry. I found myself chained, spread-eagled, to stone altars, alternately caressed and skinned alive by scaled, fish-like demons. Each dream ended with me, naked and afraid, falling through water. Deeper and deeper I sank, pulled by something I could not see, until total darkness enveloped me. Then I would wake, gulping at the air and clutching at my bed sheets.

The day I took it upon myself to visit the Kelwich Museum in person, since this H. Casimir was my only lead, was bright and oppressively hot. I fanned myself with my notebook as I alit from the tram in front of the pillared steps to the imposing edifice. Inside, the cool and shade of the high-ceilinged gallery provided a welcome respite. Hands and notebook clasped behind my back, I began my perusal of the collection. I had gone there occasionally as a student, but as with any good museum, there was always more to discover.

I was leaning over a case containing a Roman goblet, comparing the bas-relief and my sketch of the statue, when *she* materialized over my left shoulder.

"This piece is billed as the pride of the collection," I jumped at the sound of her voice, deep and melodious but with an edge of ice. I whipped around to find a woman about my age, of a beauty all the more intense for its departure from convention. She was tall and slight of figure, with dark eyes set wide over sharp cheekbones, full, rouged lips, and along, elegant neck accentuated by a high collar. Her dark tresses were piled neatly beneath a wide-brimmed hat, with a ribbon that matched her azure promenade dress. "But I find the fourth dynasty Chinese brasswork to be far more fascinating in its implications." The corner of her lips turned upwards into a small smile, as though she were amused by my surprise."Don't you?"

Though I had studied Chinese brasswork extensively, my mind was suddenly empty of all cogent thought and I stammered some idiot, half-formed response.

"Elizabeth Casimir," she announced herself, still smiling as one might while watching a child charmingly try and fail some simple task.

"Dalman..." I replied, gathering my wits again and wanting to kick myself for my ineloquence. "Edgar Dalman."Certainly I was shocked to find that E. Casimir was a woman, but the twisting in my gut could not be attributed solely to surprise. I found my eyes wandering over the angles and curves of her form, and something stirred, unbidden, in the core of my being. Suddenly the room was too hot, my collar too tight.

"Hmm... The name is familiar to me. That's it... You're on the faculty at the University, are you not? Department of Antiquities?"

"Yes, and I've also heard your name, Mrs. Casimir..."

"Miss, actually."

"My apologies." I indicated a nearby plaque which bore her name, and explained the research that had brought me to sift through the museum's sales receipts.

"Alas," she sighed,"I must sell an artifact every now and again in order to maintain the rest of my family's estate. A pity, money is such a vulgar thing to trade for such treasures. I feel sullied each time I do it. Still, the private collection remains formidable."

"If I might ask, how did your family come upon such a collection?" She had the eye and tone of one well-versed in antiquities, observations which only fueled the growing heat in my core.

"My grandmother was an antiquarian and explorer who, because of her gender, never gained the respect she was due in the field." She frowned at the goblet I'd been examining. "Museums even refused to buy from her, suspecting her finds of being artful forgeries. She refused to use a middleman on principle."

I decided then to take advantage of the encounter luck or fate had provided me, and inquire about the statue. I opened my notebook, but as soon as I showed her my drawing of it, something in her countenance changed. She gazed at it for a long moment, during which I hardly dared breathe. My legs felt numb, and... other parts of me, far too sensitive. When she looked back up at me, I thought I perceived a spark in her eyes that had not been there before.

She produced a cream-colored calling card from her purse, and extended it to me, clutched between two slender, gloved fingers. I took it, perhaps faster and more forcefully than I should have, in my anxiety.

"Mr. Dalman, I am hopeful that I shall be able to help you in your research. Perhaps we can arrange a private tour of my family's collection at Warriton Hall." She gave me another of her small, half-smiles, and the pit dropped out of my stomach. "Good day, Mr. Dalman." And with that, she was gone.

That night, my dreams took a disturbing turn. Instead of impossible cities or alien beings, it was Miss Casimir who appeared to me. Her hips swayed as she stepped towards me out of the shadows of my unconscious, the nipples on her pert, full breasts flushed and erect. She was completely naked and achingly beautiful. My gaze followed the lines of her collarbones to the delicate curve of her waist and down over her hips and the triangle of dark hair covering her most intimate of places, exploring all the planes and valleys of her creamy skin. I was pinned by the intensity of her gaze, the hot, unfettered desire in it.

She reached out to press her hand to my chest, and her touch was warm and substantial. She ran her fingertips over my skin, and I realized that I too was naked, my skin flushed and my cock stiff between my legs. Elizabeth Casimir (or my dream of her) leaned in close and pressed her lips to mine, parting them with a gentle swipe of her tongue. She kissed me, first delicately, then with increasing hunger.

Effortlessly, she pushed me backwards, laying me out on the marble altar I had visited in past dreams. She knelt over me, looking down her marvelously sculpted nose and smiling the way she had in the museum — as though I was some kind of student in need of her tutelage. Her hands found their way back to my chest, fingers brushing over my nipples. I could feel the heat of her sex against my thigh. Slowly, deliberately, she lowered herself over me, sliding down onto my cock. I felt her beautiful, slick tightness close around me, and I gasped as she settled into place. Every thought driven from me, a being of pure sensation, I thrust up into her. We fell into rhythm, and while she rode me I forgot how to breathe. I felt a knot of energy forming in my abdomen, blood pounded in my ears while she clawed at my ribcage and threw her head back, clenching down around me. Just as I felt myself about to tip over the edge, I froze, horror-struck, as Miss Casimir transformed into a mass of writhing tentacles and glaring eyes, the very monster depicted on the statue that lead me to her.

I woke in a mess of my own ejaculate and cold sweat. Terror and guilt clutched at me, for I am not prone to those sorts of dreams, nor to sexualize a woman upon first meeting her. But dreams are not obedient creatures, and they returned the next night, and the next. Soon I could hardly close my eyes but the image of Miss Casimir would coalesce, and I would feel myself growing hard in my trousers.

It was these dreams that kept me from pursuing my one lead — Miss Casimir and her family's collection — for nearly a week. I buried myself in aimless reading and side projects. But the more I tried to drive the terrible statue from my thoughts, the more it played upon my mind. At last, I resolved to get to the bottom of this, hoping that by uncovering the truth about the statue I might exorcise whatever demon it had set upon me.

My jaw clenched until it ached as I strode to the telegraph office down the street, the calling card Miss Casimir had given me burning in my breast pocket. I did not have to wait long for a response to the message I sent her. The next day, a man in a butler's black suit appeared on my doorstep and wordlessly handed me a delicate ivory envelope. Inside, I found the following note, handwritten in a lilting script:

> Dear Mr. Dalman,
> I will be available to show you the collection at 8 in the evening, tomorrow night at my estate, Warriton Hall. Bring your statue. I shall expect you.
> E. Casimir

Thus I came to Warriton Hall.

I swallowed the lump that had formed in my throat while I stood on the stone doorstep, awaiting the appearance of Miss Casimir. It was a manservant who answered when I worked up the courage to knock at the door, the same blank-eyed manservant who had delivered her letter the previous day.

He showed me to the parlor, where Miss Casimir was waiting. I suppressed a gasp. She was dressed in a robe of red brocade, which lay luxuriously across her shoulders, exposing her delicate collarbones. My alarm at finding her so dressed came out in an awkward, barking cough. She nodded in greeting, but said nothing.

The lights in the house were dim, save for a lantern set upon the parlor table. Picking it up, she led me to a heavy door which opened onto a set of stone stairs disappearing downwards into the dark. The bobbing pool of light cast by the lantern threw long shadows against the walls of the narrow stairwell. Looking at my feet and the curving flagstones beneath them brought on a minor bout of vertigo, so I kept my gaze fixed ahead of me, on my guide. Her footsteps, delicate but decisive, beat out a steady rhythm like a hypnotist's drum. Her thick, mahogany hair was twisted and pinned into a loose bun at the back of her head. Red fabric draped from her shoulders and over her hips, which rocked gently as she descended the stairs. From the way the light played on the curves and folds of her robe, I began to suspect that she wore nothing beneath it. I shook my head, admonishing myself for thoughts of such impropriety.

As we descended, the walls of brick turned to earth, which gave way to cobble, then to solid stone. I felt as though I had been walking for hours. I clutched the statue in my sweating hands.

"How much further is it?" I asked. My voice echoed uncomfortably.

Miss Casimir continued on without answering or looking back at me. Her pace remained steady. When I had almost made up my mind to insist on going back, a heavy door of cedar and wrought iron appeared in front of us.

Miss Casimir produced a ring of keys and fit one into the keyhole.

"You have been expected," she said. "My guests are waiting."

"Guests?"

But I received no response. There was the click of a lock, and Miss Casimir pulled open the door with ease and stepped inside, turning to hang her lantern on the wall.

Having come this far, with the darkness closing over the stairs behind me, I could do nothing else but follow. I stepped out into a twilit grotto of enormous height, stretching farther away into darkness than the eye could see. The massive cavern was illuminated by braziers mounted to stone pillars which looked much like stalactites, but were so evenly spaced around the central antechamber that they could not possibly have been naturally formed. The cave walls dripped and glimmered, moss or fungi creeping from every edge and corner. Some meters from the doorway there began a series of pools, and the torchlight reflected green on the surface of the water, which was rippled by some wind I could not detect. The cavern opened out over what must have been a massive pool of water, though our corner of the chamber was the only part that was lit, and I could not see how far it extended into the dark nor could I fathom its depth. In the center of the circle of light stood a stone dais carved with the same skill and style as the statue in my hands.

While I marveled at the sight, its mystery and suggestions, Miss Casimir turned and approached me. I started as something in the shadows over her shoulder shifted. It was then that I saw the figures in the darkness. One by one, they stepped forward into the torchlight, each one hooded and robed in the same red brocade as Miss Casimir. I felt a knot of apprehension form in the pit of my stomach as the silent figures formed a circle around us, their faces concealed by the shadow of their hoods.

"You were chosen," Miss Casimir intoned without acknowledging them."The statue brought you to us, as He knew it would. As it always does."

She stepped toward me, letting the red robe fall from her shoulders into a pile behind her. My breath caught in my throat. She stood before me, naked and radiant. Her ribs rippled against her skin as she reached up to unpin her hair, letting it cascade down her back. I felt heat rising again to my face — it had been a long time since I had seen a woman naked, let alone been close enough to touch her, outside of dreams. She reached out and placed a hand on my hip, and I was suddenly and acutely aware of the tightness of my trousers. I wanted to step back, I should have run, but something held me in place. She took the statue (now quite warm) from my hands, and I did not resist.

"Every cycle," she said, stepping closer,"He selects a champion and draws them here. We are His disciples." She motioned to the hooded figures. Though I could not see their eyes, I felt them burning into me, into us. Elizabeth caressed my jaw, and I shuddered beneath her touch. "You stand among the Enlightened, those who have seen the wonders that lurk in the dark places of the world, who have walked the hallowed corridors of Dream, who have given themselves over to all the beautiful and terrible things of this world and what lies Beyond, and have made sacrifice in the name of ultimate Pleasure." Light-headed with fear and desire, I reached out for her waist, but she stepped away.

"Now, Mr. Dalman," she called over her shoulder as she walked towards the altar, "it is your turn."

There was a moment of silence that seemed to stretch on into eternity. I felt the collective gaze of the congregation fixed upon me, heavy and hungry. I could hear nothing but the pounding of my own blood in my ears.

I sensed something stir behind me. The water in the greenish pool began to bubble, the surface breaking in angry ripples. Though I recognized it from its statue, to accurately describe the heinous thing that rose, slick and dripping, from the water is beyond human ken. It was a writhing mass of tentacles and unblinking eyes, gnashing mouths and extended tongues. Its shape shifted and undulated even as I looked on, petrified, displacing the water around it so that it gurgled and sloshed over the rocks at the edge of its pool.

I must be deliberate now, and choose my words.

I turned and ran for the door, but something lashed out for my ankle. I tripped forwards, but before I could hit the ground I was hoisted, feet-first, into the air, losing a shoe and a sock in the process. I thrashed and kicked to no avail; thick tentacles wrapped around my chest and shoulders, while others grasped my wrists and ankles. The monster's flesh was wet and clammy against me, the suction cups lining the underside of each tentacle mouthing at my skin.

The muscled tentacles righted me and held me up, as though displaying me to the assembled crowd, spreading my arms and legs. I wrenched against it, but I could not move.

"Struggle if you wish, Mr. Dalman," Miss Casimir smiled, "There is no escape. But after tonight, you will have earned your robes, just as we all did. You should be honored."

To my horror, one of the appendages slid its way up under my shirt, another down the leg of my trousers. With a mighty rip, the things tore my clothing to ribbons, sending buttons ricocheting off the walls and plinking to the damp floor of the cave. It ripped off the scraps of fabric that still clung to my body, along with my remaining shoe, until I was stark naked in its grasp.

I opened my mouth to scream, but a tentacle pushed its way past my lips until I felt it scrape the back of my throat. I gagged as it withdrew, only to plunge in again. I sputtered as it took a few long, slow strokes, an assisting tentacle wrapping itself around my neck and holding my head in place. I dare not struggle, lest it tighten its grip. The one in my mouth set up a steady, pulsing rhythm as I fought to find my breath again.

My skin burned under the gaze of every eye in the cavern. Unable to look down, I felt a pair of tentacles weave their way up my legs. One of them brushed over my testicles and down the length of my manhood, which twitched in response. I tried again to scream, but I could not, around the tentacle penetrating my mouth. One of the appendages exploring between my legs wrapped around my scrotum and sucked gently, while the other lay its suction cups against the underside of my prick, as though teasing me. I was terrified to find myself growing hard under the monster's ministrations; before long I stood fully erect, a tentacle wrapped around the base of my cock, another wriggling up and down the shaft.

No sooner had I reached full mast than two more tentacles (there was no way of knowing how many the creature possessed, or even how many were touching me) wound around my thighs, pulling them apart and exposing me completely. The tentacle in my mouth withdrew long enough to permit me a gasp of horror before plunging back in. I felt one of the slick appendages trace down my spine and over the curves of my buttocks before coming to rest. I struggled, I tried to pull myself away, but it only tightened its grasp.

Bright stars of pain exploded in the corners of my vision as the slimy, muscled thing thrust into me. My cry was stifled by the other limb having its way with my mouth, but hot tears sprung up in the corners of my eyes.

I was no champion — I was a sacrifice.

The tentacle wriggled inside me, pushing deeper, until it brushed against something that sent a jolt of electricity up my spine.

Sensation ripped through me such as I had never experienced before, and, as I was sure I would die there, thought I would never experience again.

The tentacle around my neck loosened, allowing me enough motion to look across the cavern. Elizabeth Casimir's eyes caught mine, and a wicked smile broke across her features. I tried to look away, but I could not. She held my gaze like a vice as she spread herself over the altar, lowering the statue between her legs and slicking it against her sex. There was hunger and reverence in the way her body enveloped the carved form as she slid it into herself. She gasped and threw her head back in pleasure, but her eyes never left me. Beneath her hungry gaze, I was but an instrument.

Taking this as a sign, the rest of the congregation doffed their robes and fell upon one another without regard for gender or jealousy, mouthing and groping like animals. Fingernails scraped down bare backs, teeth closed around throats, buttocks were grasped and thighs flung open until one form could not be distinguished from the next and they had devolved into a heaving pile of flesh. The crowd took up a low chant in a long-forgotten language, punctuated by gasps and moans. I could do nothing but watch them rut against each other, fucking and being fucked on the cavern floor. The orgiastic conglomerate encircled the altar, on which Miss Casimir lay, reclined and queen-like above the fray, fingers playing over her clitoris while she pushed the statue in and out of her wet, crimson cunt. Her moans rose above the others, like an intoned prayer.

All the while, the tentacles worked my body, some caressing my skin delicately, even as others pounded into me without mercy. The tentacles restraining my arms and legs tightened their grip, while the others quickened their rhythm. Miss Casimir cried out in climax, as she had so often in my dreams, but it was as if I was hearing it from a great distance. The moans of the rutting congregation echoed throughout the cavern. I felt a desperate heat pooling in my groin, I found myself thrusting into the creature's grasp, but I was too far gone to be horrified by the implications of it.

My eyes rolled back as I exploded in orgasm, impaled on one tentacle and choking around another.

I heard nothing but a distant ringing in my ears as the creature slowly withdrew from me and deposited me gently on the cold stone floor, my limbs trembling, with tears drying on my cheeks.

I blinked through the haze clouding my vision to see Miss Casimir standing over me, smiling, arms extended.

"Welcome home."

I must end here, for night has fallen and the red moon casts its light through my open window like a dread signal. Now that this account is complete, I will burn these pages, lest they fall into the hands of some poor soul and burden him with their terrible secrets, or worse, spark in a reader a desire to investigate them.

It is time. I go now to don my robe of red brocade and join my Brothers and Sisters in celebration. He waits for us in the roiling pools beneath Warriton Hall.

If you enjoyed this story, you can sign up for a free membership at ForbiddenFiction and discuss it with other readers and the author at the *The Facts in the Case of Miss Casimir* story page at http://forbiddenfiction.com/story/mel-1-000301.

Lady Sally and the Automaton Horse

Chapter 1:
Gracious In Defeat... If Fairly Beaten!

The sound of hooves thundered on the turf. Two horses galloped around the bend of the track, and as they headed for the final furlongs, a black stallion edged in front. With two sharp slashes of the riding crop, the brown horse close on his hooves accelerated past him. The jockey of the black stallion crouched over his mount, bellowing encouragement. His hooves kicked the turf and with a surge of speed, he nosed ahead again. The whole race course roared. As one person they rose to their feet, the gentlemen tossing their top hats into the air with excitement.

In the grandstand a table went flying, a cut-glass flute and bottle of vintage champagne went spinning in the air as Lady Sally leapt to urge her horse across the finish line. Her maid, despite the encumbrances of layers of petticoats and a huge bustle, jumped and caught the champagne glass in one hand and bottle in the other, without spilling a single drop.

With a succession of savage slices of the riding crop, the brown horse was forced into one final spurt of speed as its nose edged past the finish line. The crowd let out an exuberant roar; never in the history of York Races had there been such an exciting finish.

The cogs and wheels of the giant clockwork course board in front of the grandstand clicked and whirred into action. The letters spun into place until they announced the results of the 1907 Ebor Shield: *Winner–'Pride of Rock', owned Lord Melchiot, ridden Duggleby Howe; Runner-up–'Nemesis', owned Lady Sally Rudston-Chichester, ridden Vaslen Nano.*

"I'm sorry Madam," said Victoria, Lady Sally's maid, a transvestite dressed in a French maid's uniform and tottering on high-heeled shoes. "I know how much you wanted to win the Ebor Shield again this year."

"Yes, Victoria, it's a great disappointment to me. I'm gracious in defeat if I'm beaten fairly, but I believe Lord Melchiot treats his horses cruelly and that makes my loss bitter. It upsets me to see such a splendid beast treated so abominably. I may treat my male submissives in that way, but never an animal," complained Lady Sally turning to her maid and gesturing her to pour another glass of champagne. "Oh and by the way, Victoria, splendid catch! I could do with another drink before we go down to the enclosure."

Lady Sally's jockey, in her ladyship's black and purple silk livery, was leading the magnificent stallion into the paddock, its flawless black coat steaming and its head tossing with the exertion of the race. Lady Sally stroked hair on his muzzle and offered her horse a piece of apple.

"I'm sorry, Mistress," said the jockey. "He did you proud. I really thought we had it Madam. I can't think how the other horse found that last spurt of speed."

Lady Sally looked thoughtful, "Yes, I too am surprised my prize stallion is not the better of any horse at York today."

There was a commotion as the winning steed entered the enclosure, his hind a bloodied mess, covered in deep gashes. The horse was clearly lame, and in great pain. Before the winner's rosette could be put around his neck, the horse collapsed in the enclosure, to the shock of the on-looking race goers. His owner, Lord Melchiot, looked on carelessly smoking a cigar, the winner's takings stuffed in his pocket. Lady Sally's blue eyes narrowed and her elegant eyebrow rose. Oh yes, she'd make him pay for his arrogance.

"Congratulations, your Lordship," said Lady Sally through gritted, pearly teeth. "It's a great shame about the horse though. You must tell me the secrets of your success."

Lord Melchiot looked down at the horse collapsed on the ground with disdain. "I've plenty more where that one came from. Treat them cruelly and make them work for you; that's my motto." He took Lady Sally confidentially to one side, "And some wire spikes wrapped around the riding crop to drive them to go faster."

"How intriguing," replied Lady Sally, expertly disguising her disgust. "But Lord Melchiot, let it not be said Lady Sally Rudston-

Chichester is not a gracious loser. You must come and visit me at Rudston Hall sometime, and we can discuss racing. Perhaps you would be gracious enough to pass on some of your tips. And you must bring along your riding crop."

"Here, have it," he said passing it to her. "I've plenty more where that came from."

"Thank you, that's most gracious of you. I'll be delighted to add that to my collection. But seriously, you must come and visit me. Rudston Hall is a most commodious country house—and its mistress an exacting hostess," she added, a mischievous twinkle in her eye. "Also, I have something I believe will capture your imagination, both as an owner of horses and a person I know to have an interest in mechanisation. My personal artificer and engineer have constructed an automaton horse for me. It's not only a technological marvel, but also a thing of great beauty. You are welcome to view it at any time, your Lordship."

Lady Sally smiled and handed Lord Melchiot her calling card. Her bait had been laid. If that wasn't enough to interest him, she had other means. Lord Melchiot glanced down at the card and noticed the curious coat of arms; a purple and black shield with the letters 'L', 'S', 'R' and 'C' in its quarters, surmounted by two crossed whips, and the unusual title, *Lady Sally Rudston-Chichester, gentlewoman and strict dominatrix.*

He twisted his ginger moustache as he contemplated the card.

"A most intriguing invitation Lady Sally, I shall certainly ponder on it."

Lord Melchiot looked up to meet her eyes, before his gaze strayed down to her heaving décolletage. With that one look Lady Sally knew she had him captured. Oh yes, he would come... and then the fun would start.

Lady Sally gave Lord Melchiot a brief tour of her country residence before they returned to the drawing room for tea. He was impressed

by the quality of the house, grounds, and stables, and also by her workshops, where her team of artificers and engineers were working on all manner of projects, developing clockwork mechanisms.

"Would you like another cup of tea, Lord Melchiot?" Lady Sally asked.

"Yes, thank you, your Ladyship. It has a very distinctive flavour. What blend is it?"

"It's Lapsang Souchong from my own tea plantation in the foothills of the Himalayas."

Lady Sally's transvestite maid was in her element, serving mistress and her guest, pouring the tea, fussing over them, and offering the smoked salmon and cucumber sandwiches (the fish caught from Lady Sally's own river in the Scottish Highlands, naturally), and delicate fancies.

Lady Sally observed how transfixed Lord Melchiot was by her voluptuous figure. She was wearing her crimson velvet dress with a huge bustle and a cameo brooch at its neck. Her black hair was tied up, and perched on top of it was a fascinator decorated with two pheasant feathers. The dress was demure, in its way, but its modesty was belied by the sensuality of the figure occupying it. The dress was cut so expertly that it hugged Lady Sally's hour glass figure. It was the kind of modesty that enticed an admirer into speculating what pleasures awaited beneath the thick velvet. She noticed Lord Melchiot ogling her magnificent bust as she leaned over him with the sugar tongs.

"One lump, or two?" she asked.

"Two, please," mumbled Lord Melchiot.

He held out the cup; from Lady Sally's Ming dynasty tea service. Two sugar cubes plopped into the tea.

"Lord Melchiot, I know you are a gambling man. I will offer you a little wager. I propose a game of poker. If I win, well, you are aware of my predilections, I will require that you submit to whatever punishment I desire. If you win, then I will provide you with a demonstration of my automaton horse. How does that sound, as a wager to make our afternoon a little more interesting?"

Lord Melchiot laughed, "Your Ladyship, that hardly seems a fair deal. Indeed, I seem to recall the offer of viewing your clockwork horse was part of your invitation."

"Of course, you are quite right, your Lordship. I can see I must offer something more alluring to entice you into my game. I shall raise the stakes. If I lose, then I will permit you to take me to my bedchamber and let you have your way with me. It's rare that I offer my body up in this way. Is this not a tempting offer?"

"That sounds rather more interesting," he agreed, his eyes lighting up lasciviously at the prospect of an afternoon of sex with her.

Lady Sally's maid gasped, "But madam..."

"Hush, Victoria, don't be such a fuss-pot. I shall rather enjoy the adrenaline of the risk I think."

"Yes, I agree to your terms—but I will make one stipulation." Lord Melchiot added, "The wager should be based not on one game, but best of five. Anyone can win a game with the right hand and some luck, but it takes skill to win a series. You do know that I'm an expert poker player, your Ladyship?"

"Yes, of course." Lady Sally had done her homework and knew of his prowess at the card table. "I trust those odds would make my proposal more appealing to you. So you will join in my little bet?"

Lady Sally smiled. She knew appealing to Lord Melchiot's vanity would pay dividends. How could he turn down a game of poker with a mere woman? He would be the laughing stock at his club if word got out that he was afraid of losing a game of cards to a weak female.

Victoria produced a pack of cards, wrapped in wax paper and sealed, from her apron pocket and presented it to Lord Melchiot. He opened the pack and spread them onto the table, studying the deck fastidiously to ensure there was nothing untoward with it. It was a distinctive pack, all the picture cards had a leering skull where the face should be, and it was decorated with strange symbols.

"Yes, they are highly amusing are they not? I own a sugar plantation in Haiti and my land agent there has these decks of 'voodoo' cards made especially and shipped back to me."

Victoria dealt, and the two antagonists were soon intensely absorbed in their game. Lord Melchiot won the first two games. Lady Sally observed how he sat back in his chair smugly, confident his skills at the gaming table would exceed hers. It was all the better for her if his concentration was affected by considering what he might do to her if they were to retire to her boudoir. Did he really think she would allow him to win, just so he could boast over brandies and cigars at his club about how he got a dominatrix to suck his cock?

Lord Melchiot had grown over-confident and distracted. He lost the next two rounds to Lady Sally, making the fifth and final hand the decider. Victoria dealt and cards were exchanged from the deck. Lord Melchiot looked smug; Lady Sally inscrutable. He laid his hand on the green baize of the card table.

"Four kings," he announced.

"An excellent hand, your Lordship," she said as she set her cards down. "Four aces. I believe that makes me the winner."

Lord Melchiot was furious at this defeat. He was, after all, a skilled poker player, and he looked bewildered at how she managed to get the better of him. His ruddy face darkened in frustration until it looked as though it was going to burst and his knuckles tightened into white balls. Lady Sally was delighted. It served him right for paying more attention to the swelling of her bosom than what was happening at the card table. Or perhaps he secretly harboured a desire to lose the game so he could submit to her commanding presence?

"First, as I have promised, I will give you a demonstration of my automaton horse. It's an object of which I'm very proud. So, let us retire to my trophy room."

Victoria led the way, opening the teak doors and gesturing them into Lady Sally's grand trophy room. Dominating the room was the life size automaton horse, fashioned from gleaming brass. The magnificent mechanical device ought to have been the main focus of Lord Melchiot's attention but Lady Sally's alert gaze followed his reactions as he surveyed the contents of the room. Yes, he could not fail to register the marvellous automaton but his eyes soon shifted to take in his surroundings.

Where would they alight? Would it be on Lady Sally's trophy cabinets with their lines of sliver cups and bowls acquired from race meets at York, Doncaster, Epsom, Goodwood, and other race courses across the country? Did his look betray envy at the evidence of her equine triumphs? Would his eyes fall on the portraits of the Rudston-Chichester stallions that filled the longest wall in the room? In particular to the huge canvas by the renowned artist George Stubbs of *Nemesis I*, the magnificent black stallion who sired generations of race horses for the family's stables, each horse blacker and sleeker than the other.

No, they didn't. They fell on Lady's Sally's collection of antique riding crops. She smiled. How interesting that he would be drawn to these objects above all others.

"Lord Melchiot, I see you are intrigued by my collection of crops and whips. It is indeed a magnificent assemblage, is it not?" Lady Sally said, gesturing with a sweep of her arm at the implements hanging on the wall in neat rows.

She observed him gazing at the whips with studious interest, "Yes, it's a most excellent collection," Lord Melchiot complimented "I've never seen so many crops in one place."

"It's taken me years to build it up. There are some choice examples of the art of saddlery here. Every item is hand-made by skilled craftsmen and many are antiques of considerable value. You see this crop here," said Lady Sally taking one down from its mount on the wall and slicing it through the air. "This was the riding crop of the Duke of Wellington, used at the battle of Waterloo, no less. I have my favourites of course."

She showed Lord Melchiot a whip with the head of Nefertiti carved in ebony and another with its handle moulded into the shape of a horse's head and a third with a serpent in Celtic design made from the purest silver.

"They are beautiful objects, Lady Sally, I'm most impressed."

"Yes, I can see how intrigued you are by my collection. And it's not just the design and craftsmanship of the handles I admire. I feel there's as much artistry in the canes and straps. You see, each crop and whip is different; each has its own personality, and when I use them I feel the character of every crop. Each one has a different width and flexibility and will deliver its own quality of sting, don't you agree?"

"Why, yes Lady Sally, I'm an aficionado of the riding crop. I believe that, used mercilessly by a jockey, it will drive a steed on to exceptional bursts of speed, as I believe you witnessed to your cost at the Ebor Races the other day," Lord Melchiot boasted as he stroked his ginger moustache.

"Ah, yes," replied Lady Sally, "that was indeed an impressive sprint to the finish line by your horse. And *Nemesis* is one of my finest stallions, one in a long line of pedigree race horses. It would take something exceptional to overcome him. But, 'tis no matter, as I've said, I'm not an ungracious loser, Lord Melchiot. However, I do divert from you on this point, your Lordship. You see, I've never used any of these crops on a horse. I only ever use my whips to administer punishment to men."

Lady Sally observed the look of shock on Lord Melchiot as the full possibilities of his defeat in the bet finally dawned on him.

Chapter 2:
An Excellent Afternoon of Entertainment

Lord Melchiot was furious. How had he allowed Lady Sally to get the better of him? He had grown over-confident and allowed her to get back into the game and, undeniably, he was distracted by her commanding sexuality on the other side of the card table. And the final game came as a shock. He had a winning hand; what were the odds that four kings would be beaten? And now, having lost the wager, he was facing the prospect of having to submit to his opponent. He had mixed feelings about this. Part of him rather desired the opportunity to pit himself against Lady Sally, yet the sadistic glint in her eye and the dark hints at what was to follow unsettled him.

"Come now, I don't believe you could be so naïve as to not realise I will punish you. You have seen my calling card. You must have suspected, surely?"

"Well, yes, I was intrigued by your card, Lady Sally," he muttered.

"Yes, 'tis often the case. Men are fascinated by the possibility of surrendering themselves to a strict dominatrix. I could see that in your eyes, the moment you saw that card, and your gaze diverted to my breasts and shapely frame. Am I not right Lord Melchiot?"

"Yes, Lady Sally, I can't deny that," he conceded. "How could a man not be attracted to such a handsome figure?"

"You see, you are so easy to read. I believe you came here expecting, even desiring, this. I could read your lack of concern on losing the wager. Indeed, I suspect you were quite satisfied to lose it. Am I not right, Lord Melchiot?"

He shuffled uncomfortably, mumbling an acknowledgement. He could not deny he was drawn to Rudston Hall, and into the wager, by the prospect of testing himself against this self-styled dominatrix. And from their very first meeting he was aroused by her; by her stunning figure and the commanding tone of her voice. He had gone away from that meeting curious as to what it would it would feel like to submit to her.

"And you will surrender to my will, I know it; not only because you lost and it would be ungentlemanly not to honour your debt, but also because you secretly want it. Am I not right?"

Lord Melchiot grunted. He felt his face flush as Lady Sally's words exposed his innermost secret desires.

The timbre of Lady Sally's voice rose slightly, just enough to show her displeasure at his refusal to acknowledge her, "I said... am I not right, Lord Melchiot?"

"Yes, Lady Sally," he replied clearly now and in an appropriately submissive tone.

"Excellent, then let me demonstrate the object that will be the implement of torment for you this afternoon."

Lady Sally gestured Lord Melchiot forward to the automaton horse in the centre of the room. It was constructed entirely of burnished brass, which glowed with a reddish hue in the light of Lady Sally's trophy room. The metal on its hind and along its back was smooth and flawless. The horse's features were perfect, almost life-like. The body rested on the horse's haunches where there were a series of smooth plates that hid the mechanism that worked it. The automaton was designed to rock back and forth on its legs with the inner workings hidden behind the plates discreetly placed on the horse's joints.

Lady Sally brushed her painted finger nails along its shiny haunches and invited Lord Melchiot to do the same. He ran his freckled hand across the horse's body. The brass was as smooth as sea-buffed pebbles and unnervingly chilly to touch.

"She's exquisite, isn't she?" said Lady Sally, before appearing to spot something on the surface of the brass. "Victoria, come here."

Victoria shuffled across the room with a concerned expression.

"Look at this," she said pointing to the slightest blemish on the gleaming brass. "You know it's one of your duties to polish my automaton horse. Do you see, you've missed a bit. That's not good enough; the brass must be kept spotless."

"I'm very sorry, Madam. I'll get some polish and do it now, Madam."

"Well, there's no point now, Victoria, is there? In any case, once Lord Melchiot's sweaty body has been on it, it will need a thorough polish anyway." She turned back to him, "It's a wondrous object, is it not?"

Lord Melchiot noted the strange comment but could only gasp in admiration now he had studied the automaton more closely, "It's a beautiful thing, Lady Sally."

He felt his cock twitch with arousal as he wondered how the brass might feel against his naked skin and speculated as to the role the automaton horse would play in her game. Lord Melchiot felt a tingle of anticipation at the ordeal he'd committed himself to.

"She's a mare, of course, designed by my own fair hands as you would expect. I provided the sketches and my arcane engineers set to work on constructing her. I get the brass supplied from my mine in Zanzibar."

"A brass mine?!" spluttered Lord Melchiot in disbelief.

He was no expert in metallurgy, but even he understood this to be an extraordinary claim, though he chose not to question Lady Sally further on the matter as she appeared to be convinced she owned such a mine.

"Why yes, of course; it is a most singular place and very profitable, brass being so much the fashion of the age. You are welcome to invest in it if you wish."

"It's a very fine offer, your Ladyship, but I think I'll decline."

"Well, that's your loss. I believe the productivity of my brass mine has never been higher. Anyhow, my own artificers moulded the brass into the shape of the horse, and my arcane engineers created the clockwork inside that generates the movement. I use only the finest and most skilled craftsmen for my enterprises, as you would expect. I have a vision that one day soon it will be a breed of mechanical horses that race and we will bet on the skill of our engineers and craftsmen. Come, let me show you her inner workings."

He crouched with Lady Sally underneath the belly of the brass horse. Kneeling so close to her; Lord Melchiot could not help but be overwhelmed by the power of her scent and the proximity of her breasts, hidden inside the crimson velvet. Lady Sally unscrewed a plate in the horse's underbelly so she could reveal its inner workings. Inside, Lord Melchiot examined an intricate network of well-oiled cogs and shafts that made the horse move on its haunches.

"By what means is it powered?" asked Lord Melchiot.

"I will demonstrate in just a moment, but first I think it is time for me to cash my wager."

Lady Sally faced him, a riding crop in one hand tapping it menacingly against her other.

"First of all, I expect you to strip naked for me," she commanded. "Victoria, come over here and take his Lordship's clothes for him."

He was nervous. Now the time had come to submit to the terms of the bet, yet there was something about Lady Sally's formidable presence and the tone of her voice that made him need to surrender. The atmosphere in the room was intoxicating and he could feel the swelling in his cock in excitement at what Lady Sally might do to him.

He began to hesitantly remove his jacket and unbutton his shirt.

"Come now, your Lordship," said Lady Sally, using the tip of the crop to lift his chin up, "I expect you to enter into the game with a little more enthusiasm."

He felt Lady Sally watching him attentively as he shed shoes, breeches, and knickerbockers and dropped them into the waiting arms of her maid. He was conscious of her revelling in the removal of each item of clothing until he stood naked before her. He felt exposed and vulnerable. He remained silent as he stood there and Lady Sally ran the tip of her crop down his skinny torso, covered in wispy red hair, finally lifting his swelling penis up with it.

"Look at this object," she said with disdain as she manipulated his hardening cock with the crop. "So, does my presence arouse you, Lord Melchiot?"

"Yes, Lady Sally," he replied, secretly relishing the humiliating treatment of his manhood.

She laughed. "Then it's time for you to feast your eyes on my ravishing presence."

He became a spectator as Lady Sally set about revealing herself in all her dominatrix glory. She removed her cameo brooch and started to undo the ivory buttons of her velvet dress. With the tantalising release of each button, she revealed a little bit more of her flesh, and the attire beneath the folds of thick velvet. First her elegant, milky neckline, then just the hint of the rounded curve of a breast with its exotic phoenix tattoo. Lord Melchiot looked on, mesmerised, unable to pull his eyes away from Lady Sally's seductive display. The undoing of the next button revealed her naked breasts, the nipples covered by pasties with silk tassels hanging from them. Lord Melchiot gasped at the delicate beauty of the deliciously curved orbs revealed to him.

She flaunted her sexual power over him and he could only succumb to it as he gazed on in admiration at her voluptuous beauty. He felt his cock tighten as it reached a full erection.

Lady Sally smiled, "You men are so predictable. There isn't one amongst the male of the species, from street urchin to lord of the realm, who would not be captivated by my ravishing display of dominant femininity."

Lord Melchiot could not disagree with that statement.

With the opening of the next few buttons, the dress parted to reveal the corsetry hidden beneath it. He admired the panels of black and purple silk strengthened by stays of whale bone that pulled her waist in and thrust her breasts upwards. She looked magnificent in her sumptuous and erotic corset.

Lady Sally ran her fingers tantalisingly over the material.

"I brought the silk back from a visit to Samarkand," she explained, "and had my personal couturier make it up. It feels deliciously divine to wear and looks stunning, don't you think?"

Seeing Lady Sally revealed in her corsetry, he gasped and felt his cock throb with sexual tension.

By now, Lady Sally had undone the buttons, pulled the dress off and held it out expectantly for Victoria to collect. She stood there in knee high leather boots with silver buckles, the epitome of the strict dominatrix she was. Finally, she removed her fascinator, pulled out the hair pins and let her dark hair tumble over her alabaster shoulders and breasts. Now she was ready.

"On to the horse, now," she ordered.

"But..."

"I said now!"

Now the moment to mount the horse had arrived, Lord Melchiot felt any resistance to the formidable Lady Sally and her calmly authoritative voice, melt away. He wanted to surrender himself to her. And this feeling was deeper than any mere matter of honour at having lost the wager; he desired it. His need to submit to her was overwhelming.

He stepped onto a footstool Victoria had set down for him and heaved himself onto the back of the horse. The brass was smooth and cool against his skin, and surprisingly sensuous as he felt his hard cock press against the shiny metal. Lady Sally set to work with leather straps and buckles. His ankles were fastened to the back legs of the horse, his arms were hung over the horse's neck, with their wrists strapped together. Lady Sally produced more wide leather straps and pulled them around Lord Melchiot's torso, fastening them onto the horse's back. She stepped back, seeming to admire her handiwork. He could not move and could do no more than surrender himself to the bizarre game Lady Sally had set up and which he had knowingly walked into.

Lady Sally held a shining brass key before him.

"This is what works the clockwork mechanism. It tightens the coils and the springs inside the horse, and when they are fully sprung, the mechanism is released and a gear works the speed of the movement of the horse. It's most ingenious, don't you think? Victoria, will you do the honours please," she said passing the key to her maid.

Victoria lifted up the burnished tail of the horse and inserted the key into its anus, where it slid in perfectly, and turned it. Lord Melchiot heard the grinding of the key and felt the tension of the mechanism as the springs within the body of the horse tightened underneath him.

He was jolted by the crack of a crop against his arse.

Lady Sally laughed; she had stepped back by his side. "Just a little warm-up before I start the mechanical horse."

"That was a warm-up?" gasped Lord Melchiot at the sharp pain from the strike.

"Oh, come now, your Lordship, that was merely a little tap," she laughed, her hair caressing his face as she leaned against him to show the implement she had used, a crop with a piece of spade shaped leather at its end. "This is one of my favourites. It's not really so bad, after all the pad of leather diffuses the strike. A little."

She returned to a position at the hind of the brass horse and gently ran the leather pad against his backside with a sensuous touch before delivering another three hard strokes. Lord Melchiot grunted. The feeling was a heady mixture of pain and pleasure that left him reeling. He knew he could do nothing now other than submit to Lady's Sally's punishment.

He heard a click and a whir and felt a strange sensation of movement underneath him—Lady Sally had set the automaton horse into action. The horse's movement was smooth, quiet, and most disconcerting. The well-oiled cogs and wheels inside its mechanism were drawing the horse's body back and forth across its haunches in a smooth, rocking motion. The sensation against his hard cock as it rubbed against the shiny metal, combined with the delicious punishment from the crop, was arousing. It was like his penis was being masturbated by a cool metal glove. He felt come oozing out of his cock as each motion pressed it hard against the horse's back. He was ready to burst, but tried to hold it back, believing, with justification, that Lady Sally would not be best pleased if he befouled her sleek brass horse with his spunk. With each backward movement the horse lifted it haunches slightly so that the unfortunate rider's backside was lifted invitingly upwards to be welcomed by the crack of Lady Sally's riding crop.

"Hmm, let me try another implement," said Lady Sally, dangling another object before his eyes, taking great delight in showing off her tools of punishment to her hapless victim. "This one is more of a strap than a crop. Do you not see what I mean when I say how each crop has its own quality? This one is made from finest calf skin, I believe. You can see that the width and flexibility of the strap will deliver a different quality of pain."

Lord Melchiot grunted. He felt himself caught in a strange nether world, on the one hand humiliated at his predicament, but on the other secretly longing for it. Suddenly he had acquired awareness of what the term *gentlewoman and strict dominatrix* really meant. Being strapped down with his cheek pressed onto the brass horse, gave him a unique perspective. Lady Sally's breasts, thrust up by the panels of purple silk, were at eye level. He could fully appreciate how the stiff stays of her corset moulded her body into voluptuousness. Stunned by this physical presence, and overwhelmed by the combination of her exotic scent and the smell of the calf skin strap, how could he not submit to her?

"There are several gears, of course," she said, "and I simply must try all of them out on you."

He looked back over his shoulder and saw Lady Sally flick a switch by the horse's tail. The motion remained smooth and even, but the pace increased sharply.

Lord Melchiot watched as Lady Sally steadied herself and lifted the strap high above her head, timing every stroke to perfection so that each raising of his derriere was met with a strike from the strap. He heard the strap slap against his backside and felt its flesh ripple with the force of each stroke. He could imagine how red and sore the skin must look. It was a punishing series of strokes that left him gasping with pain, but a pain tinged with pleasure, and a need to receive more.

Lord Melchiot let out a cry. "Oh no, please, that hurts."

"Of course it hurts," she said firmly. "Come now, my Lordship, let it not be said an English gentleman cannot take his punishment. It's most distracting to hear cries and pleas. If you carry on like that, I'll have no option but to gag you, and I'm sure you wouldn't like that humiliation, would you?"

"No, Lady Sally," said Lord Melchiot.

He forced himself into receiving the ensuing strokes in resigned silence.

He was just beginning to come to terms with his predicament and the pain of the strokes against his arse when he heard a click and whir. He sensed the coils and springs inside the horse release, and the speed of the automaton accelerated again. The brass horse rocked with a swishing sound as the mechanism pulled it back and forth. This was more than slightly alarming as the sudden movement disorientated him.

Lord Melchiot experienced a loss of control as the horse moved swiftly underneath him. This, he surmised, was very different from the feeling one of his jockeys would have when riding, as they were in control of the beast. It was closer to the sensation a rider has when a horse bolts. It was not lost on Lord Melchiot that he had surrendered control to the automaton, whose gears dictated the pace of the movement. Every other part of his body being strapped into immobility he could only respond by tightening his fists. The speed of the motions forced his cock hard against the brass haunches of the horse causing him to grunt. It was a gloriously heady experience as the swift movements propelled him tantalisingly closer to orgasm.

Lady Sally laughed at his predicament. "Yes, it's an interesting sensation, is it not? I use my automaton horse to help train my jockeys. It reproduces that sensation of the surge of speed a refined stallion makes, which is so hard to reproduce, except in race conditions. I hope that cock of yours is not getting too aroused," she added. "I shall be most displeased if I detect any traces of spunk on my horse. Remember this is not being done for your pleasure... but for mine."

She moved in front of him again and the feeling was strange. One second his face was practically pushed against her cleavage; the next it was being driven away from it at considerable pace. Focusing on those beautiful orbs of milky flesh helped him adjust to movement of the horse. He noticed Lady Sally was now holding another implement. She was flexing a long thin cane with a strand of cord attached, which he recognised as a dressage whip.

"Yes, this little thing will deliver a nice little sting, I believe," said Lady Sally. "This is quite a challenge for my skills as a dominatrix. It will require great technique to time the lashes of the whip to inflict the optimum sting."

Lady Sally retired to the back of the horse. Lord Melchiot craned his head around to see her standing well away from it, holding the dressage whip high, to give her enough space to create a long circling motion with her arm. He watched as she assessed the speed of the automaton and the lifting of Lord Melchiot's backside. The tail of the whip came swishing down on his arse, and Lady Sally, skilled as she clearly was in delivering such punishments, immediately achieved a momentum whereby after each strike the long tail circled above her head and came slicing down just at the optimal point as the automaton propelled his backside into the air. He felt his pale skin glow red with the stroke marks. He could see her maid in the corner of his eye watching in admiration at the perfect timing of his mistress.

Lord Melchiot let out a scream of pain. The thinness and delicacy of the whip's cord delivered such a sharp sting he could not prevent himself from letting out a cry despite Lady Sally's strictures to take his punishment with controlled restraint. His head was reeling and his body was aching. The pain was excruciating, but Lady Sally did not relent with the stinging whips of the cord and was concentrating too much on the timing of her strokes to show any concern for his suffering. Yet, strangely, the more strokes Lord Melchiot received, the more he yearned for them as he drifted into a state of mind where pain and pleasure melted into one another.

"That was fun, I enjoyed that," she said when she had finished with the dressage whip. "When I finally release you and let you go home, you must admire my handiwork in a mirror. There are some rather lovely long welts on your arse, your Lordship. I do so love to see that. You see, I like to add some artistry to what I do."

Lord Melchiot's head was spinning with the whirring rocking of the horse and the pain that radiated through his backside, and through his body. Lady Sally's seductive physical presence and commanding tone of voice combined to provide her with an uncanny ability to subdue his in-bred arrogance, and control him. The sheer physical exertion of the whipping sent his head spinning in a whirl, rendering him open to receive any manner of punishment and humiliation which pleased Lady Sally to inflict. He wanted to submit. He was overcome with the desire to give himself up to her.

"I think I'm ready for the final implement, and to run the automaton at its fastest pace. You know, Lord Melchiot, you are privileged, for this is the first time I've had a submissive on the horse at its highest setting. Do you recognise this, Lord Melchiot?"

Lady Sally stood before him, a splendid figure of a dominatrix with her exquisite corsetry and long leather boots. The horse was still moving at some considerable pace, and it took him a while before he recognised the object held out before him as it rushed towards him and then receded again at speed. He had a flash of recognition. It was the riding crop he had given Lady Sally after he had won the Ebor shield, still muddied and stained with the dried blood of his horse. The true purpose of this session struck him. Lady Sally stood there with the crop in one hand and two playing cards, the two of hearts and five of diamonds, in her other. These were the cards which had earlier been replaced with aces by the maid's deft hands whilst Lord Melchiot was admiring Lady Sally's bust. He had been tricked and the full menace of Lady Sally's intent revealed.

He had been duped and manipulated. Though he felt he should be furious at her cheating, oddly enough, it only increased his admiration for her. And the sight of his riding crop brought home to him that Lady Sally had planned everything. She knew he could be enticed to visit her at Rudston Hall, she rigged the card game and always knew she would win it and, lastly, he realised, she planned all along to get her retribution for the defeat of her horse. The whole scenario had been meticulously devised and he had fallen into her trap. He acknowledged Lady Sally had got the better of him and now he faced the final denouement as she extracted her revenge. What a formidable woman she was. She deserved the title *strict dominatrix* and, now, he understood what it meant. He was ready to submit to her and receive his final punishment, a deserved whipping with his own riding crop.

"Did I say I was a gracious loser, Lord Melchiot? Well, that may be true if I lose fairly. Your final, and most severe, punishment will be with the implement with which you so cruelly treated your horse, and cheated me out of the Ebor shield. You see, Lord Melchiot, I don't take kindly to being beaten unfairly, and it's not wise to anger a vengeful dominatrix. I am still too generous, your Lordship, as I have at least spared you the metal spikes you inflicted on the poor animal. This, I feel, will be an appropriate punishment for you, and will give you cause to reflect on your behaviour."

At those words Lady Sally retired to the rear of the horse and moved the switch to its final setting. The gears clicked. Every spring, sprocket, cog, and joint whirred into action to achieve the full capacity of the clockwork mechanism. The rocking movement of the horse accelerated to a speed considerably beyond what any real horse could achieve. The force of the movement pressed him hard against the smooth brass automaton, no longer cool but, as Lady Sally had anticipated, hot and sticky with his own sweat. The speed of the movement was dizzying now as the brass body slid effortlessly and speedily. His cock was no longer erect, the combination of Lady Sally's command not to come, the savage punishments and giddiness caused by the speed of the horse all conspiring to dampen his libido. He was now resigned to his fate. He almost desired the strokes to start, so the pain could distract him from the nausea inducing motions.

However, with the first stroke, he regretted thinking that. Lady Sally had revealed her hand. Her strokes were harsh, vengeful, and relentless. She kept pace with the dizzying speed of the horse, raining down a series of hard whacks onto Lord Melchiot's backside. He gasped with pain. He could feel his arse glowing with heat at each savage stroke. Lady Sally kept her unremitting pace for what seemed like an age. Lord Melchiot wondered how long he would be able to endure, until at last the strokes stopped and Lady Sally worked back through the gears to bring the automaton to a gradual halt.

The transvestite maid unstrapped Lord Melchiot, and he was brought down to his knees before Lady Sally. His derriere was sore and throbbing and he could barely walk with the pain.

"I am returning your riding crop. It's a good implement of punishment, and worthy to be added to my collection, but I prefer you to keep it as a reminder of your unnecessary cruelty and my retribution. I expect you never to use such cruel methods on your horses again. I will find out, of course, and then you will be summoned here again, and you will come, won't you slave?"

"Yes," he said, his mind and body too broken to summon up any more than this mumbled assent.

Her eyebrow raised, her look pierced through him and her voice assumed a subtle but menacing tone.

"Yes, what?"

"Yes, Mistress. Mistress's punishment is fair," he replied, pulling himself together to show he understood why Lady Sally's punishment and humiliation of him was just.

"Indeed, and you will come when I summon you because you have tasted Lady Sally's whip and you will submit to me, is that not so, my slave?"

"Yes mistress," Lord Melchiot acknowledged, completely subdued and kneeling before this formidable woman.

He had been cheated, controlled, punished, and humiliated. But, despite all that, he respected her ingenuity and skill in planning the afternoon's scenario. The title *strict dominatrix* was well earned. The feeling he had after everything was a sense of euphoria. She had gotten inside his head and he still wanted to submit to her.

"Please, Mistress, may I attend you again?" He asked.

"Yes, I think that can be arranged. It would give me pleasure to find yet more ways to punish you. Excellent. You may get dressed now and Victoria will show you the door."

Lady Sally retired to the drawing room to partake of a well-earned cup of tea and a chocolate éclair from her favourite patisserie.

Her maid leaned forward to pour the tea for her mistress whilst Lady Sally wiped some cream off her lips with a napkin. Lady Sally had a self-satisfied smile. It had been an enjoyable afternoon. She had done more than exact her justly deserved revenge on Lord Melchiot, which would have been satisfaction enough, but she had also wielded her power over him. How she loved it when that happened. She got a rush of pleasure from exercising her feminine dominance over men and to have Lord Melchiot so completely succumb to her was a source of great satisfaction. Her control over him was so complete that, by the end, he had willingly submitted to her. Oh yes, she would have some more fun with him when he returned. Having tasted her skills of sadistic dominance, she knew he would not be able to resist them.

Lady Sally turned to her maid, "That was an excellent afternoon of entertainment for me and a most felicitous outcome. Did Lord Melchiot really think he could get the better of Lady Sally Rudston-Chichester? I think he has learned his lesson and is suitably chastised."

"Undoubtedly so, Madam," her maid agreed.

"And I don't think he will risk abusing his horses so abominably again because, if he does, well then, I will get my engineers to add some more gears to my automaton and he'll really get a whipping!"

If you enjoyed this story, you can sign up for a free membership at ForbiddenFiction and discuss it with other readers and the author at the *Lady Sally and the Automaton Horse* story page at http://forbiddenfiction.com/story/sn1-1-000229.

Live Performance at the Grand Guignol

Live Performance at the Grand Guignol

In the hallway of the boarding house, Coral tied her black hair into a respectable bun and covered it with a mini top hat. She smoothed her mauve ankle-length skirts and pulled up her laced gloves.

"Good luck, dearie," said her landlady.

"Thank you, Mrs Cranlow," said Coral demurely before opening the door onto the streets of London. She held back a smile; to her landlady and any strangers she was a respectable woman, and that was how it would stay. The bad times were over: her beginning at Madame Chavelle's, the times she found herself penniless on tour with theatre companies. She knew the looks the other performers gave her the morning after a night of fundraising on filthy streets. Well, no longer. Now she was a real actress in the *Grand Guignol*.

She had seen the *Grand Guignol* only a few times, once in the original Paris theatre. She and the other patrons had made their way down a terrifying, dark, cobbled street to *Le Théâtre du Grand-Guignol* to be tortured with spectacles of graphic violence, raving mad women, and rivers of blood. It was wonderful; everyone was breathless when they left and spent the rest of the night reliving the more gruesome parts.

She stepped daintily between clumps of horse muck, hansom cabs, growlers, and street vendors wailing the latest headlines. Men tipped their hats and women offered uncertain smiles. *They have no idea of who I once was*, she thought. *If they knew the things I had done they wouldn't smile at me so. If they knew I had performed in one way or another—from Italy to America—they wouldn't offer such pleasantries.* Still, she thought with a flutter of pride, all that was over.

Past the costermonger's vegetable barrows she went, and past the butcher's dangling meats. Past the piano tuners and sweet shops she marched until she reached the dark streets of Soho. She passed Caldwell's dancing rooms, a nightly haunt for the working men and women of the area, quiet as a stone at this hour. A pickpocket boy circled a group of lost looking gentlemen unaware of his advances. It was this small side road she needed. The winter sun was weak and the air filled with choking smoke, and the path looked as though it could do with some gaslight already. Excitement and fear fizzed in her blood like lemonade and she stepped down the dark alley towards the peeling doors of the theatre.

Two men stood on a vast stage at the far end of a gaslit room, a younger in a grey frock coat and striped trousers and a mutton-chopped older fellow. They turned to her as she shut the door. The place smelled of a grandmother's house. Or of how Coral imagined a grandmother's house to smell, having never had one.

"Ah," said the younger man, leaping to the floor and striding towards her, "here comes our dear sweet Nancy, cut down in her prime by the brutish McHaggard."

"The very same," Coral curtseyed, playing along. The man before her was fair haired and tall, handsome and self-assured, with a small beard and moustache. She had met those like him a thousand times before, and failed to resist their fleeting charms just as often. This time, she told herself, would be different; the box office doors would remain firmly closed.

"I was just saying to Old Albert here, it's not quite Drury Lane, is it?" The young man grinned at her. "My agent was not entirely forthcoming with the facts, it seems."

"Oh, really?" said Coral, "mine was quite honest." So excited had she been at a change from burlesque comedy that she had practically forced her agent to let her audition. With those flimsy pieces, she often felt she had only to walk onstage and utter the words "private parts" for the audience to fall about laughing.

"Well," said the older gentleman, "it all adds to the effect. This is *Grand Guignol*, after all, not the Royal Shakespeare Company. The original theatre in Paris measures its success by how many people have fainted." He lowered his voice for the last few words, infusing them with drama.

"Indeed they do, and I hear tell they have boxes beneath the balcony to rent for those whose passions have been... aroused." The fair-haired man leered at Coral and she decided it wouldn't be difficult to keep away from him after all. She turned away in disgust, delighting in his shock. Evidently he had mistaken her for another type of lady. The older man spluttered.

"Well, that sort of thing may be acceptable in France but it is most definitely not going to occur here, just a good clean performance."

The younger man bellowed with laughter, "Yes, good clean strangulation, mutilation, and murder."

Coral couldn't help but laugh herself, and the older fellow straightened his waistcoat and offered to show her around. "I am Wilfred Hodgkins, and this fellow is our resident murderer, Richard Morris," Mr Morris tipped his hat. "Now, the audience this type of fair can get somewhat rowdy; are you certain you can take it?"

"Oh, yes," Coral smiled. "You'd be surprised at the things I've seen." Morris' ears virtually pricked up and Coral inwardly chided herself.

"Er, quite," said Mr Hodgkins. "Now, if you'll come this way."

The stagehand platforms above the performers looked none too safe, and the ropes and pulleys were coated in dust. The stage itself was tall enough to protect them from grasping hands in the front row and very wide. The changing rooms were the actor's water closets, luckily at least separated into ladies and gentlemen. The previous floral wallpaper had almost peeled off completely, revealing the dank wall beneath. Coral hid disappointment that her newfound respectability looked very much like her old, squalid life, but she assured Wilfred she'd be quite at home.

By the time she had changed into her Duchess costume of inexpensive ruffled material and glass pearls, two more murder victims had arrived with baskets of clothes. One was another young woman, Maud, who changed into a bawdy house dress and the other, Penny, would play Coral's elderly aunt. Both women were more theatrically experienced than Coral, despite Maud being younger. Coral's earlier pride deflated like an old balloon. Waiting for them onstage was Hodgkins in a policeman's outfit and Morris in a long black velvet cloak. Coral decided to forgive his earlier insolence, unwilling to engage in any more backstage squabbles.

"Let the rehearsal commence," bellowed a dandy with large, curly, dark hair from a seat in the front row—the director, Mr Hill.

The first run-through was a painful experience. Each actor at some point forgot several lines, and the trapdoor Morris would spring from—to surprise Maud—creaked like an old man's bones. "That," boomed Mr Hill over the giggles, "will be oiled tomorrow; just please ignore it for now."

The murder scenes were practiced next and Maud giggled shamelessly while Morris' hands crept about her. When it was Coral's turn, she remained professional, ignoring his rough fingers and close proximity. However, when Hodgkins pulled him from her during the arrest scene, the phantom of his body was still on her for some time, and the look he gave her as he strutted back to the changing room invaded her thoughts that night.

The second morning Coral rose early, with a mind to be the first one there. She made short work of the kedgeree breakfast while her landlady wittered on about her relative's cholera. Truly, thought Coral, we could be having the most darling conversation about flowers, and as soon as food is before me it's death and disease.

"You want to get out o' that acting game," the landlady flashed her brown teeth, "find yourself a nice husband before it's too late." Coral smiled politely, ignoring the indigestion burning her throat.

She caught the early omnibus but, of course, Hill and Hodgkins were already there. She couldn't help but feel a sense of childish glee when she saw how impressed they were by her early appearance. Rehearsal began as usual, all atop the stage reciting lines and practicing blocking, and then something odd happened.

A knock came from the front doors, softly at first, and then insistent. Hills opened up, revealing a messenger boy holding tightly onto a missive. It was, no doubt, one of his first and he swelled with pride when handing it over. Hills paid the boy a farthing and read aloud, "Richard Morris." A storm brewed on Morris' face, and he strode at once to tear into it. Gradually his composure was punctured and he seemed to wither, until finally he looked like an uncertain young boy.

"God damn them all," he bellowed, making for the men's changing rooms. The others followed him and Coral heard the handle turn again and again, but he had locked himself in.

"Morris," each person called in turn.

"Morris, my love," Maud ladled honey onto her voice, "why don't you let me in and I can help you?"

"Morris!" yelled Hills, "we have a play to do."

Every second he didn't emerge was another second Coral felt herself falling back into Madam Chavelle's. She tried to breathe calmly, to assure herself that he simply needed a moment or two, but after half an hour she had nail indents on her palms. She flew to the room and pounded on the door. "Morris," she barked, "we have a show to do; come out this instant." To everyone surprise they heard the lock draw across. The door opened slightly and they glanced at each other, unsure of what to do. Maud pushed to the front expecting to walk straight in, but opened her mouth in shock when a croaky voice issued from within.

"Where is Coral? I want to speak to Coral." She laughed nervously at the look of hatred burning from Maud.

"Come," said Hills, "let them speak and we shall rehearse the scene where Duke discovers his wife missing." They tramped towards the stage, Maud staring back as she went. Coral sighed, unsure how she had gotten mixed up in trouble yet again, and stepped inside.

On seeing him hunched in a wooden chair, his head in his hands, all her anger dissipated. "What's happened?"

"My wretched family," he held out the note, now ragged and bent, "has announced their intentions to do for my allowance. If I," he read from the page, "insist upon keeping close quarters with misfits and ne'er-do-wells, I must support myself while doing so." Here he placed his head back in his hands.

Coral bit her lip—that was all? Every day folks avoided the workhouse by any means necessary, and he was afraid of surviving on a performer's wage? Still, she couldn't help feeling sad at his helplessness, and the thought of him doing his parent's bidding by leaving the show terrified her.

She placed a hand on his shoulder and he gripped it with his own, tickling her inner wrist with his thumb. Her body, asleep for so many months, sparked with life. She knew she should leave but she didn't. Instead, she let his fingers stroke her arm beneath her sleeve. Surely she didn't want this job so badly that she would debase herself again? No, she thought as she wrapped her arms about his head and lowered her lips to his, I would debase myself because I simply want to.

He unbuttoned his trousers while she lifted her skirts, sliding down on his erection. Desire hit her like a feathered whip and they sighed together, she writhing against him while he gripped her rump tightly. Too long it had been since she felt such heat, such wetness between her thighs and such pleasure. She pulled his hair and he moaned as she rode him faster, faster, until too quickly she felt the satisfying tingle swimming inside her.

She removed herself from his lap and straightened her skirts. The situation at once seemed horrifying. The others were efficiently rehearsing and, once again, she had snuck into a dark corner with a man. Morris grinned like the cat in Alice's Adventures in Wonderland and it repulsed her. "We are never to speak of this again."

"We're not?" His face again resembled the lost child.

"I am a respectable woman," she said, hearing a jeering audience in her head as she spoke the words.

"I'm a respectable man," he shrugged.

"Respectable men and slumming dandies are two very different things." She regretted her sharpness once she saw the hurt in his eyes.

"I, too, am simply trying to make my own way," he said coldly, throwing the door open and striding onstage. He embraced Maud, who smirked at Coral. Coral looked away, eager to begin her scene. She reasoned that the hollow feeling in her stomach was nothing but disappointment in herself, and nothing to do with the kiss that Morris planted on Maud's lips or the need she still felt between her legs.

"Well done," Hills whispered; "whatever you said worked marvellously."

In the two weeks that followed, Morris and Maud's open affections managed to offend almost everyone's sensibilities, except for Mr Hill, who didn't care as long as they remembered their lines and turned up on time. "You're a good girl, aren't you," muttered Penny to Coral one afternoon whilst eyeing the giggling couple in the corner, "not like that strumpet."

"Youngsters," griped Hodgkins, "They have no sense of propriety." By the same token, Coral was delighted at the ease with which she now lived her life. There were no desperate lovers' scenes, no guilt over the pain she caused the wives of her male co-stars and directors, and nothing to distract her from her work. Despite this, she couldn't help the sting she felt when Morris shared secrets with Maud in the corner, and envied the flush of the other girl's cheeks that was so like the one she must have had on the second day. Morris' response when he noticed any outrage was to tip his hat and grin, confirming Coral's first opinion of him.

On the day of the dress rehearsal, he approached her. She had been the first to change, and now watched the stage hands clear the room of dust. "Won't you join us at the Crown for refreshments later?" He was the Morris she had seen in the dressing room, defenceless, somehow smaller.

A thousand replies circled Coral's mind, but only the correct one left her lips, "I'm terribly sorry; I must be at the boarding house by a reasonable time or I'll be locked out."

He nodded slightly, shifting his focus onto the wall to appear nonchalant, "Very well." At that moment Maud appeared with Penny, the younger girl's venom apparent when she saw the two step apart suddenly. Coral wanted to shout at the girl that he was all hers, that she had more important things to concern herself with, but instead she made her way to the spot on stage where she would be murdered after her husband, the Duke, discovered her missing from the parlour.

In the changing room, Coral's hands shook, pricking her lobe as she inserted the pearl earring. She replied when spoken to by Penny and Maud and laughed on cue, but all she could think of was the audience waiting in their seats. Would they simply laugh? Would they think she was terrible? She ran her hands over her skirts to rid them of their terrible clamminess. "Of course," said Maud, "at the Old Vic, there was a much larger audience. We could hear them calling for the show to begin all the way down the hall; it was terrifying!"

"It was the same when I toured with the Dulston players," said Penny, not to be outdone. "Oftentimes it was the same faces night after night; that's how loved we were."

Coral tried to shut out their voices, but they became a roaring steam train. She had to get away, to find a quiet place just for a few minutes. "I won't be long," she muttered, not caring that as soon as she left they would strip her bare with acid tongues.

The hallway outside the changing rooms was cool and peaceful. She leaned against the wall and closed her eyes, thinking of nothing except her warm bed which waited for her at the end of tonight. She jolted when the door to the men's room opened. Facing her was Morris. She considered slipping back inside but decided to remain where she was. "I thought you might be Maud," he whispered.

"Sorry to disappoint." Coral wished she didn't sound so bitter.

"Far from it." He reached out to touch her arm. Coral frowned at the impropriety, but didn't move.

"What would your sweetheart say if she could see you now?"

"It's nothing more than a fleeting thing."

"I'm not sure she agrees. I believe she has intentions to marry."

Morris huffed and rested against the opposite wall sullenly. "She isn't the one for me. Could you see me introducing her to mother?" He grinned wryly, but also a little sadly.

"I don't think you could introduce me either." Coral wasn't sure why she said it and promptly wished she hadn't. Morris looked her full in the eyes.

"It wouldn't matter," he said, leaning towards her. Silence followed while they gazed at each other. Coral wanted to speak, to say something, but the changing room doors opened and the others emerged, and it was too late. The others rushed to head for the stage while Coral darted back into the room to check herself in front of the mirror. Before leaving she pulled up her skirts and, for reasons she couldn't quite explain, removed her pantaloons. The very gesture made her flesh tingle, and she revelled in the air between her legs as she made her way behind the curtain.

Blinking against the limelight machine in the wings, she took a breath when her cue was spoken and stepped onto the stage. The men cat called and the women shrieked with laughter. The Duke—

Mr Hill—waited. She swallowed. Her mouth was dry. "Husband, are we to remain indoors day and night 'til the murderer be caught?"

Quiet fell over the onlookers until Morris made his first entrance. The Duchess—Coral—argued angrily with her husband and ran out into the night—stage left—where she passed a working girl. Maud savoured every innuendo, tipping the wink and rolling her hips, provoking whistles and shouts. Coral saw the girl's anger towards her and felt an odd thrill.

"What's that?" Maud whispered loudly. "Does someone approach? Anyone wishing to sample me wares?" The audience responded vocally and Coral took her cue to hide behind a papier-mâché bush upstage. Morris burst through the trapdoor, filling the theatre with shrieks. He flung his black cloak from his face revealing kohl-rimmed eyes, whitened skin, and smears of blood. He looked ghoulish, but passion for his role burned in his eyes, further wakening Coral's sleeping senses.

Pig's blood and meat covered the stage, and Maud's screams sent sharp pains through Coral's ears. Maud slid to the ground more dramatically than a real corpse, and Morris' eyes met sharply with Coral's. She was dizzy when he grabbed her, feeling both his eyes and the audience's tickle her skin.

"Oh, help me, help me; I have been so foolish," she cried as his fingers closed about her throat. They sank to the floor, her skirts crumpling around her thighs in the struggle and Morris' black cloak covering them both from the shoulders down. She feigned fighting weakly as the Duke and the policeman began their scene to the right.

Morris's left hand was about her neck while the other slid beneath the cloak to her waist. Coral tried not to think about his fingers on her hip bone, his breath on her ear lobe, or the gentle flower scent of his pomade.

"Your wife is missing?" boomed Hodgkins in the parlour. "Why, she may be being murdered this very second." Morris' hand crept lower, tickling the flesh of her thigh. Coral glanced out to the audience, but the lights were too bright to see anybody's reaction. What would they think if they knew what was happening? Would she be finished as an actress? Or arrested, even?

Her nipples hardened into points. She shifted slightly to allow his hand further access and she felt his breath on her face quicken.

Elsewhere, Penny arrived in the Duke's parlour revealing a gory missing eye, but the only thing Coral was truly aware of was Morris' fingers stroking the wet lips between her legs. His touch rolled back and forth over her clit, and Coral pursed her lips to keep from moaning.

Heat rushed to her cheeks while Morris' finger traced its way over her hardening button. She rocked her hips as gently as she could, finding it harder and harder to hide the paroxysm building inside as the sensation bubbled up from Morris' fingertip and flooded throughout her body. She groaned, unable to stop herself, though the other actors continued their performance.

"We must find the brute!" declared the Duke, and Coral was pulled back into her situation—Morris would be pulled from her to reveal her skirts crumpled about her waist. They appeared all too quickly, grabbing his shoulders.

"No!" cried Morris, resisting their violent wrenching. Coral attempted to make her face a mask as, beneath his cloak, they both pulled her skirts as hard as possible. Coral felt as though she would burst into flames with horror.

"Come, fiend, your time is up," yelled Hodgkins for the second time, he and Hills seeming concerned that their target refused to be caught.

"Yes," hissed Hills, "the fiend's time is up."

Morris was dragged from her, leaving her a crumpled corpse on the ground, her dress safely hiding any sign of misdeeds. Hills picked Coral up and carried her into the limelight, weeping and wailing theatrically. It was all Coral could do not to laugh.

The room thundered with applause and the actors bowed, Coral's body limp with relief and her thighs aching deliciously. They filed offstage congratulating each other. In the corridor Maud clung to Morris; "You were wonderful, darling."

"Yes," he grinned. "You were superb, yourself."

Maud sashayed into the dressing room, leaving them alone. Sense told Coral to follow the other girl and leave him behind, but she faltered, watching the door close. "What are we to do?" said Morris. Coral turned to him.

"I don't know." She couldn't think of anything else.

"I need to see you again." It was a line she had read many times in books, yet now she sensed the heaviness of its meaning.

"We have no future," she said.

"I've no need of my parent's money; we'll make do."

Coral raised her eyebrow. "We both know that won't happen." Morris looked down at his feet. "Will you meet me in the churchyard behind the theatre?"

"Yes." He left for the men's changing room and Coral entered hers, smiling merrily at Maud.

If you enjoyed this story, you can sign up for a free membership at ForbiddenFiction and discuss it with other readers and the author at the *Live Performance at the Grand Guignol* story page at http://forbiddenfiction.com/story/ms1-1-000242.

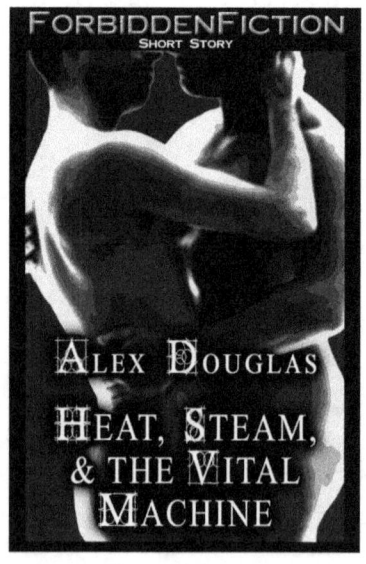

FORBIDDENFICTION
SHORT STORY

ALEX DOUGLAS

HEAT, STEAM,
& THE VITAL
MACHINE

Heat, Steam, and the Vital Machine

Chapter 1:
What Hides in the Dark

We only had three hours of light today, but that's okay; I'm used to the darkness.

Two paces from the bed and I'm at the wall touching the bar where my uniform hangs, freshly pressed from the launderer, smelling of faded flowers. It's the one thing I don't like about my job. Every night I have to squeeze into this thick, blue material and button the shirt and coat right up to the neck. It feels just a little bit like being strangled. The machine I'm responsible for guarding is hot, and I often have to walk right through its sighs of steam, returning to my cubicle in the morning almost completely saturated with sweat and damp and mad with itch.

I adjust my hat and smooth the fluff from the front of my coat before grimacing at myself in the mirror to check that my teeth are clean. In the dim emergency light, my cubicle looks smaller than ever. Just a single blue-covered bed that's a good seven inches too short for me; a small table to one side and a metal bar at the foot that stretches from one wall to the next, upon which I hang my spare uniforms and few free time clothes. The toilet hides behind a blue curtain, and on the ceiling I've stuck an old poster that Perri drew for me when we were still in primary education. A curly-haired boy and dark-skinned girl touch heads while they draw eights in the sand with their fingers, and behind them the sea stretches far away. Over the years, the colours have faded completely, so now it's just outlines. The blues and yellows are just a memory, but I love how much space Perri has in her imagination, since neither of us has ever laid eyes on the beach, or the sea for that matter.

It's good to know that one version of me has seen the sky, at least.

After giving my boots a quick once over with my cuff, I'm ready for duty. I lift my ID and hang it around my neck. The door opens automatically and I step out into the dark corridor. My heels clink against the metal as I make my way along, past the doors of all the other single people who live on the bottom tier, to the locked door at the end through which only I and the other guards can pass. It still excites me, the fact that I have access to an area that many others don't. On our recreation days, when I first started my job, Perri used to beg me to tell her about the machine, but now she's lost interest because as huge and wondrous as the machine is, it is unchanging.

Perri's been my friend for as long as I can remember. Our friendship works because she likes to talk and I like to listen. She works in another restricted access area, where the cataloguers copy and preserve old books. Like most other precious things, books are rationed to the public, but she tells me some of the fragments of the stories she gets to read. She's an expressive storyteller; her gestures and excitable voice open for me these gateways to ancient and wonderful worlds. People ask us when we'll have a baby, but that's the sort of thing people always ask when they see a man and a woman together. Maybe we will someday; it's our duty after all.

My thoughts turn to the night ahead as I swipe my card at the thick metal door and hear a click before it creaks open, and I step into the moist, dark cavern. My heart's starting to beat a little harder as the lock slams into the rock once more behind me. Keeping my hands on the rails of the walkway, I close my eyes and let the hot and humid air fill my lungs with the smell of scorching oil, as if the machine is greeting me. After so long in its clanking presence, I feel like we've become intimate. I know all the secret spots where it wheezes when it's tired, where the cogs click more slowly than they used to and where the thick metal cords are fraying; I know where the tubes are too hot to touch, and where it feels just right to flatten my palm against it and let the vibrations surge through my body.

It's a thing of chaotic beauty for sure, but I have no idea how it works. That information is on a need-to-know basis, Zhan likes to say, as if he's one of those who knows. But even I can see that the engineers will eventually run out of space to make their modifications and additions. What then? I tug fruitlessly at the itchy neck of my coat with a sigh and a shrug. Such problems aren't for me to solve, for I haven't the brains. But I'm powerful and tall which makes me an ideal guard. We all have our place and until recently, I've been content with mine.

I follow the walkway to a convergence where the other guards are assembled. We nod greetings to each other and I notice a new recruit among our ranks. A scrawny youth, red hair already plastered to his cheeks and neck with sweat, is gazing around goggle-eyed. I learn that his name is Gahan, and his presence brings our number to ten. It's nowhere near enough to be effective against the Saboteurs, but we do what we can and leave the engineers to do the rest.

Zhan, our captain, fills us in on the locations of the latest non-functioning components so we don't waste time filling out forms unnecessarily. Then he nods a cursory welcome to the new guard before running through the alphabetically-organised duty roster from his usual position on top of a box. He's shorter than everyone else and compensates by wielding the little power he has in a ferociously pedantic manner. I'm not afraid of him, but I defer all the same; there's no point making life more difficult than it has to be.

I'm the last on the list. "Zakkary, James. Sector 3." Zhan tucks his clipboard under his arm and begins the little speech I already know off by heart. "Be vigilant, one and all. If you see evidence of sabotage or its perpetrators, tread with caution. These people are armed and dangerous and our priority is to protect the machine from harm. But it's also vitally important that we learn how they're getting in so first cue, then pursue. And good luck."

Trying to hide my sudden happiness at my night's assignment, I turn towards the flight of steps that will take me to the long and lonely walkway around the bottom of the machine. Sector three means I'll be completely alone, and won't intersect with any of the other patrols. It means the freedom to dawdle and pause, and most importantly it's the darkest sector and most vulnerable to attack. Zhan usually sends people down there as a punishment. If there's no one to be punished, it's usually me. Perhaps because I'm bigger and stronger than all the others, and Zhan wants to have some muscle where it counts.

The muttering of the others fades as I descend into the belly of the cave. I'm hot now, hot with excitement and anticipation of the night ahead, hot in my belly and groin as I've been every night for months.

I'm the only guard to have caught a Saboteur, and I'm not planning to let him go anytime soon.

From the walkway I can reach out and touch the damp walls of the cave. It's noisier down here, right at the base. The machine is smooth on the outside, but something's battering away inside the metal. They say this is the oldest part, and that back in the early days the machine was small and compact, not the behemoth it is now. It gives us most of the energy the complex needs to function, and filters out the toxins from the air we breathe. It's why it could never be switched off. I pause to stretch and press my hand against a panel covering one of the sections Zhan mentioned had gone dark. Still warm. I whisper words of encouragement, feeling stupid even though no one could possibly hear me through the noise. Unable to build a new one, the engineers just have to keep tinkering and adapting. Some of the new additions are thanks to me as well, when I suggested that the machine should have some dummy gears and levers to fool the Saboteurs.

The Overseers were pleased with my idea and gave me extra light in my room and double dessert tickets for a whole month.

I turn a corner, feeling my skin tingle with excitement. It was here that I saw him for the first time, crouched over a small pipe with a wrench in his hand to harm the machine, much as a flea bites an ankle. All Zhan's warnings about armed and dangerous people flew out of my head. My vision clouded with rage at the thought of someone damaging the machine I'd almost come to think of as my own.

He didn't hear me approach until I was almost upon him and when he stood up, I launched myself and grabbed at his body. We thudded down on the metal walkway together, me on top, panting with effort as my hat rolled off into the darkness. He didn't seem afraid of me. He'd rolled his balaclava up so he could breathe more easily in the heat, and as I glared down at him through the steam and the dim light, I saw him smile.

He had a curved, sensuous mouth and a few days' growth of dark stubble on his strong chin. He was shorter than me, but wiry and slippery, and I pinned his wrists at either side of his head with difficulty. Fighting for purchase, I drove my thigh between his. He moaned as he continued to struggle beneath me until—to my shame —I felt my cock grow hard. He must have felt it too, because his smile grew wider and he stopped struggling suddenly, and parted his legs. My body slid into the space and I ground against him, trying to maintain my hold. But his skin was damp with moisture and my palms were hot and sweaty and eventually he twisted his wrists from my grasp with a triumphant laugh.

I expected him to claw at me, to gouge at my eyes, and I was about to put up an arm to shield myself. Time seemed to grind to a halt as we assessed each other. His eyes were dark and lined with thick lashes, slight crinkles at the corners that told me he smiled often. He murmured something and took my face in his hands, closing the distance between our lips in a second. I froze in momentary surprise. Unused to such intense physical contact, I found that the struggle had unleashed a passion inside me that I'd long since thought was dead. I was panting, alive, cock hard and burning in my pants – a flesh and blood man, not a piece of the machine I'd almost come to see myself as. At the firm touch of the Saboteur's lips against mine, desire swept through my whole body, burning away the guilt and shame. He smelt of sweat and oil, a tangy masculine aroma that rose intoxicatingly from under his clothes.

I kissed him hungrily, tearing at the shirt he wore until his heaving chest was half-exposed. Breathless, I took a moment to gaze at his perfectly-muscled chest, dusted with thick dark curls. His skin glinted gold in the dim light and I took a long, delicious lick over his nipple, savouring the taste of his fresh sweat and the tickle of his hair against my chin. His back arched and he groaned, then he kissed me again and worked his hand between our bodies to rub at my swollen cock through the rough material of my uniform. It had been a long time since I'd had sexual release with anything other than my hand and each of his hot kisses seemed to suck the sense from my mind. This dark spot was as good a place as any to find release once more.

I could always arrest him afterwards.

Fumbling mindlessly at his pants I freed his cock and balls and then my own which mashed against his almost painfully. I shifted into a more comfortable position and the feeling of the two cocks together, hard and leaking against our clothes, was incredible. He pulled up my jacket and his shirt until our hot bellies were just flesh on flesh, then he wrapped a hand around our dicks and began to move it up and down. His palm was as rough as his cock was smooth. I found his mouth again as my hips began to move with him and he gasped and grunted, clearly as lost in the moment as I was. It didn't take long for me to come, crying out helplessly as I soaked his belly. He wasn't far behind and we lay where we'd fallen together, gasping.

When I rolled off him, he buttoned his pants and kissed my cheek before stumbling off into the dark. Clever boy. I was in no state to pursue him. As my senses—and breath—returned, I eased myself up slowly and dusted myself down, bewildered by the maelstrom of feelings that had seized me and ashamed that I'd failed so utterly to do my duty to protect the machine. I re-adjusted my uniform as best I could and felt about the material for any tell-tale stains of what I'd done. As I fixed my fallen hat into position, I touched the machine apologetically and vowed to it that if I should ever run into that Saboteur again, I would surely do the right thing and bring him to justice.

The next time I found him, he didn't even have any equipment. He was waiting for me in the dark and fell to his knees before me before I could even speak. All thoughts of arrest flew out of my head as he sucked my cock into his hot mouth, and his tongue was so wickedly agile that as I roared my release into the all-engulfing noise of the machine, trembling at the knees, I vowed never to make stupid vows again.

He's not always waiting for me; there are nights when I pace up and down and around the walkways and find nothing, like tonight. By the fifth hour of my shift, my heart begins to sink and my pace slows to a dawdle. I still haven't figured out how he's getting in and out of the cavern. They say there are tunnels, built long ago, big enough for a man to crawl through. Zhan was all puffed out like a rooster when we managed to find one, and it was blocked up pretty fast. But still the Saboteurs keep coming.

As do I.

The next day is a recreation day. I used to look forward to them, but now they're little more than time to kill before my next shift. I get up late and wander to the shower room, where I scrub myself hard as if I can wash last night's disappointment from my mind. As usual, I've arranged to meet Perri for lunch in the canteen. There's nowhere else to eat so we make do with what we have. There are hydroponic gardens in some other part of the complex that I'm forbidden to enter, and the produce is usually fresh and delicious, if not exactly copious in quantity.

Today there are roasted vegetables on the menu, as well as the usual pack of powdered supplements to be dissolved in water. Perri and I sit together as far from everyone else as possible,and I ask her what books she's managed to read since the last time we met. She tells me about a page they've found, tucked away inside another book. There's a list of items handwritten on the back—potatoes, carrots, condensed milk, digestive biscuits and tea. She's very excited about the list because it tells us a lot about how people used to live.

"Can you imagine eating all that at the same time?" She curls the tip of her black braid around her finger with a wistful sigh. "I wonder who wrote it, what they were thinking at the time. It's not often we find these relics, but it's amazing all the same. Isn't it? To think that it's someone's actual handwriting. A real person wrote it, sat there and planned an everyday meal on a piece of paper! And to think that person's long dead and yet to touch the impression of their pen on paper… it gives me shivers. You know what I mean."

"Wonderful," I agree half-heartedly, my mind still patrolling the machine, looking for him.

She sighs and pushes her empty plate away. "What's up with you these days, James? You're even more silent than usual, and that's saying something."

I sip my drink. "Nothing's *wrong*. I'm just… restless. It gets boring, doing the same thing all the time at work."

The lie slips from my mouth easily. If what I've been doing comes to light, I'll surely be imprisoned for treason. And that'll be *after* the Overseers are done making an example of me. The thought of a public flogging should rouse me from this madness, but it doesn't, somehow.

"Yeah, I get that. I worry about you sometimes, you know. You're always so *alone* at work, pacing around that machine again and again with no one to talk to, but I suppose you can't talk, can you, in all that noise. I'm so lucky with my colleagues, they're a great bunch. There's a guy I work with, quite good-looking. Actually, I thought you should meet, so I told him we were going to be here so he might join us. I hope you don't mind."

Nice colleagues. I think guiltily of the new guard. It never entered my head to befriend him. Then again, I've always believed that guard duty appeals to like-minded people. Those of us who get sick of the constant presence of others and listening to their banal chatter; men and women who don't like being monitored and bossed about, who enjoy solitude and the time just to think and dream. I have little interest in meeting this colleague of Perri's—it won't be the first time she's tried to set me up, and we clearly have differing opinions on what constitutes *good-looking*, but when he finally shows up she gives him a warm hug and ushers him to sit beside me so she can look at both of us.

"So James, this is Luca. Luca, James. Now we're all caught up, didn't someone say they had some spare dessert tickets?"

I glance sideways at Luca. He looks a few years younger than me, slender and dressed casually as Perri and I both are, in patched grey sweatpants and a white t-shirt. His hair is black and curly and his eyes are blue, like my uniform. His cheeks are pink from a recent shave and he smells of soap. His handshake is dry and firm.

It's only when he smiles that I realise who he is.

I stare at my hands, stunned, willing myself to show no reaction as my body begins to respond to his close proximity.

"Nice to meet you, Luca."

It sounds as if someone else is speaking, someone terse and unfriendly.

"Likewise," he says, and moistens his lips with the tip of his tongue.

The same tongue which, not four nights previously, had been lapping at the streams of spunk that jetted from my swollen cock into his mouth.

I focus on Perri and dig my wallet from my pocket. "I have some extra dessert tickets."

She snatches them from my hand joyfully. "Great! Double sweet softies, coming right up!"

When she's gone, Luca leans closer and whispers in my ear. "You have no idea how pleased I was when Perri mentioned she was best friends with one of the guards. When she said you were so tall you needed to stoop in your own cubicle, I *knew*. God, I was so happy. I've been angling to meet you properly for ages. We need to talk. Do you want to come to my place?"

"Yours or mine, it doesn't matter."

I don't want to *talk*. I want to strangle him for appearing in my perfectly ordered existence and throwing it all up in the air like dice that haven't landed yet. I want to punish him for making me feel as if my life isn't good enough as it is; we're all supposed to know our place and be happy with it. Most of all, I want to fuck him senseless, right where he sits. But I do none of those things, and when Perri comes back to the table with her tray groaning under the weight of multiple softies, I take mine and lick the creamy drops from the side of the glass and go about eating it, deliberately not looking at Luca because I don't know if I could control myself if I saw him doing the same.

Perri chats away brightly, apparently oblivious to the tension between us. When we've finished eating, she returns the tray and suggests going to the games room to play cards. I decline, feigning exhaustion after my night shift. She doesn't seem surprised, and says she'll see me again same time next recreation day.

I don't stay around to find out if Luca's refused her offer too, because I'm sure he will, and I know he'll be knocking on my door soon enough.

Chapter 2:
What Hides in the Light

He steps inside with a shy smile and glances about. Suddenly I'm conscious of how bare my room is. I lift my dirty uniform off the bed and toss it into the corner. There's no chair so I sit down on the mattress and pat the space beside me, which he fills gracefully.

"So talk," I say.

He clears his throat. "You can't imagine how much I've wanted to talk to you, but that damn machine is so noisy."

I shrug an agreement. I'd certainly found it hard to talk to him, since my mouth was otherwise occupied on every occasion. Our little fingers are almost touching and I can feel the warmth of his skin radiating against me.

"You're probably wondering why we do it."

"Sabotage the machine? The thought had crossed my mind."

He takes my hand and touches his lips against my palm. "I'd rather show you than tell you, to be honest. You're on again tomorrow night? Bring a change of clothes if you can. I'll be waiting."

That's all I want to hear. I pull him into my arms and kiss him. His mouth opens like a flower and a helpless groan escapes from me as his tongue touches against mine. I realise that I don't care why he does what he does. I only want to know that he'll be waiting for me in the dark, in the heat and the steam and noise.

I pull his t-shirt off and run my hands over his chest, tweaking his nipples and brushing my fingertips through the springy hair. Now I have proper light, I can really enjoy the incredibly arousing sight of how he melds to me, how his gorgeous body responds to my touch almost involuntarily. His pupils are enlarged, his breathing shallow and his cock is starting to tent his sweatpants.

"James," he murmurs, stroking the side of my face tenderly.

"What do you want?"

He smiles. "Everything."

Even though we have all night to be together, I skip the preliminaries. The aching need to be joined to him at last is so strong that my hands tremble as he hands me the little jar of oil he's got in his pocket. He watches me with heavy-lidded eyes and a half-smile on his face as I get him ready. Then he rolls over and I straddle him, pausing to stroke his shoulders, to admire the sweep of his spine and the faint outline of the muscles at his sides, as my slippery cock comes to rest inside his crack.

His buttocks are firm but pliable under my fingers as I slip inside him and he lets out a groan. I spread his cheeks so I can drink in the sight of his hole stretched around my cock. He whispers something and I lean forward to hear it, buried inside him to the root. He's so warm and tight I'm glad of the distraction because I have a feeling I won't last long.

"What did you say?"

"*Ssh*. Just fuck me. Hard."

Then, with a distant whine, the power dies and we're in the dark.

He spreads his legs and I slip between them, remembering our struggle the first time I encountered him. He's not struggling now, just pushing back against me as much as he can as I begin to move. Trying to prolong the pleasure, I force my mind away from the wonderful sensation of his muscles clenching around my dick and listen to his quickened breaths, the stream of whispered expletives and the sound of my balls slapping against him. I ease myself forward so our whole bodies are touching, and nibble and lick his ear. Like one of the pistons on the machine I begin to fuck him hard and rhythmically until I feel my orgasm building deep inside, then it travels through my balls to an explosive climax that wrenches a cry from my lips as semen bursts out of me in great waves of excruciating pleasure.

When the blinding passion fades, the strength drains from my muscles and I flop on top of him, still buried deep inside of his body. He's mine now, and the feeling of possession is a clench in my guts. I know I can never let him go now, no matter what he does.

And the most wonderful thing is that the feeling appears to be mutual. With so few of us around, folk settle for what they can get. Someone they can tolerate or learn to like. I can't believe I'm so lucky to have found Luca, even if he is an enemy of the people.

When he finally rolls over to face me, I feel his warm breath in my face and the heat of his palms cupping my face as he kisses my nose, my forehead, my cheeks. My mattress is alternately damp and wet from our sweat and his semen. He hooks his leg idly over mine and I touch my forehead against his. Unable to see him I content myself with stroking his face tenderly, feeling the emergence of stubble on his cheeks, the sweep of his upturned nose, the softness of his full lips.

Mine.

The next morning, the light comes back on, and Luca excuses himself to go to work.

He pulls back the blue curtain and lets me watch him shower. The water travels over his firm body, and I wish fervently that there was room enough for two, because I would love to trail my tongue over the little rivulets that wend their way through the hairs on his chest and then sink to my knees before him to catch the stream of water pouring off his cock. When he's done he towels his hair vigorously and then grins at the sight of my burgeoning erection.

"Four times wasn't enough for you?" he says with a laugh as he begins to pull on his clothes. "Don't forget what I told you about tonight. Change of clothes. I'll be waiting."

Reluctantly I watch him leave, knowing that if I get up to kiss him goodbye he'd be in danger of getting flung onto the bed and fucked once more. The Overseers don't like it when we're late for work. Ignoring my hard cock, I turn off the light, determined to get another few hours' sleep so I'll be wide awake on my night shift.

When I finally get to work—wearing my change of clothes under my uniform, which is now tighter than ever—I learn that last night, while Luca and I were fucking to blissful oblivion in the darkness of my cubicle, something terrible happened. I stand with the other guards, open-mouthed, as Zhan gives us the grim details.

The new guard, Gahan, encountered a Saboteur while on patrol. In the subsequent scuffle, he plunged over the railings. Presumably to his death, because he was on a set of stairs a good thirty yards above the base of the machine.

They haven't managed to recover his body.

It must have been an accident, surely. In my bones I know that Luca would be as horrified as I am. He couldn't possibly support the killing of men who are just doing their job. Could he?

And to make matters worse—now we are to make our patrol in pairs.

"It's for your own safety," Zhan says, tucking his clipboard under his arm with a sigh. "Pairing you as partners certainly diminishes our ability to monitor the machine for Saboteurs, but on the other hand my priority has to be your safety. Remember Gahan if you see any of these traitors, and spare no effort for their capture. You will be rewarded."

There's a muttering among my colleagues. Their faces are stiff with shock and fear. They shuffle their feet as Zhan goes back to the safety of his guard room, leaving them in the dim light and noise with the prospect of meeting a murderer on what should have been a routine walk around the machine. I'm assigned to patrol with Mak, who's fifty-something with a substantial paunch, ten-to-two feet and the worn-down expression of one who's unhappily partnered. He looks as thrilled as I am to be assigned to the upper level where Gahan met his death.

"Fuck this," he bellows into my ear as we step upwards, away from the others. "I've got a daughter to think about."

I turn to him and hold out my hands in a what-can-we-do gesture, my eardrum ringing from his shout. His shoulders are slumped and it seems to be an effort for him to climb the steps. He grips the handrail with a glum expression on his reddened face. My heart's thumping with trepidation and sweat is already starting to run down my back thanks to the extra clothes and the heat emanating from the machine.

Luca's not expecting two of us. What if—despite his apparent apathy—Mak decides to be a hero? What if Luca simply melts back into the shadows and I don't see him at all?

Hours pass and my heart is in my boots. There's no point trying to ease the tense boredom with conversation amid the noise. As we reach the top of the steps for the third time and turn the corner onto the long walkway ahead, a movement ahead catches my eye.

He's there, in the shadows at the end of the walkway.

I look sideways at Mak, but he obviously hasn't noticed, grumbling to himself under his breath as he walks with his funny feet splayed out. While he's obviously not the fittest of men, he's certainly not stupid. I consider what's about to happen with some anxiety. There's no way Luca could convincingly overpower me unless he has a weapon. Fervently, I hope he has thought to bring one. It'll certainly spur Mak into a run—hopefully in the opposite direction. I feel helpless as I walk, dragging my feet, worrying the whole time.

Does Luca know I've seen him? Is it even him, lurking there around the corner in the dark? What if it's not Luca at all, but the actual murderer?

I'm so preoccupied with anxiety that by the time we reach the corner that I barely notice the black-garbed figure springing out from the shadow and swinging a length of pipe in my direction. My shoulder takes the brunt of the blow which then glances off my head. It's not a powerful hit, but it's enough to hurt. Mak shouts something and begins to back away. The pipe swings again and I duck, hearing it clang against the handrail. Just then the machine emits a huge sigh and blows steam around us, and for a second all I can see is Luca's slim body in black, shrouded in white. Clever boy, perfect timing. He knows the machine almost as well as I do. Under the cover of the steam he grabs me and pulls me ahead and out of the cloud. I glance around and see that Mak hasn't followed me in.

"Run!" Luca bellows and I sprint after him until we're out of my partner's line of sight.

It's almost pitch black here, close to the cave wall at an intersection of the walkways. I can't see what lies beneath us, always assuming it was a steep drop down to the bottom of the cavern. Luca throws down his length of pipe, vaults the handrail and clings to the other side for a second. "Follow me," he mouths, and relinquishes his hold on the rail before dropping down out of sight.

I take a deep breath and climb over. It's just a couple of meters onto flattened rock. My ankles jar for a second and my eyes stretch wide in the dark as I look up at the walkway I've just left. Any guard walking around it would be blind to what lies beneath.

Clever, very clever.

"Uniform off," he shouts into my ear, and I oblige. It's a relief to get the scratchy, tight material off my body and there's a breeze coming from somewhere that cools the sweat on my skin. Luca takes my uniform and ties it to the underside of the walkway before taking my hand and planting a brief kiss on my palm.

"You hit me, you asshole." I'm only half-laughing.

"You can take it, big guy. I have faith in you."

Then I follow him.

It's one of those tunnels they talk about, barely big enough for a man to squeeze into on his hands and knees. It's dusty and stale and my knees scratch against the rock as the noise and the heat of the machine fade behind me. Now all I can hear is Luca scrambling along ahead and—completely blind now in the dark—I crawl along after him, trying to ignore the feeling of claustrophobia. I'm used to small spaces, but not ones that press against my back and knees at the same time.

Eventually he stops, and I find that we're in a shaft of some sort, where I can stand up to my full height, which I do with a groan of relief.

"Where are you taking me?" I ask him at last.

I can hear his smile in the dark. "Up."

"What do you mean, *up*? There is no up from here. Unless you're talking about..."

"The surface."

I let out a disbelieving laugh. "Don't be ridiculous. The air is toxic. We'll die."

"Do you trust me?"

Contemplating his question for a moment, I find that my answer is yes.

There's a ladder behind him. The metal feels rough, and I'm sure that when I can see again, I'll find my palms covered in rust. Dust falls into my face,making me sneeze, but we carry on up for a good thirty yards before Luca pauses and I hear him grunting with effort. A crack of dim light appears above us and he flings the trapdoor back with a slam and a final squeal of hinges.

We climb out into another tunnel, but it's not as dark as the ones I'm used to down below. There's a definite breeze now, which lifts my hair from my sweaty forehead. Luca takes my hand again and leads me off to the left where the tunnel is starting to widen. The air is dry and dusty, and I notice two lines of metal cutting into the rock and running along beneath our feet.

"What is this place?" My voice has a strange echoing quality to it, which reflects my state of confusion pretty well.

"It was a mine, once."

We reach an apparent dead end where there has been a cave-in and rubble lies all about. Agile as a cat, Luca begins to scramble up the boulders and just at the top there's a small space big enough for an average man to squeeze through. I'm not an average man, however, and Luca almost has to dig me out by clawing at the rocks and pushing them away so that they clatter down back into the tunnel. "You're a big bastard," he says, puffing as he hauls me out.

"You weren't complaining about that last night," I say, then the smile fades from my face as I finally see what lies all around me.

I'm *outside*.

Shocked into silence, I fall to my knees as I look up at the sky and take a lungful of the gloriously fresh air. It's not toxic at all, and I don't die. My ears tune into unfamiliar musical sawing sounds coming from the grasses that grow high all around, and movements in the sky catch my eye.

"Are those birds?" I say weakly.

Luca sits down beside me. We're at the top of a high hill looking down at a spread of green. The sky is a rich, dark blue and the scenery before me is like nothing I have ever seen. It's as if someone has thrown a fuzzy green blanket over a series of spikes which rise jaggedly from the land ahead. The hills around us slope down majestically to the sea, which is a luminescent line of shimmering blue far in the distance.

The sea.

"Oh," I say, completely overcome with the desolate beauty of it all.

He puts his arm around me and holds me tight. "It was a city once, what you're seeing. Those were buildings, taller than you could ever imagine. The air hasn't been toxic for a very long time, that's what we learned from some leaflets we found, tucked away inside a book that someone wrote about a hundred years or so ago. The Overseers wouldn't allow them to be copied."

"But why?"

"They were old and afraid it wasn't true, and unwilling to risk lives by sending an expedition to the surface. Now the new ones are young and afraid and won't listen. You know the rumours, James. About how the machine isn't working anymore, and how people aren't having babies like they should. We're dying out down there, that's the truth. And they know it, the Overseers. That's why we've been trying to sabotage the machine. If they realise they have no choice, then we figured they would have to send an expedition someday. And the sooner, the better."

He falls silent as a bird lands on a rock just a few yards away. It's sleek and black, and surveys us with a cocked head and a beady eye, obviously unafraid. I hold my breath and hope it'll approach but it decides we aren't interesting enough and flies off into the sky.

Luca leans his head against my shoulder. "We could start again. Couldn't we? We could live here, on the surface, like we were supposed to. Wouldn't you like that? To see the sky every day? Can you imagine what it would be like to have the sea swirling around your feet and the sand between your toes?" He sighs with obvious longing, and I know that he's been imagining those very things for a long, long time.

My eyes scan the green expanse ahead, hungrily drinking in in the shapes of the trees, the beautiful colours of the earth beneath me and the shimmering sea ahead. Everything's so bright I have to squint a little. It's one of those moments that couldn't get any better. I pluck a handful of grass and breathe in its scent. I've never been so powerfully happy in my life.

Then Luca whispers in my ear. "I think I might love you, James."

I was wrong—those moments can always get better.

I turn his face to mine and plant a soft kiss on his lips. "I'd certainly live in a pile of rubble, just to be with you."

He laughs. "You've got such a way with words."

I take his hand and we sit together on the dry stony earth, gazing out at the ruins of the long-dead city and daring to dream. The sky is brighter now and some clouds have appeared above the earth, grey and streaked with pink and orange. And then the horizon begins to crack and a dazzling orange lights up the sky, casting a glow across the tops of the trees. A cloud of distant birds swoops and glides in stunning formation and I shield my eyes against the brightness and the beauty. It's almost too much for me to bear, but I hang on, my hand clasped almost painfully in Luca's. The gentle wind dries the tears on my cheeks as the sun, like a tentative lover exploring a new body for the first time, lights up my skin and my soul, and warms the world beneath with its sleepy morning rays.

If you enjoyed this story, you can sign up for a free membership at ForbiddenFiction and discuss it with other readers and the author at the *Heat, Steam, and the Vital Machine* story page at http://forbiddenfiction.com/story/ad2-1-000295.

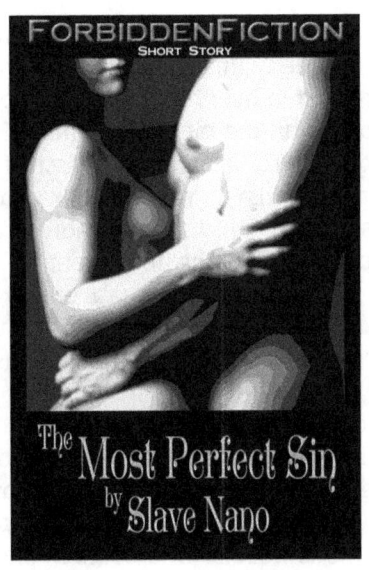

ForbiddenFiction
Short Story

The Most Perfect Sin
by Slave Nano

The Most Perfect Sin

The Most Perfect Sin

"Is God not omnipotent? Is God not all powerful? Yea, fellow creatures, how can you deny this self-evident truth? So, if it is thus, is God not everywhere and in everything? Is God not in this tankard of ale that I sup? Is God not in the pipe that I smoke?"

The notorious Ranter, Tobias Coppe, was in full flow. *The Flask Tavern* in Southwark was his church, the oak table he stood on his pulpit and the assortment of drunks, whores, and travellers, his congregation. He commanded the full attention of the revellers in the inn with the passion and persuasiveness of his voice. He preached with an arrogant swagger that had the wenches swooning with lust. His words were met with uproarious approval by his audience.

There was only one Puritan family who, looking on aghast from a discreet corner at the rear of the tavern, muttered their disapproval. They may have sided with Parliament but were now bemoaning how civil war and King Charles's be-heading had led to this explosion of radical and blasphemous beliefs. One of them slunk out of the door to alert officers of the army.

Tobias Coppe had his audience hanging on his every word. A lock of luxuriant brown hair framed his handsome features. His shirt was unbuttoned down to his navel to reveal a hairless but muscular torso. His breeches betrayed a bulge that was testament to the virility of his manhood. This was only too evident to the wenches gathered around him eye level with his bulging cod-piece. He revelled in the lust in the young women's eyes and warmed to his task.

"And doth it not follow, therefore, that God is in my cock. And that God is in your cunt. And when my tail is stiff, is that not godly? For whatsoever is done with the spirit of God inside us, is that not good and godly? And when a prick doth penetrate a quim, are we not rejoicing in God's love? For doth God not love his children unreservedly, sinning as well as praying. Indeed, art those most perfect which doth commit the greatest sin with least remorse!"

The crowd roared in appreciation at Tobias's proselytising.

"Yea, show us your cock Tobias Coppe! Let's see one of God's works," laughed one of the wenches.

The call echoed around the tavern, "Yea, let's see it, Tobias!"

"You want to see it doth thou? You want to see my quimstake?"

"I don't just want to see it, I want to suck on it!" screamed one of Tobias's buxom admirers.

"If it be God's will, then so be it!"

Tobias's hands reached down to his groin and he unbuttoned his breeches. He pulled the crotch apart and lowered his knickerbockers and a thick veined cock sprung out to the collective gasp of the crowd. Even his Ranter friends looked on in alarm that he would really go that far, whilst the group of Puritans could take no more and left in disgust.

The tavern wench was true to her word. She ran her fingers along the hard flesh before grasping the prick in her fist and closing her mouth around its tip, gorging herself on the erect penis with gusto. Her red head bobbed up and down as she sucked on his cock enthusiastically whilst Tobias Coppe attempted to continue his Ranter sermon to the raucous cheers from the crowd.

"Oh yes! I can feel the power of the Lord's spirit filling me. Ah, yes... All power and all acts are from God... Ooh... yes, yes. So there is no act whatsoever that is sinful before God. Oo, yea...! What act soever is done thee in light and love is godly. Ah, yes, yes!"

There was a commotion at the inn door. An officer from Cromwell's New Model Army, his sword raised, burst into the tavern accompanied by two pike men. The woman, in the midst of sliding her lips up and down Coppe's hard cock and anticipating the spurt of come into her mouth, was disturbed by the burst of activity. Reluctantly, she pulled her lips from his prick. On the point of reaching his climax, Tobias was frustrated at having his pleasure curtailed so dramatically. He hastily pulled up his breeches and was in the process of buttoning them up as the officer strode towards him.

They faced off against one another, and the officer was about to drag Tobias off his perch to arrest him when their eyes caught and a flash of recognition was exchanged. Before the officer could lay his hands on him, Tobias leaned forward to make a quiet, but impassioned, plea in his ear.

"John Thomas, for surely it is you. My fellow creature and friend, hath it come to this that you'd arrest a comrade in arms? Didst we not stand together at Marston Moor against the king's army? Didst we not listen to the Levellers at Putney and dream of a new order where all men wouldst be equal before God? Didst we not celebrate with tankards of ale when the king's head rolled into a basket? There was a time when we believed God's Kingdom could be built on earth, here and now! When didst you lose your faith my friend?"

"Aye, Tobias, I still carry the scars from the scrapes you got me into – the musket-shot wounds and the bruises from drunken tavern brawls," John Thomas replied.

"Ah, but would you really have it any different, my friend? And don't forget all the wenches we fucked!"

"Aye, that's true! Things have changed, Tobias. I've a wife and children now. I've a commission in the army. But look, for old-times sake, I'll give you a chance. I'll give you a couple of minutes to get out of here, but then you're on your own."

Coppe seized the opportunity offered by his friend by pushing him in the chest. John Thomas staggered and fell backwards against his men, sending them crashing onto the stone-flagged floor. In a fleeting moment, the Ranter leapt off the table and made a dash for the door beyond the bar, leaving behind a tangled heap of bodies, pikes and swords.

He escaped into a passage, hoping to find a means of escape into the dark alleyways behind *The Flask* but was thwarted. The passage only led to a staircase, the upstairs gallery and the guesting rooms of the inn. He had no choice but to take that route and trust he could find somewhere to hide, but the corridor was a dead end, leaving him trapped. He heard the muffled calls of the pike men from downstairs. In seconds he would be captured. He had no choice but to hide in one of the bed chambers.

He threw open the nearest door and closed it behind him, hoping there would be no guests using the chamber and that he could escape out of a window and onto the roof tops. But facing him was a four-poster bed, and in it a young woman who hastily gathered up the bolster to protect her modesty. Her bright blue eyes conveyed her surprise but also her curiosity.

"Sir, how dare you intrude on a maiden's privacy."

Before Tobias could reply, there was a bang on the door as one of the soldiers called out, "Open up. We're searching for the Ranter who goes by the name Tobias Coppe."

Coppe cast an imploring glance across at the young woman. His fate was entirely in her hands. One word from her and the soldiers would burst into the room, and he'd be arrested.

"No, you may not enter!" she called out. "I am in a most immodest state of undress and it wouldst be wholly inappropriate for you to come in. I would not permit any of the ranting sort in my chamber sir. I can assure you of that."

"Sorry to disturb you, my lady," replied one of the men.

Tobias listened as they shuffled along the gallery to the next bedchamber. He turned with respect to the young woman, still sat bolt upright and startled in her bed, the cover wrapped tightly around her chest. She was certainly a lovely young woman with a peach-like complexion and long fair hair that fanned over the pillow.

"Thank you, madam. I am in your debt. May I ask the name of the young woman who hath saved me from gaol?"

"It's Chastity. Chastity Clarkson."

Tobias smiled, "With that name, I wouldst guess you come from good Puritan stock?"

"Yes indeed sir, that would be true. My father is a wool merchant from Norwich and is in town on business with my brothers," she explained.

"Ah, I believe I did spy them in the tavern. So, it wouldst be your brother who sneaked out to fetch the soldiers to get me arrested. And I was in the midst of such an inspirational sermon on the nature of God's love... and so close to its climax!" Tobias laughed.

Chastity leapt to the defence of her brother, "And no doubt with good reason, sir. I can imagine what vile blasphemies you wouldst be preaching."

"What doth you know of what I believe?"

"Why, I understand well what you are. My brother was lately an officer in Parliament's army and hath spoken to me of some of the strange beliefs he encountered amongst the soldiers there. I know you are profaners; that you believe in free love, excessive drinking and swearing. I'm not so naïve that I do not know you preach debauchery and blasphemy."

Tobias put on his most charming and persuasive voice, "Indeed, much of what you say is true my lady, for I enjoy all the bounties of life. But that is because my spirit dwells with God, sups with him and feeds with him. My humanity in God rejoices in the company of my fellow creatures, and since we are all equal in the eyes of God, yes, why not publicans and whores."

It was one thing to have your cock sucked by a drunken harlot in a tavern, but to seduce a young Puritan maiden, to persuade this sweet and virginal girl that sex was a godly and beautiful act, now that was indeed a challenge worthy of a Ranter. He flung off his jerkin, kicked off his boots and jumped onto the bed beside her.

Her heart was racing. What should she do? This attractive man was full of the experience of life and love, and so charismatic. And the smell of him, now he was sat next to her, was so gorgeous and manly. She could not bring it on herself to order him off her bed any more than she could betray him to the soldiers when she first saw him burst into her bedchamber. She was confused and had never had feelings like these for a man before.

She clung onto the coverlet, shielding her womanly charms ever tighter but did nothing to ask him to leave, saying warily, "Keep your distance sir, I would not have you come so close. My brothers are in the adjoining chambers and I would rouse them if you attempt to take liberties, sir."

Coppe held his hands up in innocence, "Chastity, I would only ask for the chance to explain, for I believe you misunderstand me and my beliefs. The terms profaner and fornicator are unjust, my lady. For looking at you, I see God's gift of beauty before mine very eyes. Hair of corn field gold and eyes of cornflower blue and a complexion of such pristine beauty, you are a wonder to behold."

Chasity gazed on as Tobias reached out to stroke her hair and run his finger down her cheek.

Her heart was thumping at the familiarity of his words and touch but hugely flattered at the same time. She should order him to stop, yet she could not.

"Doth you mock me, sir?" she gasped.

"No, far from it, madam. For herein I see the work of God. Doth you not see it? For, in you, I see God's image, so why would I not desire what God hath created?"

He took her hand, prising it gently off the bolster, and pulling it towards his lips.

Chastity did not know where to put herself, so she tried to protect herself with words.

"But this is merely lust, sir, and lust is a sin, one of the seven mortal sins. If we succumb to this then we must surely be condemned to eternal damnation."

Chastity sat-up in her bed transfixed as Coppe rolled back the coverlet to reveal her buxom frame wrapped in her night gown. She reddened, conscious of the attentive gaze being directed at her heaving breasts under the folds of material and her own anxious panting.

"But wherein lay that sin, my lady? For when God is in man and nature, then heaven and hell are in the hearts of men. Then this sin is merely an imagining. Come, tell me where will I find this thing you call sin?"

He leapt off the bed, took up the candlestick and held it under the bedstead.

"This sin, is it under your bed? Is it in you chamber pot? I see no sin here."

"Now I really do believe you are mocking me sir," she replied, but with laughter not indignation.

He jumped back onto the bed, "A believer cannot commit an unpardonable sin if his conscience is with Christ and God. If this is sin on your rosy lips, then let me kiss it off for you."

At this, he leant over, cupped her cheeks in his hands and planted a kiss on her lips. Their lips pressed together eagerly and with a passion on Chastity's part that disconcerted her. She felt her resistance to his charm draining away, so tried to muster another argument to ward him off.

"But what of the devil sir? Doth you not fear eternal damnation if you succumb to temptation?"

"Yes, but the devil couldst do no evil at all if God didst not first give him the power to do so, and, therefore, the devil is not so much in the fault. For if God is omnipotent, why doth he permit evil? There can be no such thing, for the devil is an invention of man. For if not, then the devil and evil must be part of God's plan, which cannot be. So there is no judgement or eternal damnation; that is a mere fiction so men can oppress other men."

"Yes, but...." Chastity mumbled as her defences, both intellectual and physical, started to crumble before her.

Tobias leaned across and kissed her again, this time with even greater passion, his lips pressed tightly against hers as his tongue explored her mouth. Chastity lifted her hands around his back and pressed him closer to her. Whilst locked in this embrace, her resistance melted away. It was only when their lips parted again that her conscience gnawed away at her, nagging that this was against everything she'd been brought up to believe; that such sensual pleasure for its own sake was immoral.

"I wouldst see your naked body in all its glory if thou wouldst permit," whispered Coppe.

"But sir, surely this is sinful, for should not my body be saved only for my husband, for the one to whom I will be joined in the eyes of God?" Chastity protested half-heartedly, whilst secretly wishing he continue.

"But Chastity, my love, are we not all wedded to God and are not all men and women already wedded to each other through him?"

The argument was hardly necessary because, even as he was speaking, Chastity yielded and lifted her body up to allow Tobias to pull the night dress over her head until she was before him, entirely naked. Her feelings were confused. She felt wonderfully liberated yet still had a twinge of guilt.

Tobias nuzzled her neck. He gradually worked his way down to the arc of her swelling breasts with gentle kisses that sent a tingle shooting through her. The first kiss planted on her breast aroused feelings of desire and need she had never experienced before.

He gently guided her down onto the bed. Chastity noted Tobias's admiring gaze as he looked down upon the curves of her breasts and the porcelain-like delicacy of her skin. He stroked her softness with his fingers. He was the first man to gaze upon and touch the delights of her flesh.

"I cannot help but feel this is wrong, that I should lay here unclothed beside you, that this is an offence to the principles of modesty and virtue," said Chastity in a reflective mood, seeking assurance rather than objecting.

"You should recognise your own beauty. This is how God made you. You should rejoice in the glory of His creation. Didst not Adam and Eve stand together naked in the Garden of Eden?"

"Yes, but they fell from grace because they yielded to temptation."

"But if we accept God's grace, we can return to that place before the fall of man by permitting the spirit of Christ into our flesh. If we canst but do this, then we can resurrect God's kingdom here on earth. But to attain that state we must receive God's spirit openly in us without guilt or remorse and reject the mere fabrications of men."

Throughout this discourse, Tobias stroked Chastity's flesh, cupped her breasts in his hand and placed his lips all over her body, drawing ever closer to her most intimate parts. She yearned to feel his bare flesh against hers, and he instinctively responded to her need, pulling off his shirt, dropping his breeches, and idly tossing them onto the floor.

Having his naked body lay so close to her enflamed Chastity's desire. The physicality and smell of him next to her stirred the ardour of her passion. His physique was perfect, his muscles so strong and toned it reminded her of a statue of a Greek God. She reached out to touch his body. Yet there were flaws, too, that were testament to the full life he had led; a healed wound on his arm and a long scar down his side.

"How did you get those?" she asked.

"In the late wars, fighting for Parliament against the king. One is a musket wound, the other a cavalier's sword from the battle of Naseby. Doth they upset you?"

"No," Chastity replied as she ran her finger along the sword scar, across Tobias's back, "In truth, I am drawn to them. They are part of you and the history of your life. I admire your bravery."

He pulled her close, and their lips joined again. They wrapped their arms around each other and gloried in the touch of flesh upon flesh. When their lips separated, they lay in one another's arms gazing, in silence for once, into one another's eyes. Her look strayed down to his crotch. She reached out and took his erect cock in her hand. He expelled a gasp at her touch.

"And this is your manhood?" she asked, fondling his cock with curiosity.

"Yes, indeed it is lady. And a godly tool it is, too!"

"You must tell me how you want me to handle it and if I do anything wrong, for this is the first male member I've ever held in my hand."

"Oh, my love," he gasped," I would not believe that if you had not said, for your touch is so exquisite."

She wrapped her fingers around his hardness and rubbed his glans, her touch taking Tobias to a new level of passion.

"It fascinates me," she whispered, "it feels so strong and hard in my hand. I love its roughness and the thickness of the veins."

She toyed with the pulsing object gripped in her hand and was amazed to witness the reactions of Tobias as his breathing got heavier and his eyes glazed over in ecstasy.

"My lady, your touch is so arousing that I fear I will spill my seed over your fingers at any moment."

He unwound her fingers from around his cock, laid her down on her back and crouched over her, his face over her fair pubic hair.

"Permit me to show you how to receive pleasure, my love."

At that, he kissed around her pubes, nuzzling her wisps of fine hair with his lips. She moaned with longing and desire.

"Doth that not feel like the spirit of God?" he asked.

His finger parted the folds of her flesh to seek out the bud of pleasure that lay within them. Having found it, he touched it with the tip of his finger and pressed it against her pelvic bone. Chastity groaned with a euphoric, sensual feeling that was a revelation to her, her modesty having never allowed any man to touch there before.

"How can you deny that this is not godly?" he whispered.

"I don't," she gasped, "Really, I don't, my love. Please touch me there again."

He did, and Chastity moaned with desire. He leaned over her and buried his face into her muff, rolling his tongue against her clit to the sound of her squeals of pleasure.

"Wouldst you have me inside you? I will not do this without your say, for I will not enter you without you truly believing this act is noble."

"Yes, I want it, Tobias. But reassure me; let me hear your discourse. Did not God mean this act only for procreation, not for earthly pleasure? Tell me I'm not committing a mortal sin if I allow you into me."

"God is that pure and perfect being in whom we all are. That secret blood of his breath courses through our blood, yea into the veins that feed my cock. Do not fear, Chastity, for when we do this act, we return to God again to be swallowed up in him as a drop is in the ocean. And this pleasure is part of God's design for us."

"That is all I need to hear. Then I want you, Tobias Coppe. I want your manhood inside me."

He mounted her gently and eased himself into her cunt. There was a moment when Chastity expelled a gasp as he penetrated, but she only pulled him further into her until his cock nestled comfortably inside her. And when her cunt was filled and she felt him moving inside her, it felt glorious. It really did feel like God's spirit was within her and all her doubts were dispelled.

She allowed her body to move with his in pleasure, for all Tobias said was true, that an act uniting man and woman so closely in loving feeling could never be a sin in the eyes of God. And when he finally spent himself into her, she gripped tightly onto his body as it shook with his climax. She delighted in feeling the strength of his body against her and the ejaculation of his life force into her.

Chastity believed that once Tobias had released himself into her and withdrawn, they would finish, but that proved not to be so. He lay beside her and turned his attention to her needs by seeking out that nub of flesh in the folds of her sex that had given her so much pleasure a few moments ago. He rubbed it with the tip of his finger, gently at first, and then more vigorously, until a feeling of urgent need for relief welled up in her. And when it was released, a wave of euphoria burst out from her with an intensity that was overwhelming. So this is what she had heard preached against. These were the feelings she had been told would condemn her to eternal damnation. She no longer believed it could be so.

Tobias clung to her naked body to feel the final ripples of her climax against his flesh. After these had subsided, they lay there in one another's arms, exhausted and spent; their bodies sticky with sweat and sex. They held onto one another in a tender embrace.

Tobias looked upon Chastity with respect. He had intended a simple seduction of this lovely Puritan girl as a challenge, but his feelings for her were spiralling out of control. He admired her for the cut and thrust of their argument and her willingness to debate new ideas; though, he wasn't expecting her to embrace them so openly. He was taken aback by the enthusiasm with which this supposedly chaste Puritan maiden had entered into her seduction by boldly grasping his member. Her touch was so instinctive and exquisite it had left him gasping with arousal and aching for release. By the end, he was pursuing her not only for the carnal pleasure but because he liked her and desired her. How many women had he been with? Too many to recall – there were tavern whores he'd paid for but many others who had been seduced by his charisma and good looks. Yet out of all of these, Chastity had the greatest impact on him.

Tobias was the first to break their contented silence.

"Come with me, Chastity. Give up this life of prudence and modesty, for truly you are not suited to it. Come and join my group of Ranters. I would have you by my side at all times."

"No, Tobias Coppe. I do not think I could do that."

He looked surprised, "Doth you still fear of sin and that the temptations of the flesh will condemn you?"

"No, I don't believe that is it. For I want you. I desire you so much. I want the touch of your flesh against mine and to feel you inside me. I believe you when you say this is an expression of God's spirit in us and that God will not condemn me for something so beautiful. But here is my doubt. I know of the lifestyle of the ranting kind and, though having listened to your pleadings, I would no longer condemn you for it, yet I know you will lie with other women. And my problem is this; I would not desire to share you with anybody, for I would want you all for myself. So, my proposition to you is this, that you stay with me and together we will consume ourselves with our love and desire for one another."

"Can you do that?" she persisted, "Couldst you give up your ranting ways to submit to me and the earthly joys of the flesh I can offer you?"

For once, Tobias Coppe was left speechless. His discourse had been so convincing, his seduction so successful and Chastity's willingness to succumb so complete, that she embraced all his arguments and turned them back on him in a way he had not anticipated. The tables had been truly turned on him. Chastity had set him a challenge. Was she serious, or did the mischievous glint in her eye suggest she might be playing with him?

"Ah, but Chastity, that might depend on the theological basis of your argument. Do you say that it is sinful to lie with more than one lover? For wherein doth it say that it is thus, if God's love is in us all."

"Methinks, sir, that for a Ranter, you concern yourself too much with this notion of sin, for this is not a matter of sin but one of desire. For doth it not follow that if sin is a mere figment of man's construction then what one is left with is free will. So, I put it to you that it is a matter of choice and love freely given. What do you choose?"

She had put him on the defensive. He smiled in admiration at how Chastity had twisted his own words to use them against him. Indeed, her proposal held great appeal for him, and he was sorely tempted by it. But he was also too aware of his own appetites and wondered whether he could control those, even for the sake of the lovely Chastity. But the time for internal dialogue was over.

He rolled over on top of her and pressed his lips eagerly against hers. They were met passionately as Chastity wrapped her arms around his back and pulled him onto her. When their lips parted, he looked at her with longing. He whispered in her ear.

"Your arguments are convincing, my love, but I feel this is a debate we must continue into the night." he replied, his hand straying down to her still sopping cunt.

She moaned with pleasure, "And I trust our discourse will be most energetic."

Devil's Bargain, Devil's Kiss

Chapter 1:
The Miracle Medicine

It ain't easy work, getting up on rooftops and cleaning out folks' gutters, and it don't pay too good either, but Jonah don't have a lot of other choices. A little town like Ritten don't have much honest work for some orphan kid whose mama was a scandal as long as she lived. So Jonah takes what he can get, does hard work for pennies and dangerous work for nickels, and that's how he's up on the Jacobsens' roof when the wagon comes to town.

He sees it coming up the road into town, a covered wagon, dusty red, pulled by a sturdy brown mule and driven by a fellow in a black top hat. Strangers don't come to town too often, so when the fellow stops on the road to say something to Miz Hartley outside the general store, Jonah can't help creeping across the roof to get a little closer, see if he can't hear some of what they have to say.

He'd swear that what happens then can't be natural, because he's been climbing roofs like this for years and his footing's good—it feels like the house just pulls itself up short like a fly-bit horse and throws him right off. He barely has time to yelp before the ground is coming right at him.

Next thing he knows, he's opening his eyes, sputtering a little as he tries to swallow a mouthful of something that tastes red. The stranger's kneeling over him, hat off, black hair slicked straight back like a city salesman's, and when Jonah looks him in the eye he smiles so broad it splits his face right in half.

"There you are," he says, and sits back on his heels. "A sip of Doctor Nicolas Black's miracle medicine and you're right as rain. Go on, my boy, sit up. You've got these good people worried for nothing."

Ain't nobody in town going to worry about him, Jonah nearly points out, except people are staring, gathering round to gawk like he's a calf born with two heads. "What happened?" he says, rubbing at his head a little.

"You took a nasty fall just now," the stranger says, one big hand on Jonah's shoulder, "but fortunately your troubles were not beyond the means of my patented curative elixir." He gets up, and hauls Jonah up next to him. He's tall, lanky, and he seems just kind of big all over, like it's hard to look away from him. Something about meeting his green-dark eyes makes Jonah's heart speed up a little. "How do you feel, young man?"

"Fine, I guess," Jonah says. "My head don't even hurt."

The stranger laughs, loud and real satisfied, and claps Jonah on the back. His hand lingers there, just for a bit, warm and solid. "Happy to have been of service!" he says. He grins at the folks watching, like they're all in on something together now. "There'll be a more organized demonstration of the miraculous restorative powers of this recipe tonight, just outside of town—I do hope to see every one of you there."

Jonah doesn't make it to the show that night, but he figures he already got his demonstration anyway, so what does it matter? The doctor is the only thing the town talks about for days, the doctor and the girl he's got with him. Jonah didn't see any girl when he met the doctor himself, but he hears plenty about her. There's arguments about her on Miz Hartley's porch once or twice, all the boys who went to the show trying to decide where she could have come from. They're all pretty sure she ain't like any of the local girls at all.

Folks buy the doctor's medicines, either because they want to trade a couple words with the strange girl or because the demonstrations are hard to argue with. There's ointments for rheumatism and syrups for colic and tinctures for bee stings, and all of it works. The town's never been so healthy. When Doc Bennett makes it down from the north end of the county on Saturday for his weekly visit, there's not a soul in town needs his attention.

Miz Colby, who runs the boarding house where Jonah stays, says it's a blessing the doctor came by. She gets all her boarders to bow their heads on Sunday night when she says a few words of thanks. It's the kind of luck that's hard to come by, and she says they should thank the Lord for sending such a balm their way.

It's a couple days after that when Jonah takes ill. He's never felt anything quite like it, sluggish and cold like he's trying to wade through mud everywhere he goes. He don't have much to his name, but if anyone can fix him up it'd be Doctor Black, wouldn't it? So he gathers up his pennies and his nickels and trudges out to the wagon at the edge of town. By the time he gets out there his teeth are chattering, even though it's the middle of July and too hot for anyone but the grasshoppers to think it's nice weather.

"Doc?" he calls when he gets close.

"Round the back," the doctor answers, so Jonah limps around behind the wagon, finds him sitting by a little campfire with his shirt-sleeves rolled up and something bubbling in a beat up tin pot. His forearms are all ropy muscle, a match for his broad hands. "What can I do for you, my boy? If you'll pardon my saying so, you don't look well at all."

Jonah shakes his head. "No, sir," he says. "I feel pretty rotten, to tell the truth."

The doctor gives him one of those wide, knowing smiles—the girls in town are probably talking about him as much as the boys are talking about his lady friend, Jonah realizes—and reaches into his waistcoat. "I do believe I have just the thing," he says.

"I hope so," Jonah says. He's got his hands stuffed in his armpits by now, and that don't help him feel any warmer.

"Have a sip of this, then," the doctor says, getting up from his cook fire, uncorking a little brown glass bottle. He comes right over and puts it to Jonah's lips himself, so all Jonah has to do is swallow. It's the same red taste he remembers from the day the doctor came to town, and it warms him up like moonshine, straight down to his belly and spreading out from there.

"Damn," he says before he can remember his manners. "Thank you, sir."

The doctor chuckles. "Good for what ails you, isn't it?" he says. His hand's on the back of Jonah's neck, big and warm and solid. It feels good there—feels good to be touched, when usually there ain't a lot of that to go around in Jonah's days.

"Sure is," Jonah says, trying to push the thought away. He licks his lips. "What do I owe you?"

"Not a cent," the doctor says. "I wouldn't hear of it, not when my good fortune here is owed entirely to you."

Jonah smiles, a little stiff. "Really?" he says.

"Truly," the doctor says. "If you must provide me compensation, my boy, tell me your name."

"It's Jonah. No last name or nothing," he says, and maybe the doctor will think less of him for that, but it's too late to lie now.

"If Jonah from the Bible could get by with no last name," the doctor says, with a twinkle in his dark eyes, "then I'm sure it'll do you no harm, either."

"No, sir," Jonah says, grinning back, and heads back to town that afternoon feeling better than he has in a damn long while.

The gossip dies down a little over the next week, 'cause what is there to say when it's all so-and-so feels fine, so-and-so is doing great? No juicy details in that kind of news. Mister Jacobsen's wife is finally pregnant, but folks figure that can't be the fault of the doctor's miracle cures—or anything else, and ain't nobody even joking about that where Mister Jacobsen might hear—because how would she know so soon? Jonah does some fetch-and-carry work that week and repaints somebody's barn, and feels fit as a fiddle for days.

When he starts to feel a little less ship-shape, a little slower and achier than normal, he don't waste any time before he heads straight on out to see the doctor again. The cure was quick and easy last time, wasn't it? A little of Doctor Black's miracle medicine and he'll be on his way.

It's around sundown when he gets out that way, the sky streaked purply red over the mountains to the west, the air still thick with heat. Jonah wonders if he'll catch the doctor having dinner, if he'll finally meet the mystery girl.

Turns out neither, not this time. The brown mule is grazing near the wagon, not fenced or tethered, just staying put. The doctor's sitting in a folding chair and watching it, smoking a pipe.

"Got him trained pretty good, don't you?" Jonah says by way of greeting.

"He knows who he belongs to, that's all," the doctor says. Jonah's starting to think he smiles at everything, treats the whole world like a joke only he knows the punch line to.

"Ain't a lot of creatures you can say that for," Jonah says.

The doctor nods, pulling on his pipe so the coals glow bright. He sits there for a second looking satisfied, then blows out a long stream of smoke. "If you tell me you came out here to discuss animal husbandry, Jonah, I'm going to be quite surprised."

Jonah laughs, ducking his head a little. "No, sir," he says. "Wish I could say this was just a social call, but—."

"No need to apologize, my boy," the doctor says. He sets his pipe on the arm of his chair and gets up. "A medical man grows accustomed to the feeling of being ever on call, I assure you."

"Still," Jonah says, "I don't mean to trouble you. You must be wanting some supper, and it—it can't be easy on your lady friend if you're working all the time."

The doctor shakes his head, coming over to where Jonah's standing. "You're a fine young man, Jonah, but don't you worry. Eve's out just at the moment anyway. I promise she won't begrudge you this."

Jonah frowns, because that kind of sounds funny. "I wasn't trying to make it sound like..." he says, and the doctor lays a heavy hand on his shoulder.

"Now, I have what you need here, Jonah," he says, "but I think I'm going to have to ask you for payment. I promise it'll be nothing you can't spare."

"I would have paid you last time," Jonah says. He reaches into his pocket for his coins.

"I wonder," the doctor says, and his tone makes Jonah stop and look up at him. "I'm not asking for money, my boy." His smile gets wider. "I'm asking a kiss."

"You *what*?" Jonah demands. He goes real still. Sure, he might have liked the way the doctor talked to him like he was special, and he might have liked being touched, even, but that didn't mean he wanted this. Did it?

The doctor shrugs. "I can get money from any of your townsfolk," he says. "They're happy enough to part with it, given what I can do for them. But not a one of them is as handsome as you."

Jonah shakes his head. He keeps looking at the doctor's mouth, no matter how much he tries to look away. "You can't be serious."

"As the grave," the doctor says. "Think carefully before you turn me down, Jonah. You're starting to feel unwell this evening. How serious will it be by tomorrow? Can you work when you feel so ill?"

"You knew I was going to get sick again," Jonah accuses.

The doctor nods slowly. "It's a sad truth," he says, "that some maladies can be treated, but not cured."

The chill down Jonah's back just then is probably something else than sickness. "What do I have?" he says.

"I fear the diagnosis would cost you more than the treatment," the doctor says, cool as a cucumber, "and I would still ask payment in advance."

"You son of a bitch," Jonah says. He bites his tongue before he can say something like *I might have said yes easier if you hadn't been a bastard about it.*

"I promise to be gentle," the doctor answers.

No wonder he goddamn well smiles all the time. He's a cheating bastard. "Get it over with," Jonah says.

He tries to glare when the doctor comes back over, but it's a little scary—that feeling of bigness the doctor always has around him is stronger than usual now, and Jonah catches himself balling his hands into fists at his sides.

And then it happens, just as easy as that. The doctor leans down and claims Jonah's mouth. He smells like good fancy tobacco and maybe a little like medicine. He slides his arms around Jonah's waist, slips his tongue into Jonah's mouth and oh, Jonah wants to stay mad at him for being a bastard, but it feels like being the center of the world, just for a minute. His hands are hot on Jonah's back, hot and so big, and his tongue teases against Jonah's in a way that makes little shivers of sensation crawl up and down Jonah's skin. It's a breathless sort of feeling, the slick heat of that kiss crowding out everything else. He closes his eyes and kisses back, lets himself go along for the ride just for a minute.

Still, if he's getting dizzy by the time the doctor lets him go, Jonah's going to put that down to the sickness and not anything else. "You got your payment," he says. "Now I want that medicine." He wonders how much the doctor would charge for the whole bottle instead of just a sip, figures he don't really want to hear the answer right now.

"Of course," the doctor says, and pulls out the bottle. He still holds it himself, feeds Jonah the medicine, tipping the bottle up just long enough for Jonah to get a mouthful of it before he pulls it away.

"That's it?" Jonah says, swallowing again, the taste still red on his tongue. "That's as much as I get?"

"No man prospers by greed, my boy," the doctor answers, and Jonah decides that when he smiles it makes him look like the devil. "How do you feel?"

"Pissed. But better," Jonah allows.

"Then I couldn't hope for more," the doctor says. "Do come to see me right away if you suffer another such spell."

Jonah frowns. "We'll see about that," he says.

He ain't going back out there, he decides. If he gets sick, he gets sick, and he'll sweat it out like usual. Town got by just fine before Doctor Nicolas Black and his fancy medicines rolled in.

There's a bad storm comes in that week, pours for two solid days. Ark-building weather, people call it, and shake their heads when they talk about the harvest. Once or twice Jonah hears somebody wonder out loud how the doctor's making out, but nobody ever says a word about inviting him in to stay until it clears. For his part, Jonah sort of hopes the storm just washes the doctor's wagon clean away, and all his bargains with him. He makes everything too complicated, with his miracle medicine and his warm hands and that kiss that Jonah does his damnedest not to think about all the time.

After the storm clears out, there's plenty of work to do, fixing up fences that got knocked down in floods, hauling out stuck wagons. Jonah's mostly too busy to worry about anything weird going on around town.

He does notice, though, when Jack Greene, the sheriff's son, starts coming around in the evenings to ask after Millie, who does chores around the boardinghouse. Most everybody's always figured Millie would grow up to be an old maid, since she ain't got a fortune and she's plain as they come. But Jack comes by twice that week, taking his hat off all proper, talking sweet like he means it. Millie, well—if he's being honest, Jonah thinks probably Millie's never looked so sweet herself, with a bit of a blush to her cheeks and a sparkle in her eyes that weren't there before.

By Saturday afternoon Jonah's starting to feel a little chill again, even in the summer heat. Fortunately it waited until the work week was just about done, and it ain't so bad as it maybe could be. He grits his teeth and puts his back into the ditch-digging work he's got that day and tells himself it ain't nothing, and that keeps him going fine enough. After supper he thinks it must have been all in his head. He got a little spooked by the doctor last time, that's all.

In the middle of the night he wakes up freezing. He drags himself out of bed to pull the heavy quilt out of the closet, but wrapping himself up in it don't help much. He lies there and shivers about until the sun starts to come up, until he can hear Miz Colby rattling around in the kitchen to make breakfast before folks head over to church. He feels numb when he gets up, stumbling down the hall. She's got to have more blankets somewhere, or maybe a cup of coffee would help, warm him up from inside.

Two steps down the stairs he slips, and falls the rest of the way. He can barely hear the noise he makes—everything sounds far away and muffled.

Miz Colby comes running, though. "Gracious, boy, what's happened to you?" she says when she finds him on the floor.

"S-sick," Jonah stutters out. "F-f-freezing."

She lays her hand across his forehead, warm and dry. "Cold as the grave," she says, and Jonah closes his eyes. She's still talking after that, but it's hard to make out words.

There's more noise, and hands on him, picking him up and carrying him somewhere. He doesn't know quite when they put him down. He feels like he's floating in the river, only it's so cold, everything so cold and dim.

Somehow he can still hear the doctor's voice just fine, though, when he shows up. "You've called me just barely in time. ...Of course, I'll do everything in my power to help the poor boy. ...No, no, there's no need for that, madam, and I'd hate to keep you from the rest of the flock on a Sunday morning. ...A shame indeed. I do hope you'll give the reverend both my regards and my regrets."

There's a click like the door closing, and then Jonah feels the bed dip under him. He opens his eyes and everything looks gray and just a little fuzzy. He can barely make out the expression on Doctor Black's face, but he'd swear it's another one of those awful satisfied smiles.

"You're damned stubborn, my boy," the doctor says.

Chapter 2:
A Change in the Wind

Doctor Black lays his hand on Jonah's forehead. He feels so warm, Jonah makes a little sound in his throat. "Yes, you're cutting it quite close, aren't you?" he goes on. "Here, now, that blue to your lips isn't fetching at all."

He pulls his hand away and it's hard to focus but Jonah thinks he's going for his bottle of miracle elixir again. He don't hold the bottle to Jonah's mouth this time, though, just wets his fingers and rubs them over Jonah's lips. It's a huge relief and an awful tease both at once, just enough heat to make sure Jonah knows how cold he is.

"More," he says, croaking like a damn bullfrog. "Please."

"That's why I'm here," the doctor says gently. "I've taken an interest in you, my boy, and I want to help you out." He pulls back the blankets, and it don't make any difference to how cold Jonah feels. Then he's pushing up Jonah's shirt, and if his hands weren't so warm Jonah would complain.

Warm or no, he still says, "Wait," when the doctor leans back and starts to unbuckle his own belt. "I don't want...."

"Most importantly, Jonah," the doctor says, and his voice is still soft but it ain't actually kind at all, "you want to get better, don't you? And you know you can't expect something for nothing in this world."

In the gray cold fog filling up Jonah's head, it make sense enough. He don't *like* it, maybe, but it makes sense. But he tries to shake his head when the doctor climbs onto the bed with him.

"Here, this is simple enough," the doctor says, and he sounds like he's almost laughing. "I wouldn't ask you to exert yourself when you're feeling so out of sorts." He takes one of Jonah's hands and puts it on his cock. "Both hands, my boy," he says, pulling the other one down too. Jonah feels too slow and weak to really fight him, and besides that the doctor stretched out over him is the first thing that's really felt warm since last night. He shivers, and his breath comes short. The doctor wraps one big hand around both of his, holding them there around his cock, and rocks a little on top of him.

"Why," Jonah gets out, and then has to take another breath. When did talking get to be so much work? "Why—this?"

"Because you're a handsome boy and I want to," the doctor says. His voice is low like thunder, his breath warm in Jonah's ear. "Because I never take payment in coin if I can help it." His cock slides in Jonah's hands, smooth and thick and so hot. "Most everyone has more interesting currency to offer, if you only take the time to ask."

"You're—a bastard," Jonah tells him.

The doctor laughs. "Could be," he says. "You can curse me for it, if it'll make you feel better. There's nobody left in the house to hear you."

They've all gone to church, he means. Miz Colby's real particular about that, don't let anybody stay in her house who won't go. And here's Jonah missing church cause he's freezing to death in July, and the only man who knows how to help him won't do it unless Jonah jerks him off first.

Jonah squeezes his eyes shut. The doctor's still talking, telling him how sweet he is, calling him pet names. Telling him how much he could learn to like this, if he stopped fighting it so much. He tries not to listen real hard, 'cause he don't have the strength to argue.

The rest of him is going all tingly and cold, back into the icy river, and only his hands curled around the doctor's cock feel real. Everything else blurs, and all that's left is the doctor rocking on top of him, using him. Sometimes a little flicker of sensation curls up from the base of his spine at a hard stroke and he gets muddled, starts to think that somehow the doctor's *inside* him. It's got to be the sickness making him confused, he knows that—he can still feel the hot smooth skin sliding between his hands. But those flickers of heat inside won't go away, and he thinks maybe he doesn't want them to. Much rather have that than the awful empty cold, wouldn't he?

He's starting to fade out again when the doctor finally comes, shooting all over his stomach, thick hot spurts of fluid. He'd be furious if he could find the strength for it, but damn, when he's so desperately cold like this it kind of feels good. The doctor sits back, then, sets Jonah's hands down at his sides.

"You're such a good boy, Jonah," he says. He runs his fingers through the mess he's made, rubbing it into Jonah's skin. "I'm going to have to keep a closer eye on you, until you learn to take better care of yourself."

"The hell are you doing?" Jonah asks. He tries to squirm, tells himself he's trying to pull away, but it's like there's lead in his veins and he can't do much more than tremble. It feels like the doctor is drawing letters on him, smearing his seed into strokes of heat that last even when he takes his hand away.

"There's power in anything spilled for another, my boy," the doctor says, "whether it's blood, or tears, or something more intimate." He finishes up whatever he's doing and brushes his hands together like he could wipe them clean that way. "I want to be able to find you if you should let yourself reach a state like this again."

"You laid a hex on me," Jonah says. His skin crawls.

"Nothing of the kind," the doctor says. "That would imply I intended to harm you with it, and I assure you this will do no such thing. It'll just let me know if you're in trouble."

Jonah shakes his head weakly. "Don't want you coming round," he says, but already those few drops of the medicine are wearing off and he feels fuzzy again.

The doctor hums, doing up his belt. "My dear boy, I do believe you're becoming delirious. Let's see what we can do to assist in your recovery, shall we?" He pulls out his medicine bottle and takes a swig for himself, and just for a second Jonah wants to kill him with envy.

And then he leans right down to kiss Jonah's mouth. His lips part and he hasn't swallowed, so the medicine floods into Jonah's mouth from his, wet and warm and bitter-sweet. Jonah don't even mean to, but his hands just move, reaching up and grabbing the doctor's crisp white shirt-sleeves. The strength comes flowing back into him and he pushes his tongue into the doctor's mouth, trying to get as much of it as he can. He chokes out this little moan that sounds way too needy, but he can't help it. The medicine makes him feel so much better, all the way alive again. When the doctor tries to pull back out of the kiss, Jonah sits up after him, not letting go of his mouth until he really has to.

The doctor laughs, and Jonah could almost swear there's fire in his eyes. "There, you see?" he says. "Looks as though you'll make a full recovery after all."

Jonah lets go of him in a hurry. "Until next time it wears off, you mean."

"Indeed," the doctor says, but he's still smiling a little, the bastard.

"Can I have more?" Jonah asks. He might as well, if he's already been through this much for it.

The doctor nods like he figured Jonah was going to say that. "If you'll take it in the same fashion, I suppose I could allow you a second dose."

Jonah looks at the doctor's mouth, watches it curve into a big smile again. "It's the only cure in town, ain't it?" he says. He wants to spit. "Fine."

"Sensible," the doctor says. He takes another sip and just waits there, watching, until Jonah realizes he's going to have to do it himself this time.

So he does. He stretches up and kisses Doctor Black, fitting their mouths together as best he can so the medicine won't spill, and he swallows and swallows and it tastes better than anything in the world. His teeth scrape the doctor's tongue and he feels *hungry,* heat flooding his limbs and pooling at the base of his spine. The doctor makes this little sound into the kiss like he's trying to laugh, and a tiny trickle of the medicine runs out the corner of his mouth. Jonah grabs him by the shoulders to hold him still and licks it up, don't want to lose any of it—

And pulls back after that, his cheeks hot and other parts of him starting to seriously get the wrong idea. "That's it, right?"

The doctor looks down at his lap, and Jonah pulls the blankets over himself but not fast enough. "For now," the doctor says, "yes, I think that should do." He gets up, but stops before he makes it to the door. "You know, if you hurry, I imagine you could make it to church in time for the second half of the good reverend's sermon."

"Get out of here," Jonah says, rolling over toward the wall. He's jittery and sweating and his cock is hard, and he can smell the stink of the doctor's come on his skin. Like he'd want to go to church when he feels like this.

"Not interested?" the doctor says. "Well, I can't say I blame you one bit, my boy." The door creaks when he opens it. "Plenty of miracles happen outside the church's doors, after all."

Jonah doesn't really let himself breathe until he hears the door close again, and then he's trying hard to just will himself calm. The doctor's a creep and a bastard, but it's *done* now, isn't it? Except for how his cock hasn't gotten the news. He tries to breathe through it, tell his body to cut that out, just let it go. His body ain't listening.

He tries to hang onto how angry he felt, how shameful it was to let the doctor use him like that, how pissed he was that the doctor had to go and make it a trade when he was helpless, instead of asking if he wanted to. It doesn't do him any damn good. He's still *hard*, and with the medicine waking his body back up he's tingling all over and can barely hold still. He can feel the ghost of the doctor's touch on his skin, and he can't quite push away the memory of the doctor's cock sliding through his hands.

It feels like losing another standoff when Jonah tugs his pants down to get a hand on his cock, but he can't stop himself. He tries to keep it quick, tries not to think about how different it felt to touch the doctor instead of himself, the smoothness of skin and the thick heaviness of the doctor's cock, the way that touch was all he could really feel. He wonders what it would feel like to do it now, when his body's all alert and sensitive all over like this—having those hands on him and that voice in his ear when he could actually feel it all, when he could move too and it wouldn't be so one-sided.

A little whine escapes his throat and he tries to clear his mind, tries to think of anything else, think of nothing at all, but he can taste the doctor's medicine in his throat and smell the doctor's come on his skin and he thinks *that bastard probably knew his stupid medicine would do this to me* and that's when he comes.

"God *damnit*," Jonah says to the empty room.

That's gotten rid of the worst of the jitters, at least. Jonah curls up real small and sleeps like a baby, straight through the heat of the day. He washes up real good when he gets up, but he don't think the doctor's mark is going to come off that easy. Miz Colby says she's glad he's doing better, at supper time, and Jonah says he figures he must have just needed to sleep it off.

137

Monday he goes down to the store and unloads the truck that comes in with new stock. Miz Hartley says he's growing up strong as an ox, and Jonah realizes he ain't even worn out from carrying in that whole truckload of boxes. Still fresh as a daisy, like he could keep going for hours. Doctor Black's a creep, but that stuff he brews is pretty good.

That night Jonah don't sleep so great, mostly cause he just don't feel tired enough. But he gets a little shut-eye eventually, and that turns out to be enough to get him through the next day anyhow. Still plenty of medicine to keep him running.

Tuesday night Jonah's still awake when Jack Greene comes sneaking in Millie's window downstairs, and after a minute he wishes he wasn't. He can't help listening for the noises they're trying not to make, and that makes a warm night even hotter. *So much for waiting until they saw the preacher to make it official,* Jonah figures. They're whispering together and there are cloth-shifting sounds, and then some wet noises that make Jonah squirm. Millie whimpers, says something soft and breathy. A couple seconds later Jack groans, low and overwhelmed and grateful. Jonah chews on his lip, listening for the squeak of bedsprings, his hips trying to rock in sympathy.

When he gives in and reaches down to take care of himself, though, he forgets about the two of them pretty much right away. Instead he catches himself thinking about the doctor, on top of him, so big in his hands. He lets go of his cock, don't want to think about that while he's doing this. He can't get the doctor out of his head, though, imagines it's him in Millie's room, big hands on her everywhere and—he shoves his hands under his pillow, squeezes his eyes shut, don't want to think about it. No way he's going to jerk himself off to *that.*

So he dreams about it instead, the doctor with this black-haired woman in his lap, so much like him she could be his sister. His hands touch her all over, and her nails scrape down his back, and everything's on fire. She rocks in his lap, slow and rippling, her breasts swinging full and heavy. He slides his hands up her sides and cups them, rolling her nipples between his fingers, kissing and biting at her throat. She glances over at Jonah and says something that sounds like a cat purring, and the doctor laughs.

Then everything slides sideways and it's Jonah in the doctor's lap, sticky-slow like honey and so warm everywhere the doctor touches him, warm and heavy, while this huge rattler curls around them both and watches. It feels like he can only breathe in time with the doctor moving, and he don't want to look down, cause what if he's the girl now? What if he's not and he's getting screwed anyway? He don't want to think about it, wants to just let the sensations wash over him. The rocking feeling pushes right up inside him, makes him feel open and helpless and full.

He closes his eyes but somehow he can still see, watching himself from the outside as he arches his back, as he curses the doctor for not giving him *more*. The fire's rising around them, and the heat's all pooling down between his legs. His breath comes in stutters and the rocking pressure building up inside him makes him ache. *Beautiful, beautiful*, the doctor keeps saying, staring at him with bright yellow snake eyes. Jonah pushes down against him and shudders and wakes up sticky.

Wednesday a stray dog that nobody's ever seen before comes wandering up Main Street, sniffing at doors, nosing in people's garbage. It's an ugly dirt-colored thing, skinny and wild-eyed, with a torn ear and a nasty set of teeth. Just past noon it limps up onto the Jacobsens' front porch and drops a litter of dead puppies practically on the doorstep, slimy little half-formed bloody things. When it starts to eat them, Miz Jacobsen screams and hollers for her serving girl to drive the bitch off.

There's a little talk that evening about whether it's cause of Mister Jacobsen going after the doctor's girl. Some folks are saying it's a sign, a warning about how sin always comes home to roost. Miz Colby won't have with that talk in her house, says it's the Lord's own business when to punish sinners and how, and ain't nobody doing themselves any good trying to tell Him how to go about it. Jonah hopes the gossip ain't true, but he ain't sure anymore. Under his clothes it burns where the doctor drew on his skin.

Jack Greene don't come back that night. Sounds like Millie was expecting him, cause Jonah can hear her crying a little through the hole in the floorboards. He tosses and turns, feels funny in his skin. Not cold, though. Not yet.

He has more dreams like before. The doctor holds him, holds him down, shoots all over him—and feeds it to him this time, messy fingers pushing into Jonah's mouth. His come tastes sharp, like smoke, like his medicine. Jonah struggles, but not like he's really trying to get free of those hot greedy hands—all he's really doing is rubbing himself up against the doctor and making little hot bursts of feeling run tingling up his spine. He licks the pads of the doctor's fingers, lips and tongue all swollen and tender.

The doctor pulls Jonah's head down, rubs his cock on Jonah's face, and there's something cold and heavy sliding around Jonah's arms, weighing them down. He don't have to look to know it's the snake from before. Every little touch and every breath winds him tighter, leaves him this wound-up shuddering mess of hunger. The doctor's fingers pry Jonah's mouth open wide, so he can get his cock in there with them, all the way in, and all the edges go funny in the dream so it's like all of him goes after it, filling up all the space inside Jonah's skin as Jonah swallows him like a snake himself, until all he knows for sure is he wasn't full before and he is now.

He wakes up so hard he thinks he's going to die, and every sensation, the sheet falling back when he sits up, his own fingers tugging at his hair, all of it makes him harder. He can't get that dream out of his head—having his jaw forced aching wide, having that thick heat heavy on his tongue, the slide of snakeskin and the feeling of being *full*. He shoves his shorts down and the friction makes his cock ache. Getting his hand around it almost finishes him right away—all it takes is a couple rough strokes, his mouth open and panting, tongue tracing his bottom lip like he could still taste the doctor there, and then he's shooting all over himself with a sob.

He takes a second to just catch his breath, listening to the rasping sound of it and the way his heartbeat hammers in his ears. Then he goes to wipe up the mess, and stops dead. He can see the doctor's mark burn-red against his belly, glowing just a little like the afterimage of looking right into the sun. It ain't like any letters he's ever seen anywhere, looping and doubling back on itself. After a minute of squinting at it in the dark he can't see it anymore. He's still got the shivers thinking about it, though.

Thursday he's expecting something to go wrong already. So it ain't a surprise but it's still no good when Betsy Campton has a fit, just as she's walking up the steps to the reverend's house. Jonah's working when it happens, but he hears about it plenty later that afternoon: how she was twitching and foaming at the mouth, going blue in the face, how she nearly swallowed her tongue before somebody managed to get a little of Doctor Black's Patented Tonic down her throat. It's a turning point, the change in the wind before a storm rolls in. Nobody's talking about what a blessing the doctor's cures are no more.

When Jonah comes home for supper he can hear Miz Colby saying, "And you know, he hasn't been right either, since—" before she sees him coming in the kitchen. His ears burn, but it's true, ain't it? He's been pretty bad off since the doctor first came to town. Feeling good some-times, but not right.

He don't really want to go to sleep that night, not with more of those dreams to look forward to. Feels good when it's happening, sure, but that don't mean he's okay with it all. And he ain't too tired, so it's not too hard to stay up. He's lying awake when he feels something catch him round the heart and pull. He needs to go outside, right now. It's important.

The whole house is dark but Jonah don't have any trouble seeing where he's headed. His heart's pounding when he steps out the back door, barefoot, the grass wet with dew. There's a heavy fog come in all at once—somewhere up there the moon's full, but it's just a hazy smudge of far-away light. Jonah walks out toward the road, and he thinks he knows what's calling him there.

The doctor's wagon is sitting in the middle of the road, and he's up in the driver's seat, his top hat on, the reins in his hand. The mule has its head down, waiting.

"There you are," he says when Jonah steps out onto the road. "Right on time."

"You're getting the hell out of town, huh?" Jonah says. "Before people figure out how much trouble you made."

"Now, most of them brought that trouble on themselves," the doctor says. "But it's true, there's not much more I can do for them now. So don't dawdle. Once Miss Eve gets back, we'll be off."

Jonah snorts. "You think I'm going with you?"

The doctor puts down the reins and spreads his hands. The mule don't go anywhere. "My dear boy, I should think you've realized by now how much you need my help."

The hairs are all standing up on Jonah's neck, but he says, "I can get medicine somewhere else."

"I promise you," the doctor says, and for once he ain't smiling at all, "any place else you could find a similar formula would be equally unpalatable." He takes the bottle out and holds it up. "Do you know what this is, Jonah? What you owe your good health to?"

Jonah shakes his head. He's got a sick feeling in his gut.

"It's dead men's time," the doctor says, real quiet. "When a man's life is cut short, the time he had left must go somewhere. I've collected quite a bit of it in my travels, and it's thanks to that you're still with us now."

Jonah thinks back to that first day the doctor came to town, and how he never should have fallen off that roof. "You son of a bitch," he says.

"Turning me down?" the doctor asks. "Think carefully about that, my boy. If you don't find some way to replenish your lost life, and quickly—ah, excuse me." He holds out one arm, and a big old owl comes swooping down out of the mist, lands on his arm hard enough to shake the wagon. It came from the direction of the Jacobsens' house, didn't it? "Good evening, my dear," the doctor says. "Good hunting?"

The owl shakes out its wings and shrugs, and then it just stretches out and gets longer and taller, feathers melting away until it's a woman, standing next to the wagon and holding the doctor's hand. "As always. She even thanked me," the woman says. She licks blood off her mouth. She's the woman from Jonah's dream, and the snake, too, he's sure of it. It's all true.

"Well?" the doctor says to Jonah. "Time is precious and we've miles to go tonight. Are you prepared to face Hell, or would you rather come with me?"

"What makes you so damn sure that's where I'm going?" Jonah says. His hands are shaking and his stomach is twisted up in a tiny ball. He makes fists, but it don't help.

"It's a mortal sin to steal another man's life for your own," the doctor says. He don't have to sound so damn pleased about it.

Jonah takes one step toward the wagon. Feels like he's a fish on a line getting hauled in no matter how hard he tries to stay back. "It's a choice between bad and worse, ain't it?" he says. "All that stuff from the dreams...."

"Will be much more pleasant than anything you would experience down below." Not even pretending he ain't going to do it. Not even pretending that what Jonah wants has anything to do with it. "You've been to church at least enough to know that, haven't you?"

"I guess I have," Jonah says. The woman climbs up on the front seat of the wagon, next to the doctor. She stares at him with cold cat eyes and don't look like she has any sympathy at all. He takes another step, trying to think how he can get out of this. There's always a way to trick the devil, ain't there? Some way to get out of a deal with him, some way to win. Only Jonah can't see what it is.

He don't take the hand the doctor's offering as he climbs up onto the wagon. "Where we going, anyhow?" Rather think about that than anything else right now.

"Oh, we follow the wind," the doctor says, smiling as he picks up the reins. The mule gets moving right away. "Anywhere we go to sell, we always find somebody willing to buy."

If you enjoyed this story, you can sign up for a free membership at
ForbiddenFiction and discuss it with other readers and the author at
The *Devil's Bargain, Devil's Kiss* story page at
http://forbiddenfiction.com/story/lh2-1-000085.

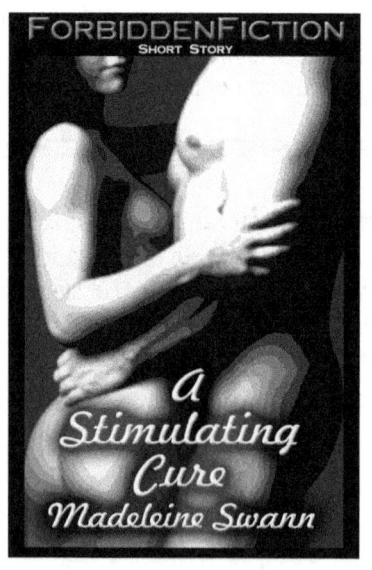

A
Stimulating
Cure
Madeleine Swann

A Stimulating Cure

A Stimulating Cure

"Do drink your phosphates, darling," said Mr. Alfred Symmonds, pointing to the glass of noxious chalky medicine on the bedside table. His wife Helena opened her eyes. She was in the same room with the same mahogany furniture and china wash basin she had seen non-stop for the last three weeks. The light that shone beyond the floral curtain was golden and so were her husband's handsome features. She wished she could reach out to him physically and emotionally whenever she wanted but knew it wouldn't do, that he wouldn't appreciate her 'fussing.' She wondered whether he would complain if she were more beautiful.

Helena drained her glass of phosphates as quickly as she could before sinking back into the Egyptian cotton bedspreads. She felt like Ophelia with her hair spread around her before reminding herself bitterly that Ophelia's wasn't mousy brown and she wasn't wearing a white nightdress. She imagined she could feel the breeze on her face and smell the Hydrangeas from the garden. "Remember what Dr MacManus advised," Alfred would say if he caught her out there, "you must have complete bed rest or your nerves will never recover." Alfred gazed at her now, his eyes full of genuine tenderness. She knew he didn't yet regret their marriage, but it had only been a year and she was already causing problems.

He turned to leave as the housemaid arrived to clean the ashes from the fireplace. Her waist was smaller than Helena's would be, even with a corset, and the sleeves of her uniform were rolled up to reveal creamy skin. A look passed between them, a look that lasted less than a fraction of a second—Helena turned on her side and willed the phosphates she now felt crawling down her gullet to numb her hysteria as quickly as possible.

145

Alfred returned in the afternoon, reminding her of yet another doctor's appointment they had to attend. "He's entirely new, but his father's been around for years," he chattered excitedly as the maid tightened Helena's corset. The room spun uncomfortably whenever she moved her head, and her hands shook. "The whole of London has been absolutely clamouring to see him and I managed to get us in." Helena followed him to the hansom cab waiting outside. The chestnut horse trotted on as the next dose hit her belly and she relaxed into the hard seat.

"Perhaps it won't be too awful," she murmured.

"That's the spirit," Alfred smiled.

The horse stopped outside a smart set of West End buildings. Helena stepped sloppily out of the cab door, holding onto Alfred's outstretched hand. "Oopsie daisy," he chuckled, his smile a little too fixed. An aging female housekeeper answered the door.

"If you would like to follow me," she said in an East End accent, "Dr Britestone will see you next." Helena caught the look in her eye, so slight most wouldn't have seen. Another hysterical woman, it said, causing trouble for her hard-working husband.

They stopped in a small, airy waiting room. A light wooden door with an oval window set near the top was situated at the back. They sat in waiting chairs next to a fellow who repeatedly pulled a watch from his waistcoat pocket and tapped his foot. A maid dusted the books on a nearby shelf; Helena pursed her lips when she saw Alfred's eyes caress her curves. She pulled her hand from his and he lowered his head silently.

Within a half hour the wooden door opened and a red-cheeked woman appeared, floating to the nervous man as serenely as a swan on a crystal lake. He took her hands and led her from the room, their bodies melting into each other.

"Mrs Symmonds?" said a young man from the doorway. He was a touch shorter than she, slightly built and dark-haired with a lively and interested expression. Helena rose and accepted his warm handshake. "Good day, I'm Dr Britestone, very pleased to make your acquaintance." The smell of old books in his room comforted her. He shut the door and led her past shelves of skeletal creatures underneath glass bell jars and puffy white objects lurking in containers of darkened liquid. He requested she sit in a musty, brown leather chair. He spoke calmly, like a scientist preparing a subject for testing. Helena placed her finger in a crack on the chair's arm. "Oh dear," smiled the doctor, "Please forgive my current possessions. One day my findings will permit me to buy the plushest of furnishings but, sadly, that day hasn't yet arrived."

Helena shook her head. "I couldn't possibly bear thoughts of such an ugly manner." As he filed through pages on his desk she looked upward—and wished she hadn't.

"Oh, fear not," he said as he followed her gaze after her sharp intake of breath, "that metal contraption is merely a vibration device for easing back ailments, nothing a lady with a hysterical womb need concern herself with."

"A hysterical...."

"Well, yes," Dr Britestone seemed taken aback that she didn't know her own prognosis. "A lady's womb can cause fits of nervousness and knows only one cure."

"Complete bed rest," said Helena bitterly.

"Of course not," laughed Dr Britestone, "that is the very last thing it needs. If you'll permit me to say, a woman as handsome as yourself should not be shut away. Oh, I've embarrassed you." A blush had crept over Helena's cheeks and she rubbed the side of her face, willing it to turn pale again.

"Oh, no, doctor," she said, "I was merely a little... taken aback."

"No, a problem such as this needs regular intervals of... attention. If you lean back in the seat I will proceed."

Dr Britestone reached behind him and lifted a contraption from inside his lower desk drawer. Helena studied it dubiously, her nerves getting the better of her. He pulled out a small, though no less monstrous, mechanical thing. He held it by a short black grip at one end and pointed the other—a tiny, flat rubber plunger—toward her. At the side of its thick silver body was a handle for turning. "This is the Pulsocon Hand Vibrator," he announced proudly.

Helena felt the hairs rising on her entire body and began shaking with fear. She wondered if a great needle would pop out of the end, filled with opiates that would knock her to the ground. "No!" she squealed, rising up and backing away.

"Please, Mrs Symmonds, there is nothing to be afraid of," the doctor assured. It was too late, Alfred was standing panicked in the doorway.

"He means to inject me," Helena whimpered, pointing accusingly.

The doctor shook his head. "Mrs Symmonds has mistaken my intention. I do not deal in prescriptions here. It is a tool merely for applying pressure to the affected area."

Helena felt her cheeks burn. "Will you be content for me to leave you?" Alfred asked her, his eyebrows knitted together in worry.

Helena nodded. "I'll be right here." The door was swiftly shut, leaving the pair of them alone once more.

"I assure you once again, you will come to no harm," said Dr Britestone.

"Yes, yes absolutely," said Helena quickly as she sat down, wanting to move past the whole business.

He knelt to the ground before her in a way Helena thought most eccentric. When he raised her skirts above her ankles she leaned forward sharply. "It is quite necessary and in no way low minded I assure you," he said, "though it may feel a little strange." Unwilling to create another scene, she leaned back, focusing on a leaflet for Dr Coling's Cure for Colic.

She held her breath as his hand crept upward, his fingers reaching beneath the hem of her bloomers. "Relax and breathe," he soothed, his touch seeking out the places only Alfred had been.

"Are... are you certain this is decent?" Helena asked.

"Men of my profession, Mrs Symmonds," he said with a tone of infinite patience, "must adhere to those nooks and crannies not discussed in polite society. If one ignores them completely who knows what may happen? Why, just the other week a lady was taken ill and rushed to hospital, only for them to find her womb had travelled the length of her body up to her brain." Helena shivered at the ghastly story and resolved to stop questioning him. Dr Britestone bit his lip in concentration as his fingertip discovered her lips, her private ones. "Oh good," he whispered, "it's so much better when there is wetness." Helena glimpsed down while he traced a line up her lips with his fingers and felt a hotness flush through her. "There you are," Dr Britestone muttered to himself, keeping a finger in place whilst applying the flat rubber nozzle. He held it in place with the grip at the back and began to slowly turn the handle. "How does that feel?"

Helena wasn't certain how to answer. The rubber nozzle plunged gently back and forth against her private area whilst rotating gradually. The effect left her feeling somewhat foolish and she wished to tell him just that, but for the odd sensation that was creeping upward from the nodule being manipulated above her lips. "It's, oh," she had meant to explain the prickling feeling on her skin, the heat spreading through her extremities, but instead this breathy reply was all she could manage.

"Marvelous," said the doctor, "that means it should be working." Despite his claims it was not low-minded, there was an unmistakable bulge in his crotch area. Helena was shocked, but instead of being enraged she felt an intense wave of excitement.

"Goodness," he said in a low voice, "it's very wet down there now. We must take care it doesn't slip."

Helena sighed, laying her head back in the chair. A prickle of warmth spread over her groin, almost as though she had spread her legs before the fire at home. The indecency of the image almost made her laugh, but instead she shivered and felt the heat gather momentum. It was a pleasant sensation, not one she was used to.

A slight movement by the door caught her eye and she jolted slightly; Alfred had evidently stood on a chair and was peeking through the oval glass in the door. She glanced again at the doctor whose body was crouched down in front of her. He wouldn't be able to see the doctor's excitement and would be unable to see his probing fingers under her skirts, but the expression on his face said he knew. He knew that her private lips were slick and hot, that she was opening her thighs to allow him better reach. Far from looking horrified, though, Alfred's pupils were large pools and his lips and cheeks were as flushed as hers.

Dr Britestone stopped turning the instrument and Helena felt an odd frustration, a sense of things left unfinished. She wanted to shout at the doctor but, to her relief, he reached into her undergarments with his hands. "I feel we would reach the consequence faster with a hands-on method," he murmured quietly. He slid a finger inside her and curled it forward. "Mmm, that's it, I've found it now." The doctor's index finger alighted on the small nub above her private lips. His soft pressure was an entirely different sensation to the insistent rubs of the machine. Helena let out a deep moan, afterward looking up in shock and embarrassment. "Don't worry, that's the effect it will have, it's quite normal," he soothed.

Helena laughed slightly, self-consciously, until another wave coursed through her. She looked again at the movement in the doctor's groin area. She opened her mouth to speak but bit the words back. If she offended him he might stop his actions or, worse still, her treatment altogether. Taking such a deep breath she felt herself go dizzy, she whispered, "You appear to be in need of some relief too." He looked up at her with wide eyes and for a moment Helena thought she would be cast out. Instead he smiled slightly and, with his free hand, the Doctor freed himself from his buttons. Helena caught Alfred's eyes and held his gaze as her hand was led by the doctor down the side of the chair, secretly, out of her husband's gaze.

"Oh," he sighed softly as she tickled his bent thigh. She stretched her fingers and he moved her hand closer until her fingertips caressed the tip of a dampening erection. The doctor placed his shaft firmly in her grasp. Helena kept her eyes on Alfred's parted lips as she stroked the doctor's length.

"Oh, God," she moaned, again surprised at her involuntary vocalising. The doctor's rubbing had deepened in feeling and heat somehow, and she rocked her hips to his movement. She watched Alfred as he chewed his lip, knowing instinctively how hard he would be. In her hands, the doctor's shaft grew sticky and pumped full of blood, and she could tell by his breath and soft noises he made that he was close to spending. Still he rubbed at the nub above her private lips, and inserted his thumb inside her. She moaned, her skin prickling with waves of fire. Alfred's eyes on her acted as a second caressing hand, and soon her hips thrusted harder than before.

The doctor pumped himself discretely into her hand until he spurted, his body stiff and his erection beating with his heart. After a moment or two of peace Helena rocked her body against his fingers once more, to remind him that she was still there. He stroked her with new vigour until she felt something—a strange and overwhelming tide—rising from deep down inside and pouring from the tiny nub throughout her body. "Oh God, oh God," she moaned over and over. She was encompassed by a crash of sensation, a flood of pleasure that poured down her spine and arched her back.

She'd never experienced such a thing before that shook her entire body.

"Yes," Dr Britestone seemed somewhat disconcerted as he tucked himself away and cleared up his mess with a tissue. "That should... that will suffice for now." He rose and washed his hands in the basin next to his desk. Helena had an urge to laugh; he seemed so much more out of sorts than she felt. She politely bit her lip, however, and accepted his hand as he helped her to rise.

"Oh, goodness," she stumbled as her knees gave way.

"Ah, yes," the Doctor said shyly, "that can be the effect of such treatment." He led her back to the door where Alfred stood in the empty waiting room, the chair he'd been standing on back in place. He was thumbing through a book he held suspiciously close to his crotch area. "Ah, Mr Symmonds," said Dr Britestone in official tones, "Helena is to enjoy regular walks in the public gardens and should take up a hobby, perhaps watercolours. She is to see me once a month, and under no circumstances is she to continue taking Phosphates." Helena almost sank to the floor in relief.

"Thank you Doctor," said Alfred, shaking his hand and leading Helena outside.

"Thank you," said Helena, turning back and catching the doctor's eye before disappearing through the door. Without thinking she leaned her head against Alfred's shoulder. To her surprise he kissed the top of her head lightly.

"That's nice," he commented. "I feel wretched when you shy away from me so."

"Really?" said Helena.

"Absolutely," he replied as they arrived back at the hansom. "Now let's head for home quick."

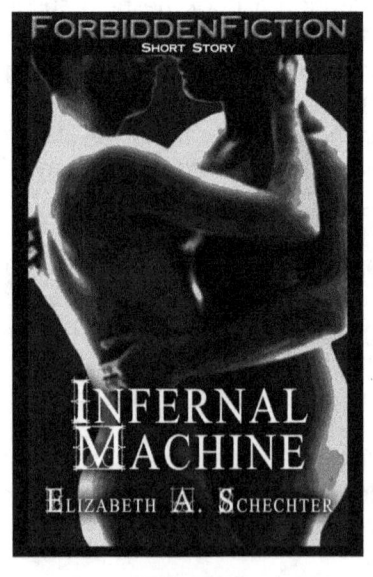

Infernal Machine

Infernal Machine

Gently, I eased my tool into the opening, easing my way down the tight passage. I made sure to restrain myself, knowing that as eager as I was, I might damage something if I simply rushed in. Instead I moved deliberately, seeking the treasures hidden within....

"Blast!" My probe clattered to the floor as I jammed my bleeding thumb into my mouth and glared at the machine in front of me. Across the room, my lover looked up from his book.

"Elijah?" he asked, clearly wanting an explanation.

"The infernal machine savaged me," I grumbled around my thumb. I turned so that I could look at Sasha, a much more pleasant view than the obstinate machine that now seemed to be laughing at me. Aleksandr Andreyevich Koslov, affectionately called Sasha, was sprawled indolently on our bed, looking very much the dissolute Russian nobleman. I'd been dizzy in love with Aleksandr since our first day at *L'Académie des Sciences Mécaniques* in Paris. And, for some reason I never understood, he loved me in return. It couldn't have been my breeding; compared to his bloodlines, my own pedigree was pure peasantry. My father was a rabbi in a small village just outside Calais, my mother a rabbi's wife and the daughter of another rabbi. I was the oldest of six children, and until two years ago, the one destined to follow my father's footsteps. Until the day I took apart the boiler in my mother's kitchen and redesigned it so that it was twice as efficient and used less than half the fuel. When my father saw what I had done, he decided that my younger brother would be better suited to the life of a rabbi. I, Elijah Moyse Saloman, was to be an Artificer, the first ever from our village. I'd arrived in Paris without even the barest hint of the world I was going to be thrust into. Wild, wicked Montmarte, with its cabarets and music halls, and its whores of either sex. And wild, wicked Sasha, whom I loved like I loved no other.

Sasha swung his legs over the edge of the bed and stood up, crossing over to sit down on the floor next to me. He was incredibly handsome, his long, dark hair hanging loose around his shoulders, his shirt hanging open to better face the heat of the summer afternoon. He frowned slightly at the machine and then poked me in the shoulder. "So what is this thing? You've not told me yet."

"I haven't?" I frowned, thinking back. Surely I'd mentioned something...?

"No. For four days you've barely said a word to me. You haven't eaten, unless I was feeding you. The only times you've come to bed was when I picked you up and put you there myself, usually after you'd passed out on the floor. So what is this thing that you are so enamored of? Other than being the most singularly ugly chair that I have ever seen?"

I grinned at his very apt description; it *was* a singularly ugly chair, if that was all it was. Surely, that was all the ironmonger had thought it, or else he'd never have let me have it for the pittance I paid. I reached out and ran my fingers over the now-bright brass. "It's a Carstairs machine."

"It isn't!" Sasha gasped, leaning closer. "How can you tell?"

"The hinges. Look at them; no one but Carstairs used that odd box hinge." It had been that detail that had caught my eye and sent me scrambling after the cart. "That was my first hint. Then I found his mark when I was polishing the brass. There, where the seat casts a shadow. Do you see it?"

Sasha nodded, "I see it... but none of his other works are this ugly. His work was always simple and elegant."

He was right, of course. Carstairs had been the Artificer's Artificer, and his work had always been simple in form. The complexity, he'd always said, was on the inside. The design on this chair was elaborate, with brass scroll-work ornamenting nearly the entire construct. "An early work, do you think?" I asked.

"I don't know," Sasha shrugged. "What does it do?"

That was the question I was hoping he wouldn't ask. "I don't know yet," I admitted. "I've cleaned and polished the entire thing, I've made certain that the boiler and the tank work, I've replaced anything that looked like it might have needed to be replaced, but I can't get into this compartment." I tapped the panel that formed the pedestal for the seat. "It does open... I think. There is a seam here, and hinges on the edges."

Sasha leaned in close enough that I could smell the light fragrance of the soap he used. He nodded, "I see. Well, that is annoying. You can't tell what it does without opening the case, and if you break open the case, it might not work at all." Sasha looked at me with his fabulously wicked grin. "Have you fired the boiler?"

I shook my head, "Not yet. I wanted to be certain that everything else worked first."

"And everything works now?"

"As far as I can tell." I glared at the recalcitrant chair. Without a word, Sasha got to his feet, fetched the pitcher from the washstand, and ceremoniously poured water into the tank.

"Then we shall fire this Carstairs' machine and see what the master wrought and what the student rescued!" he declared, throwing an elaborate bow in my direction. I laughed and went to fetch some kindling.

It took time to get a good head of steam. When, finally, the gauges showed that we had adequate pressure, Sasha came to stand next to me in front of the chair to watch the show.

Nothing happened. We watched and waited in nervous silence for nearly five minutes, then Sasha coughed and looked at me.

"Is there... a switch? A lever? Some way to turn it on?" he asked.

I shook my head slowly, "Not that I found. You look. Maybe I missed it."

He knelt down and crawled around the blasted chair, hunting for a switch that I already knew didn't exist. When finally Sasha was convinced, he sat down next to me on the floor, shoulder pressing against mine, and cursed roundly in Russian before repeating himself in French.

"Four days! Four days you've wasted on this... infernally ugly chair, and all it does is clutter the room!" he railed while I sighed and turned away, starting to clean up my tools. To my surprise, Sasha grabbed the back of my shirt and pulled me into his arms, my back against his chest. "Four days where all you've done in bed is snore at me," he whispered into my ear, tugging my shirt open with one hand, his other hand slipping into my trousers and closing around my quickly hardening cock. I leaned my head back against his shoulder, and was rewarded by his teeth along my neck, nibbling just hard enough to sting. He tugged at my shirt, pulling it off my shoulders, dipping his head down to lick the spot where my shoulder met my neck. Then he shifted, tipping me back until I was lying on the floor with him kneeling over me. He ran his hands down my chest to my waist, fumbling at the buttons on my trousers; I could see how his own trousers were bulging outwards, and moaned softly, reaching for his waist. He laughed and pushed my hands down, tugging my shirt and braces down so that my arms were tangled in them.

"Patience, *miliy moy*. You'll have that in a minute. But after four days of being driven insane by you ignoring me, I'm going to torment you a while longer." He moved down my body, tugging my trousers open and down so that my cock sprang free, then laying down on top of me, pinning me in place. He grinned down at me, his nose nearly touching mine, then kissed me hard enough that his teeth grated against mine. Sasha was taller than I, and weighed nearly ten kilos more—I couldn't move him, couldn't do anything but strain and squirm under him, growing more and more aroused as he ran his agile fingers up and down my sides. He raised himself up just long enough to unbutton his own trousers and pull his cock free, then he took his place again, this time with his cock rubbing deliciously against mine.

"Sasha... please..." I whispered harshly, before yelping as he bit my neck. He started pumping his hips, his cock hot against me, growling as he worked himself into a frenzy. Dimly, I was aware of the distant sound of the bells from Saint-Pierre-de-Montmartre, the church at the top of the hill. At the sound, Sasha froze.

"No, it can't be that late," he said softly, rolling off of me and scrambling to the table. I rolled over and sat up to see him digging around in the litter on the table-top until he found what he was looking for: his pocket watch. He opened it, looked at the time and cursed, *"Chyort voz'mi!"*

"What is it?" I asked as I rolled over and sat up, pulling my shirt up and tucking myself back into my trousers. I could tell that our fun was over for now.

"The Count is in Paris, and I'm supposed to see him tonight," Sasha answered. "I told you... oh... I told you while you were working."

I gasped in shock, "He's here? And he *wants* to see you?" I might have been one of only two people in all of Paris who actually knew the truth, who knew that while Sasha's father really was a Count, his mother was not the Countess. When Sasha had turned eighteen, the Count had given his by-blow a handsome allowance and one-way passage to Paris, the better to hide his indiscretions. Lucky for me.

"The Countess hasn't given him the son he needs. Now there's a chance that he might put her aside. In which case, he'll need an heir." Sasha hurried to the chest at the end of the bed and pulled it open, bringing out what I recognized as his best suit.

I felt my heart lurch when what he'd said sank in. "He'll bring you back to Saint Petersburg," I said softly. It was Sasha's greatest wish, I knew. He wanted to go home, and I knew that one day I'd lose him. I just hadn't expected it to be so soon.

"Not yet, I don't think," Sasha said as he hurried through his toilette, washing up, changing his clothes, brushing his hair and then braiding it neatly. "Even if he does acknowledge me, he'll probably still want me to finish my schooling. The Tsarina is said to be very fond of Artificers..." He turned to look at me, and must have seen something in my face, because he crossed the room and caught my face in his hands, kissing me deeply. "I'm not leaving you, *lubov moy*," he said gently, resting his forehead against mine. He stepped back and held his arms out, "How do I look?"

I smiled at him, and answered him with one of the Russian phrases he used on me, even though he often told me my accent was horrible, *"Vy ochen' krasivy."*

"Beautiful, hm?" he repeated, laughing. "I hope the Count thinks so. Keep yourself warm for me, *mily*. I'll be back late."

"With good news, I hope."

He grinned, "Wish me luck!" He kissed me again and almost ran from the apartment, the door bouncing open as he slammed it in his haste. I followed him and closed the door, locking it behind him and turning to look at the empty apartment. Empty except for a bed and clothes press, a rickety table, bookcases made from pieces of packing crates and bricks. And, of course, the most singularly ugly chair in France. Our only chair, really, since Sasha and I had broken our only other chair a week before.

I sighed and tugged my shirt off, throwing it onto the bed with a muttered curse. There was nothing I could do about Sasha; by the time he came back, he'd be a nobleman in truth, and from tonight on, he'd be counting the days until he returned to Saint Petersburg. And I'd be counting the days until he left me behind. After all, what could a rabbi's son offer a Count?

There was nothing I could do about that infernal machine, either. Apparently, all it was good for was, as Sasha had so aptly put it, cluttering up our room. Although... I gave it a long look and then turned to the shelf where we kept a bottle of oil. Perhaps that chair would be good for something, after all.

It was a strange affectation of mine, and one that Sasha often teased me about, but I disliked masturbating on our bed. It somehow felt dishonest. I stripped off my trousers and poured some oil into my hand, slowly smoothing it over my still-hard cock. Prepared, I sat down on the chair, finding the ugly thing oddly comfortable. I wrapped my hand around my cock and closed my eyes, thinking about Sasha, the smell of his skin, the feel of his hands on me, his cock against mine. The way he loved to tease me until I couldn't stand or speak. The way his mouth felt on my mouth, on my cock... I moaned softly and leaned back a little in the chair, my back pressing against the cool metal. Without warning, the back shifted. The seat sank, just enough to notice. I heard something click, and gears began to turn.

I had done my work well. Before I could gather my thoughts, the mechanism was working, and the ornate scroll-work snapped to life like a trap, pinning my arms to my sides, catching both of my legs, caging my head so that I couldn't turn. I struggled, unable to move at all as the gears kept on turning. The panel that I'd been so desperate to get into earlier opened, the sides rising and taking my legs with them, spreading them wide until it felt like my hips were going to snap. By the time the movement stopped, the chair had tipped back so I was helplessly reclined. I tested my bonds and cursed—I was stuck, and likely to stay that way until Sasha returned and could figure out how to release me. Then I heard another click, and the gears began to turn once more. That was when I saw movement; a pair of metal arms appeared, one rising from between my legs, the other dropping from over my head, and I caught my breath in wonder as I saw what embellished the end of each arm.

The Artificer in me saw first that there were beautifully-made wooden cocks on the arms with the finest articulation that I had ever seen. That voice was quickly silenced when one of the cocks stopped at a level with my hips, and the other lowered itself towards the cage that imprisoned my head. A cage, I suddenly noticed, that had an opening over the mouth that was just large enough to admit the wooden intruder now approaching.

"No..." I whispered. "No! Stop!" I twisted as much as I could, all the while ordering the machine to stop, to release me. It didn't accept voice commands, and soon I wasn't in any position to give them any more. It actually wasn't unpleasant— the cock wasn't too large, and the wood was smooth and warm. I ran my tongue over the surface, finding myself growing aroused again. As if it could tell what I was feeling, the movement of the arm paused for a moment, then slowly started to pump, fucking my mouth gently.

The cock in my mouth muffled my shout of surprise at the sudden pressure against my ass. That cock slid in smoothly, as if it had been greased, and started moving in a slow, steady rhythm that left me moaning and wanting more. I could feel the sweat making my skin slick under the metal bonds, allowing me to shift just enough to emphasize how completely I was bound. This wasn't my first experience with being bound for sex; Sasha had discovered a taste for it somewhere, and had taught me. Sasha insisted that we take turns, but I much preferred being bound, and the tighter the bonds, the better I liked it. It was, in truth, the way that we had broken our chair the week before.

The speed of the pumping increased, and I closed my eyes, sucking hard on the cock in my mouth, imagining that it was Sasha fucking my mouth, his cock in my ass, pounding harder and faster, making me strain against the straps as I tried to move with him, pull him deeper, silently begging him to make me scream. My orgasm was building, harder than ever before. Perhaps that was why it took several minutes for me to notice that the machine had stopped moving, and even longer to gather my wits and understand what had happened.

In the end, the answer was ridiculously simple—Sasha had only put enough water in the tank to test the mechanism. I groaned in frustration and waited for the machine to release me. Only there was no slacking of the straps, no movement, no release. After several long minutes, I realized that the straps weren't going to move, that the empty tanks meant that I'd be stuck until Sasha came home.

If he ever did. I whimpered as that nasty little thought occurred to me. Suppose the Count didn't want Sasha to finish his schooling? Suppose he wanted his new heir to return to Saint Petersburg with him immediately? What then? He wouldn't need his books any more, and any clothes he had here would never be suitable for the heir to a Count. There would be no reason for Sasha to come back to the apartment. No reason at all.

Panic struck all at once, grabbing me in its fist and squeezing. He was gone, he was never coming back, I was trapped and I would die like this. I screamed and fought the straps, lost in primal terror until at last I passed out from exhaustion, falling into a restless sleep punctuated with vague, terror-filled dreams.

I woke to the rattle of a key in the lock and the groaning of the door hinges. In the faint moonlight, I could see Sasha coming into the apartment, and almost wept with relief. He closed the door quietly, no doubt thinking me asleep. As soon as the door closed, I started to grunt, struggling weakly and trying to get his attention. I heard his breath catch.

"Illyusha?" he called softly, sounding confused. I heard the floor creak as he moved, then the lamp flared and the room filled with dim light. I could see him frowning at the empty bed. Then he turned a little more and faced me. His eyes went wide, *"Bozhe moi!"*

It wasn't hard to know what he was seeing: his lover, bound in brass, obscenely spread and presented like a two *franc* whore, impaled by a pair of wooden cocks. I grunted again, and Sasha startled, rushing forward and stopping at my side, his hands hovering over my torso.

"Illyusha, are you all right?" he asked, his eyes darting here and there, taking in all the information he could. He grabbed the gag and tried to pull it from my mouth; it didn't move. I grunted, and he met my eyes and grimaced. "Once for yes, twice for no."

I grunted once, and he relaxed. Then he scowled, "There's no way for you to tell me what happened. Or how to get you out of this."

I closed my eyes for a moment, then did my best to say the word 'water' around the gag. He looked puzzled, then shook his head.

"Let's stay with yes and no. Ah... you found how to turn it on? No? Then this was an accident. I see." He walked around behind the chair, and I heard him moving there. "The boiler is cold... Illyusha, you've been like this for hours?"

I grunted once, and he reappeared, "*Mily*, do I need to get a sledgehammer?"

I grunted twice, emphatically, and he held his hands up, "All right! No smashing the machine. But I do need to get you out of there." He glared at the chair, crouching down. Then he stood up and ran his fingers through his hair. "I don't know. Let me... let me fire the boiler. Perhaps that will make it start doing..." He gestured and stepped back, shaking his head, "I'll fill the tank to the top this time."

It took him five trips to the cistern, and then an impossibly long time crouched out of sight. Finally, he reappeared.

"It will take some time for the pressure to build enough for the mechanism to work," he said, resting one hand on my stomach. "So, shall I guess what happened?"

I grunted, and he smiled slowly, "You were being impatient, weren't you?" His fingers started to trail over my skin, skipping over the brass straps, fluttering over my nipples until I groaned. He laughed and pulled away, "So impatient. You couldn't have waited for me? Now, should I let you wait? Let this amazing discovery of yours finish you off?" He smiled at me and crossed his arms over his chest, "Or shall I entertain myself while we wait? Because you really do look very inviting like this."

Just the idea of Sasha touching me, doing whatever he willed whilst I was helplessly bound by Carstairs' infernal chair was enough to make me moan in lust, and make my cock slowly start to rise again. He laughed and moved to stand between my legs.

"I assume that is a yes?" he asked. Without waiting for my answering grunt, he grabbed my half-hard cock in his hand and slowly started to stroke me erect. He knew what I liked, what set me off like a Roman candle. And he knew very well how to keep me on the edge, keep me growing ever more frantic until at last he allowed me release. That is what he proceeded to do to me, playing with my cock and bollocks, licking my nipples with his rough tongue, then biting them hard enough to make me yell around the gag. He tried tugging on the cock buried in my ass, and found that he could get enough movement to make me gasp and moan. Then he grinned wickedly at me and proceeded to strip away his own clothing, letting the pieces fall where they would until he was naked, his erection standing out proudly. He studied me for a long moment, then stepped back, a satisfied look on his face.

"Oh, this will be interesting," he said. He turned away and picked up the bottle of oil, pouring a liberal amount into his palm. Then he moved to stand next to me, dousing my cock with the oil, anointing it like some pagan icon until it shone in the dim light. Without any hesitation, he climbed up to straddle me, my cock pressing against his ass. His eyes twinkled as he looked down at me and said, "Why should you have all the fun, hmm?"

He lowered himself slowly, and as he did so, I heard the gears start to turn again, and the cock in my ass started to move once more. I squeaked around the gag, and Sasha stopped moving, looking at me and seeing the cock fucking my mouth.

"*Bozhe moi...*" he murmured, his breath coming faster as he took me into himself, surrounding me with heat and delicious pressure. When he could go no further, when I was as deep as I ever had been, he started to rock, one hand resting on my abdomen as he used his oil-slick hand to stroke his own cock. I could hear Sasha's moans of pleasure over the music of the machine, feel his body growing tighter around me, and I knew that he would shoot before too long. The cock in my ass picked that moment to pick up speed, pumping harder and faster than Sasha ever could. The cock in my mouth plunged deeper into my throat, cutting off my already muffled screams of pleasure as I shot. A moment later, I felt warm wet splattering on my chest, and Sasha slumped over me, breathing heavily.

He raised his head and looked at me, "I wish I could kiss you."

I grunted once, tired and sore, and wondering what would happen next. I could hear the gears turning still, even though the cocks had fallen quiet. Then the chair shuddered; Sasha looked alarmed and scrambled off of my lap, looking at me warily.

He need not have been so alarmed. I felt the cocks sliding from my mouth and ass, then the chair shuddered and straightened, the straps receding until they once again resembled nothing more scroll-work on a singularly ugly chair. I stayed where I was, my head resting against the back of the chair, completely spent.

"Illyusha?" Sasha said quietly. "Can you move?"

I swallowed, feeling the soreness in my throat, "I don't know."

"Give me your hand." Sasha took my hand and tugged me to my feet, then caught me when my poor, abused legs gave out and I tumbled to the floor. We sprawled together for a moment, then he kissed me, deep and slow.

The kiss was interrupted by a long '*wheesh*' sound from the chair; we both jumped and turned to see steam escaping through the seams in the pedestal.

"It cleans itself," Sasha murmured, wonder in his voice. "Is there anything that Carstairs didn't think of?"

"A safety release," I answered wryly, drawing a laugh from Sasha. I looked up at him and smiled.

"Thank you for coming back," I whispered.

He looked puzzled, "Where else would I go?"

Reluctantly, I told him of my panic; he drew me into his arms and held me tightly.

"*Miliy moy*, I'd no more leave you behind than I'd fly to the moon. I made it very clear to my father... oh, yes, he's acknowledged me! I told him that I would marry to suit my station, but that you were going to be at my side for the rest of my days." He sobered, "If... if that's what you want. Is that what you want, Illyusha?"

I blinked, almost too tired to understand what he was saying, "You want me to come to Saint Petersburg with you?"

"Yes, if you're willing."

"I..." I couldn't think. All I could do was pull his head down to mine and kiss him. He smiled against my lips.

"I assume that is a yes?" he whispered.

"After all," I murmured back. "The Tsarina is said to be fond of Artificers."

"And I'll be bringing the genius who rebuilt a Carstairs machine into her court," he added. He looked past me at the now-quiescent chair, and a slow smile spread across his face. He looked back at me, "My turn?"

"Oh, yes!"

If you enjoyed this story, you can sign up for a free membership at ForbiddenFiction and discuss it with other readers and the author at the *Infernal Machine* story page at http://forbiddenfiction.com/story/es1-1-000270.

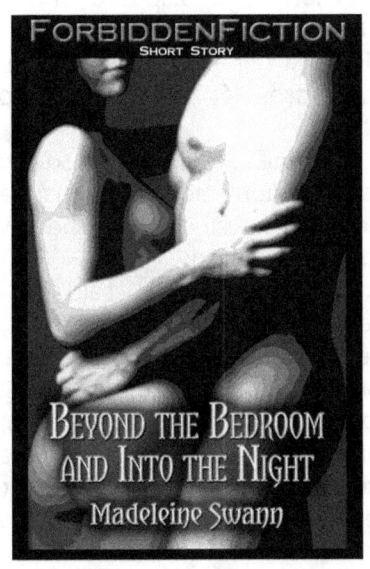

FORBIDDENFICTION
SHORT STORY

BEYOND THE BEDROOM
AND INTO THE NIGHT
Madeleine Swann

Beyond the Bedroom and Into the Night

Beyond the Bedroom and Into the Night

The gas lamp beyond the bedroom window had been lit, lifting some of the heavy mood. It also helped the three anxious men, jackets and top hats long ago disposed of, to see some of the redness seep back into Amelia's lips and cheeks. She lay in her bed, white nightdress frilling at her small wrists, when her fingers began to twitch as the moon rose. Her father rushed from his stool to her side, grabbing her hand.

He, her uncle, and the doctor were so preoccupied by her fluttering dark eyes they didn't notice the maid enter and light the gas lanterns on the wall, pausing when she saw the girl stirring, crossing herself and leaving quickly.

"The tincture must have worked," said the doctor. Her uncle folded his arms, keeping his doubts to himself.

"How do you feel, my dear?" asked her father.

"Somewhat improved." Amelia attempted to sit up, her black hair sliding over her shoulders. She did indeed feel improved, but not by any draught or poultice given by the doctor. There was something in the night air, with all its fog and filth, that restored her, and soothed the aches and shivers she'd been plagued by since receiving the odd wound on her neck.

"Your brother should be here within the hour," said her uncle, checking his gold pocket watch.

"Won't he miss his lessons?" Despite her worry, the thought of seeing her beloved Clem gave Amelia another spark of health.

"Don't you worry," her father squeezed her hand. "He's clever enough to keep up."

"Of course," said her uncle. "University isn't much of a priority when one's sister is gravely ill." He realised his mistake as soon as

166

the words left his mouth, earning a furious glance from Amelia's father.

The doctor thought swiftly to change the subject. "It's best you keep as tranquil as possible. Be still and do not tax yourself so. Why not lie down and close your eyes?"

Amelia followed his advice, accepting with good grace the fussing as the men set the pillows correctly. She listened to their whispering, voices like the wind in the grass and the breeze on the sea. Much louder in the foreground was the rhythmic pounding of blood in their veins and even the muscle constriction when they swallowed. They smelled of earth and sweat and meat. She sensed the youth and vitality of the doctor and the strength of her uncle and wished for no reason she could fathom they would step closer to her.

Her mouth watered and she tried to think of other things. She remembered the cupcakes in The Olive Branch tea rooms and riding piggy back on her brother's shoulders. She remembered the smell of the fireplace on his skin and the ease with which he carried her.

Troubled, Amelia turned her back on the others. Something flooded her body, made it tingle and prickle, and she was afraid they would notice. She was more awake than she had ever been when the sound of hooves and wheels could be heard coming down the gravel path. They heard the muffled sounds of Evelyn, the Housekeeper, cooing over the visitor before urging the maid to carry his suitcase to his old room.

Her brother, Clem, had grown taller, broader, and his chin now bristled with short black hair. His brown eyes, however, were fearful and his lips tight as he ran to the bed to embrace his sister. Beneath the attic scent of libraries, Amelia detected something deeper, something primal. She gritted her teeth while he held her hand, willing him not to notice how her pulse raced.

"What happened, Melly?" Amelia picked over her memory and sought the details she told her father before. She had gone for a late stroll in the gardens, heard a noise, and then some beast was upon her. The next moment she had awoken with two strange marks on her neck and felt feverish and weak. Her face burned with the omitted details; the stranger by the azaleas, the heat of flesh on flesh, the sensation of silk and lace and forbidden rubbings. The entire event was as misty in her mind as the sky in autumn, but its physical effects still made themselves known between her legs. Clem was looking at her curiously. "How can I help?"

She turned her head and scrutinized the hedges beyond the window. A soft voice called to her, making every hair on her body point upright. "Amelia," it called again and she closed her eyes, sighing deeply. She felt the presence withdraw and, panicked, she reached after it. The others ran to her and Clem held her other hand in an attempt to soothe her. She buried her face in the crook of his neck, listening to the tide of his blood.

"Whatever creature has poisoned her must be outside," said her father grimly. "Come. No, Clem, you stay with your sister. Tend to her needs." Amelia's father, her uncle, and the doctor hurried out the door. Clem looked momentarily aggrieved but his attention soon turned back to his sister. The stillness of the room was a salve to her wounds.

"It's good to see you, Clem," she pulled him towards her for another embrace. He removed his jacket and clambered awkwardly over her, causing them both to giggle, until he lay beside her. Outside, shouts and the soft glow of gas lanterns were a distant reminder of their troubles.

"Shall we have a game of 'I'm thinking of something'? I'll let you go first."

"Very well. Hmm..." Amelia searched her mind while she pressed herself into Clem's comforting body, burying her head between his neck and the pillow. "Thought of something."

"Right! Are you a man?" Amelia shook her head, wrapping her arm around his waist. "Are you a woman?" Clem's eyes rolled up to the ceiling while he thought. "Erm, are you a beast?" Amelia began to kiss along his neck, reaching slowly for the pulse at the side of his throat. "Melly!" Clem pulled away sharply, regarding her with large eyes, "What are you doing?"

Amelia couldn't answer; she didn't know. She was aware of a sense of shame and horror, but they meant little to her at this point. Her heart danced with exhilaration as she reached for his hand and gently pulled it towards her. Clem looked into her eyes and something unspoken seemed to soothe him; something in her scent perhaps, a new pheromone emanating from her. He allowed his palm to be placed over her breast and Amelia felt the nipple harden beneath his warmth. His tentative touch became a squeeze and then a gentle tickle. His breathing had changed, grown deeper. Amelia lifted his finger to her mouth.

"Ouch," his brow furrowed at the nip but he didn't pull away. Strength seeped into her limbs as she sucked the blood from him.

"There it is!" yelled a voice outside, her uncle. With a terrified gasp Amelia hobbled from the bed to look out the window. Clem was immediately upon her, pulling her back.

"No!" she wailed, pushing him away, her hair mingling with the net curtains in the cool wind. The gun in her uncle's hand was cocked and all three men were racing into the blackness of the gardens. In the distance, a ghostly figure flitted between the hedges, apparently unperturbed by its pursuers.

"Come along," Clem lifted her in his arms. She nuzzled into him, breathing in the aroma of dusty books and incense and that peculiar, musky scent beneath it all. He laid her on the bed and curled up next to her, the safe familiarity returning as she pressed herself against his body, feeling as though she would sink inside of him if she could. He kissed her head and she threw an arm around him, running her fingertips down the back of his crumpled waistcoat. Clem's breathing paused and the atmosphere became charged. Amelia felt every muscle movement in their bodies and heard the river of his blood pour down to his crotch. She knew it was there waiting before she reached for it, his erection straining and desperate for contact. Through the material, she wrapped her hand around it, listening to the voice in the back of her mind, a husky female voice she now knew so well.

Clem sighed and moved his hips with her as she massaged his bulge back and forth, gently at first, and then harder. He fumbled with the buttons on his trousers, catching her eye in the process. Amelia knew her gaze was steady, her actions guided as they were by her new mistress.

Clem's face was filled with confusion, disturbed at how he could allow this to happen. Mixed with it, though, were pink cheeks and enlarged pupils, hot with desire and need. His erection sprang forward. She gripped it tightly and massaged it, drawing a gruff moan. He reached once more for her breast, tugging hard this time on her waiting nipples. Amelia yelped and shocks of pleasure shot down her body. She leaned into him and found his lips with hers, sinking into the soft wetness and brushing her tongue against his. Kissing him was familiar, safe and somehow right.

She gasped and her body jolted with excitement as he reached beneath her nightgown and stroked her thighs with smooth fingers. She imagined him in gentlemen's clubs and brothels late at night. Opium smoke would curl about him as he caressed the bodies of unknown women, removing their corsets with trained hands. Amelia opened herself eagerly as he slid one and then two fingers inside her wetness, rolling her body with him. He leaned over her and found her nipples with his lips and tongue. She felt as though she were melting from such a multitude of sensations all over her body. Clem gently drove his fingers deep inside and curled them forwards to tickle a spot she had never known was there.

"Oh, yes, my brother," she whispered. He crooked his thumb upwards to stroke the button that twitched and pulsed as it begged to be touched. His lips again found hers before drawing back, his face above hers, watching and waiting.

He rubbed and tickled with his nimble fingers, each stroke bringing her closer to an overwhelming burning heat.

"That's it, carry on," she murmured, thrusting her body against his arm. All sounds from outside, and her sense of fear, disappeared as she opened her eyes to look into his.

"Something is happening," she said, and then it came, an explosion that poured through her body and flooded her brain. She moaned deeply and loudly, all the while her dark eyes on his. It lasted an eternity as he continued to rub her secret spot. Once it subsided, she removed his hand. "Your turn."

Clem's erection had grown harder from watching her come, and now it strained upwards as Amelia rolled him onto his back. She straddled him and rolled his shaft gently back and forth, kneeling to rub him enticingly against her opening. Clem watched with his mouth slightly parted, his breath quick. She teased him by nudging the tip inside and lifting herself up again, enjoying his look of need and frustration. When he could no longer stand it, she sank down, taking him in deep. They sighed together, his hands curling about her hips. She leaned over him, her hands on either side of his neck and their stomachs pressed together. They rocked back and forth slowly, she breathing in his scent once more and he gently gripping her hips.

The footsteps outside grew louder and Amelia knew the men were coming back to the house. Clem seemed not to notice, responding only when she lifted her body up on her arms and rolled her hips with a new intensity. Clem bit his lip and Amelia heard the front door opening. The men spoke hurriedly with the maid downstairs as Clem's face reddened.

"Oh, yes," he groaned; he was close. The stairs creaked as the men made their way up and Amelia felt Clem shudder as his sperm shot inside her. This was how they were when the door was opened and their uncle and the doctor entered.

At first there was nothing, no reaction and no fury, and then it all came at once.

"What is this, what are you doing?" They yelled as one, horrified. Clem blinked as if in a stupor, then seemed to realise the situation.

"What would your father say at this...this vile show?" their uncle fumed.

"What happened?" said Amelia, now panicking, "You didn't hurt her, did you?"

"Hurt her?" The doctor was wide-eyed with disbelief. "That creature was on her way here to attack you."

"No," Amelia yelled, "She would do no such thing. You must leave her be."

The horses in the stables made a furious sound, kicking against the doors and shrieking. A figure appeared at the window, white skinned and clad in a lady's golden gown. Her blonde hair was piled prettily on her head and delicate tendrils curled about her neck, but her mouth and chest were stained with a river of blood. The men shrieked in terror and Clem swooned, his eyelids flickering fitfully.

The figure hissed, revealing long fangs, and within moments Amelia's uncle was in bloody pieces. The doctor was whimpering, pinned to the floor under the creature's inhuman grip. She gestured to Amelia, who tiptoed nervously forwards. The creature bit into the doctor's neck and he wailed piteously.

"Drink from him," the creature whispered. Amelia did as she was told. With each drop her illness faded and soon she felt as though she could tear the house down with one flick of her wrist.

She sat up and laughed, freer than she had ever been. The doctor's blood seeped out over the floor towards them in an oozing, sickly pool, but they made no effort to move. The creature leaned forwards and took Amelia's cotton covered nipple in her mouth. Amelia shivered at the unexpected pleasure and reached beneath the hem of the creature's petticoats, finding her wet secrets. She did as Clem had done: rubbing, tickling and curling her fingers deep inside until her new mistress shook and shivered.

"Come, we have been here long enough," said her mistress once they were done, straightening her bloodied skirts. She strode towards Clem and lifted him in her arms, carrying him towards the window where Amelia joined her.

"Like one big happy family," said Amelia, and followed her beyond the bedroom and into the night.

If you enjoyed this story, you can sign up for a free membership at ForbiddenFiction and discuss it with other readers and the author at the *Beyond the Bedroom and Into the Night* story page at http://forbiddenfiction.com/story/ms1-1-000208.

Clockwork Dolls

Chapter 1:
The Inventor's Wonderful Toys

The planet was not Earth, but it had been built to be very much like Earth. Here, on Mundus, the city of Londinium Novum sprawled out against the uniform emerald green of the Neo-Britannic countryside like a shining brass gear set onto a jeweler's case of green velvet. Underneath the bustle of Londinium Novum beat the great heart of the world; rather than a red-hot heart of living iron, the heart of this planet was an enormous boiler. The boiler powered the factories that plugged themselves into the earth, sent heat along pipelines and into millions of homes, and set in motion an endless, interconnected system of gears that made the continents themselves drift slowly on the artificial seas. It was a masterpiece of clockwork and illusion.

In a laboratory in the middle of Londinium Novum lived an inventor, who created her own illusions for the benefit of her lady patron. Anke Schopfer had been working for the aristocratic Fitzbaine family ever since the sole daughter and heir, Phoebe, had been old enough to be introduced into society. The engineering prodigy had been plucked from the primary schools of Neue Prussia, given all the funding she needed, and ordered to make all the toys that Lady Phoebe Fitzbaine wanted. When she was younger, the toys had been marvelous creations of whimsy—mechanical horses that ran and snorted steam, giant teddy bears that gave perfect hugs, dolls that really walked and talked. Anke had passed her adolescence in the lavish laboratory, spending weeks painstakingly learning from engineering manuals and her own mistakes and discoveries, perfecting her craft. But as Lady Phoebe had grown older and her tastes in entertainment had matured, Anke's inventions had matured as well.

Anke stood watching her latest creations, a troupe of clockwork burlesque dolls that gave perfect, sensuous performances every time. Lady Phoebe was of marriageable age, but had yet to become betrothed, and her high status in society dictated that she must remain virginal and pure until her wedding day. But her sexual appetites were nearly insatiable, a secret she would only tell Anke, and so she had commissioned a fleet of dolls to perform the acts she so desired in front of her.

The dolls were all beautiful, with smooth, flawless skin, heavy-lidded eyes, soft reddened lips, graceful limbs, and delicate fingers. Anke had constructed them with terrifying steel skeletons, and then spent several weeks trying to layer rubber, fabric, and wax in a way that would perfectly mimic the feel of human flesh. Their bosoms, buttocks, and hips were lusciously padded, and Anke had personally purchased silk stockings, underthings, and scandalous dresses that complemented each doll's unique coloring.

They danced, swaying their artificial hips from side to side, twirling their feather boas and shimmying for the benefit of an audience they could not see or hear. Anke nodded in satisfaction as the dolls gravitated towards each other, guided by the magnetic elements in their skeletons, and began to gyrate over each others' bodies. Carved hands slapped padded asses, artificially wettened mouths pressed kisses to painted cheeks and breasts stuffed with sand and rubber, and jointed fingers slid into pudendas that felt no pleasure.

The dolls were working perfectly, and Anke tried to keep her pleasure in their performance limited to the satisfaction that came from testing an invention successfully. They were indistinguishable from human women, if you did not look at their glassy eyes; Anke had slipped out to study the movements of burlesque dancers and worked for hours to make the dolls move precisely like the human dancers would. She watched as they moved fluidly, naturally, and pride swelled warmly in her chest. She had imagined the dolls, had made them with her own hands, and now they were real.

Anke had modeled pieces of each doll after her patron. One doll had Lady Phoebe's clear blue eyes and long lashes, another her rosy cheeks, another her waves of golden hair, another her plump buttocks, yet another her small and ladylike hands, and another her full, round breasts that Anke longed to kiss. To Anke, Lady Phoebe was the epitome of beauty, a precious jewel forever out of her reach.Once her lady chose to wed, Anke knew that she would be let go, and the dolls she created would be the only thing of Lady Phoebe she would have left.

The inventor sighed and waited for the dolls to wind down. Anke did not consider herself as attractive as Lady Phoebe, or even as attractive as the dolls she had created. She kept her glossy black hair cut short, hid her warm brown eyes behind goggles and her high cheekbones behind a welding mask, and hid her slim waist, pert breasts, and long, athletic legs behind shapeless overalls. Her hands were large and square, her arms muscular from toting heavy pieces of metal and solid tools, for she had never felt comfortable with an assistant.

As the last doll wound down her performance, a silver bell chimed—it was Lady Phoebe. Anke hurried to the front door of the laboratory. Her space was cluttered and utilitarian, full of discarded inventions, scraps, and tools, but there was still some elegance to it —the ceiling was high and covered with gold scrolling designs, the floor was made of translucent marble, and the gas lamps that flickered on the walls were made of elegant brass and crystal. Anke had cleared a floor space in the middle of her laboratory to show her patron her designs. Her ladyship had never uttered a derogatory word towards the state of Anke's workshop, but Anke still prayed that she would find it hospitable.

Anke opened the door and bowed low. "Lady, your new toys await you!"

Lady Phoebe smiled. "My dear Anke, I'm so terribly excited! I can't wait to see what you've created. Every time I'm here, you absolutely outdo yourself." She stepped in, her high-buttoned traveling boots clicking on the floor, and shed her drab, black traveling coat. Underneath, she was wearing an elegant blue dress which set off her eyes perfectly and which was just a little lower-cut than was, strictly speaking, considered to be proper. She had put up her hair, Anke noted, which was prudent in a place where machines roamed the grounds.

"If you would follow me, my lady," Anke said, "I'll lead you to the testing floor." She stood with her hands behind her back, back straight and at attention.

Lady Phoebe sighed. "Anke, how long have we known each other?"

Anke shrugged one shoulder. "Ten years. You were seven. I was fourteen."

"And we've been friends for that long," Lady Phoebe said. "Why do you still insist on referring to me as 'my lady', Anke? It's so ridiculously formal." She followed Anke through the laboratory, occasionally stopping to marvel at a half-finished invention, the play of light on a machine. "Oh my, this is beautiful. What does it do?" Anke turned to see Lady Phoebe daintily peel off one white lace glove and run her manicured fingertips along the shining surface of a small brass gear. She imagined it to be Lady Phoebe's fingertips on her skin, and blushed.

For the past few years, she had been becoming more and more formal with her patron. It was not because she tired of her company, but quite the opposite; Anke feared that becoming too familiar with Lady Phoebe would ruin their friendship, or, even worse, Lady Phoebe's chances at a good marriage. . Although Anke was a skilled engineer, she was of common stock—even if Lady Phoebe did consent to marry her, the match would ruin her ladyship's standing in society forever, cause her friends and relations to desert her, and strip her of her dowry and inheritance rights. Anke could not bear the thought of being responsible for her friend's downfall.

"It is just a silly gadget," Anke said. "I was trying to extract sunlight from oranges."

"Is it really? How marvelous—or are you joking with me?" Lady Phoebe giggled. "You know I can never tell." She turned back to the pile, brushing her hand along the elegant curve of a curled piece of metal.

Lady Phoebe had always been impressed by the beauty and grace Anke worked hard to instill in her inventions, the marvel by which the inventor turned bits of metal and rubber into moving, working toys. When they had been younger and Anke had been less cautious, she had been eager to try to share her knowledge with Lady Phoebe, to bring her friend into the sphere in which she worked and be understood by her, to make them a little more equal.

But Lady Phoebe had had little patience for her tutoring, preferring to use their time together to gossip, giggle, and inquire into Anke's living habits. After the first few sessions saw Lady Phoebe making no real progress in understanding even basic principles of mechanics, her parents had stopped the tutoring altogether.

But Anke knew that Lady Phoebe loved the workshop. Now, her friend lifted her head, gazing at the expanse of the space, at the dusty sunlight filtering through the windows, making the steel and brass fittings and scraps sparkle and glint. "I shall miss this place when I'm married."

"Married?" Anke blinked. "So soon?"

"Oh, yes," Lady Phoebe said. "I'm almost eighteen, you know, and Mother's already lined up half-a-dozen interviews with suitors. The Countess Montbaden and her son are coming to visit tomorrow. If they don't approve of me, well, they are only the first in line." She sighed. "But let's not think of it now, Anke. I'd rather see my new toys."

Anke's heart dropped into her stomach. She could not imagine anyone turning down Lady Phoebe's hand in marriage. Her friend would surely leave her forever. Still, she kept the tremor out of her voice as she led Lady Phoebe to the testing floor. "They're just like the burlesque dancers you saw at that dance hall last year. Now you won't have to sneak out of the house when you wish to see them."

Lady Phoebe's hands flew to her cheeks, and she stared openmouthed at the dolls before exclaiming, "Why, Anke! They're marvelous!" She began to circulate among the dolls as though they were guests at a ball, touching and plucking at each one. "They feel real! How lovely!"

"Watch this." Anke produced a brass box with a lever set into it, and pulled the lever slowly downwards. A delicate grinding noise emanated from the dolls. "Pull the lever, and they wind up." When the lever had been depressed all the way, the dolls began to move, fluid and graceful with the occasional jerk or halt.

Lady Phoebe clasped her hands together, her blue eyes shining bright. "Lovely, lovely," she murmured. "Oh, Anke, I feel I shall be satisfied for a million years watching them dance."

"Just wait," Anke said, "it gets even better." She smiled, too pleased at Lady Phoebe's delight in the dolls to force herself to feel nothing. After all, this was her only real purpose, and if she could not enjoy the fruits of her labor fulfilled, then certainly there was nothing for her at all. She stuck her hands into the capacious pockets of her overalls and grinned as Lady Phoebe squealed, watching the dolls drift into each other's arms.

They watched the dolls complete their performance. Anke was proud of the way she'd animated the faces of the dolls to feign orgasm, their lips parting and their eyelids fluttering in pleasure. If Lady Phoebe stayed for long enough, she might even be able to fit them out with voice-boxes, she thought. She glanced over at Lady Phoebe to see how she'd enjoyed the show.

Lady Phoebe stared at the dolls, wringing her hands. Her lips were tight. "Anke," she said, her voice strained, "Anke, I cannot accept these dolls."

Anke felt hot tears prickle at the corner of her eyes. "Are they not to your liking?"

"They are! That is the problem." Lady Phoebe chewed on the tip of her finger, shifting her eyes away from Anke. "They are too much to my liking. I watch them, and I cannot help but long for what I cannot have. They do not satisfy my desire, but merely stimulate it. Oh, Anke, I know the work you've put into these, but they will only torment me."

Anke bit her lip. She'd put so much work into the dolls, and now her dearest friend in all the world was rejecting them as unsatisfactory. It stung, and stung hard. Would she ever be enough for Lady Phoebe? She picked up a wrench and moved towards the dolls. "I didn't mean to tease you. I'll smash them, if you like."

"No, wait!" Lady Phoebe put out a hand to stop her. "Please, they are masterpieces, and I know how much work you put into your inventions—I could not bear the thought of them being destroyed. Sell them, keep them, display them. Just do not bring them near me."

Anke dropped the wrench on the table and sighed. "My lady, is there anything I could make for you that would satisfy you? When I made you that rocking-horse that really galloped, you wanted a carousel the week after. When I made you that remote-controlled zeppelin, you wanted me to make a larger one with a basket on it so that you could ride in it. And now that I've given you dolls to play with, you want me to make them human."

Lady Phoebe covered her mouth with her hands. "Anke, I didn't mean it like that!" Her face fell, and she bowed her head. "I'm sorry, I really am. The dolls are perfect, and they are exactly what I asked for. You have satisfied every request I've made of you. I'm sorry I can't be satisfied, Anke, it's terrible of me, but I can't help it."

"Then what do you want?" Anke begged. "Lady, all I want to do is give you what you want. Just tell me."

Lady Phoebe sniffled. "I don't know! Something that will satisfy the desire, really and truly satisfy it. I'm going mad, Anke." Her face was flushed, and Anke's mind wandered to the thought of Lady Phoebe's arousal. Perhaps, under her bodice, her corset and chemise, Lady Phoebe's pink nipples were stiff and aching for the touch of a soft tongue or a firm pinch. Perhaps her cunt was beginning to moisten, was already wet and dripping, soaking her linen bloomers through—the wet fabric rubbing against Lady Phoebe's engorged clitoris, sensitive and needing touch...

Anke caught herself and bowed stiffly. "I will have something for you within the week, my lady."

"Oh, thank you!" Lady Phoebe threw her arms around Anke. Anke stiffened at the sudden warmth of Lady Phoebe's body against hers, the soft and welcome press of her friend's breasts, the heat that radiated from the space between her thighs. She put her arms around Lady Phoebe's back hesitantly, embracing her. "Anke," murmured Lady Phoebe, her lips soft against Anke's neck, "I am certain your ingenuity will save me."

Anke pressed her own lips against Lady Phoebe's white neck, trying to keep herself from placing a kiss on her friend's skin. Lady Phoebe's neck smelled like attar of roses, the scent delicate and sensual, and Anke inhaled deeply. She heard Lady Phoebe take an answering breath, as though Anke's own scent of sweat and metal were half as alluring as Lady Phoebe's perfume, and Anke could not help but press a quick, soft kiss to Lady Phoebe's skin.

"Oh," Lady Phoebe murmured, and she placed her fingers against Anke's cheek and turned her head. "Anke..." And then her lips were on Anke's, soft and warm, slick with lipstick.

Anke opened her own mouth reflexively, letting the tip of her tongue wander along Lady Phoebe's lips. She felt the wet tip of Lady Phoebe's tongue on her own, and the contact thrilled through her, making every nerve in her mouth tingle. It was the culmination of ten years of friendship, two years of wanting Lady Phoebe, watching her grow into a gorgeous, sensual young woman who would share the flower of her virginity with her.

Lady Phoebe pulled away. "Anke," she whispered, "we can't. I wish we could, but we can't."

Anke separated herself from Lady Phoebe with what seemed to her to be an act of pure will. She stood a foot away from her friend, body warm and throbbing with need. It was as though she could feel the arousal flooding her veins, making her every nerve stand on end. "You're right," she said, schooling her voice into neutrality. "You will be promised to someone soon, and I have no wish to spoil your betrothal with such a rash encounter."

Lady Phoebe bowed her head. "I am too impulsive," she murmured. "I'll leave you now. Please deliver your gadget to the house when you are finished with it." She turned and left, leaving an empty, aching place in Anke's heart.

Chapter 2:
The Cold Machine

It was only three days later that Anke sent a card summoning Lady Phoebe to her laboratory. "Invention finished," the card said, "arrive at your leisure." Lady Phoebe went straight out the door and nearly ran all the way to Anke's laboratory. The walk from Anke Schopfer's laboratory to the Fitzbaine residence was only a few blocks, but the traverse still seemed an eternity to Phoebe. She passed robot servitors out running errands for their owners, jet-powered carriages carrying fine lords and ladies, and beggars and orphans with rusty metal legs and arms, (many of which were too big or too small for their wearers, likely picked out of the trash or salvaged from scrap), barely seeing any of them for thinking of Anke. The metallic clanking of 'bots, the cries of the beggars and peddlers, and the rusty breathing of the planet under her feet barely reached her ears. Should she give in to her desires and try to seduce Anke? It wouldn't be as though anyone would know. She trusted Anke not to hang any encounter over her head, to keep it secret. Anke had only ever had her best interests at heart, after all.

She arrived disheveled and breathless, and was quite a sight when Anke opened the door. "Hello! Hello! Dear Anke!" Lady Phoebe threw her arms around Anke and kissed her on the cheek. "Oh, I've been waiting for your sign. Is the invention finished? What have you got for me?"

Anke blushed and stepped back. "It's really only a prototype, my lady—I caution you to not become overexcited." She placed the tips of her fingers on Lady Phoebe's elbow and began to guide her into the laboratory. "How was the interview with the Countess?"

182

"It went fairly well," Lady Phoebe said. "The Countess Montbaden is well-preserved, to say the least. I hadn't realized it, but she's at least my mother's age. But did you know, she's got this enormous chunk of land in New Columbia, and she owns half a moon?" Lady Phoebe chatted on about the adventures of the Countess, and Anke felt her heart sink into her stomach. She'd known the Countess Montbaden was at least twice Lady Phoebe's age, and had counted on the interview with the woman to be an unsuccessful one. But Lady Phoebe seemed very taken with the Countess, and Anke supposed sourly that she might as well run off to one of her fabulous estates tomorrow and be done with it.

"What are you looking so sour for?" Lady Phoebe asked.

"Nothing," Anke said, "I do apologize." She bit her lip. "I suppose you'll be quite happy on the Countess's half-a-moon."

"She's got an apartment here, Anke, I suppose we'll be staying there most of the time." Lady Phoebe rolled her eyes. "But not with her son. What a big, hulking brute he was! When the Countess left the room, he tried to—" She motioned to her bustline, which Anke noticed was more exposed than usual. "The dolt slipped his hand into my bodice!"

Anke shook her head in disgust, imagining the forceful, intrusive fingers of a man on Lady Phoebe's soft breasts, spreading his palms over her bosom, the rough fingertips working their way down to her erect nipples. "How awful. Do you think the Countess will send him away?"

Lady Phoebe shrugged. "I should imagine. What woman would want her son molesting her new bride? They say she's a bit of a black widow, but I hear she's only been married the once, and it's certainly not her fault her husband lost his tether to his airship and drifted away in the aether."

"Certainly now," murmured Anke. "And forgive me, my lady, but would you want her molesting you?"

Lady Phoebe giggled. "I might not mind," she admitted. "The Countess is a handsome woman. But, oh, Anke, I don't know. I've only just met her." She laid a hand on Anke's arm. "I've known you since I was a girl. Don't think I'm deserting you for her just yet."

Anke swallowed the lump in her throat. But Lady Phoebe would desert her eventually, leave Anke in her laboratory all alone, with nobody to make toys for. If the Fitzbaine family were not willing to sell Anke the property the laboratory was on, she would not even have that.

"No," she said, "not just yet." They were almost to the testing floor. Anke looked around her at her machines, the gleam of soft light on cold steel and bright brass, and she resolved to harden within herself, to make her heart like the metal she worked with. It was the only way she could imagine surviving a life without Lady Phoebe.

"I've made you a sort of mannequin," she said abruptly. "It's not as realistic as the dolls, and it's not meant to be—the form is more about the function than the style. If this works right, you won't even see it."

Lady Phoebe tilted her head and gave Anke a curious look. "Why not?" she asked.

Anke grinned, her pride in her invention quickly overriding her hasty resolution. "It's exactly the opposite of the dolls. Where the dolls were all promise, all tease, this promises nothing, and it gives everything. It will deliver the sensation I know you've been craving, my lady."

Lady Phoebe clapped her hands together with joy. "Show me!"

Anke picked up a control box from her master workbench. The box had several switches, dials, and buttons on it. Anke knew exactly what variables all of them controlled—she would have to teach them to Lady Phoebe before the invention was delivered to her house. Which would, of course, mean spending more time together; Anke pining for Lady Phoebe's touch as her deft, pale fingers worked the buttons and levers Anke had created. Perhaps it would be easier to label the damned thing.

"This controls it," she said. "But in order to activate the device, certain, er, articles must be worn."

"Articles?" One of Lady Phoebe's eyebrows went up. "What sort of articles, Anke?"

Anke fished around on her workbench and brought out a number of metal rings. "The device is magnetized," she said, "and so these must be worn around the ankles, wrists, waist—they are labeled," she added, "would you like to repair somewhere more private to put them on?"

Lady Phoebe took one of the rings and stared at it. "I believe I wouldn't know how to start," she said with a laugh, and handed the ring back to Anke. "It's your invention, Anke, surely you'll know how they should be positioned." She hiked up her skirt and straightened one leg. "Go ahead, then."

Anke bit her knuckle. She had expected layers of ruffled bloomers, enough to camouflage the shape of Lady Phoebe's limbs, but her friend was wearing sheer silk stockings that clung to her curvaceous leg. "Very well," she said, and knelt at Lady Phoebe's feet. "One ankle, please."

Lady Phoebe kicked off her slipper and extended her shapely ankle. "There you are," she said, smiling. Anke's hands trembled as her fingertips skimmed the surface of the silk stretched over skin. She carefully unlatched the metal ring and enclosed Lady Phoebe's ankle with it. It fit perfectly, the metal wrapping snugly around her.

Anke attached the matching ring to her other ankle, and sat back. "I've got to attach one to you here." She gestured, on her own body, to the place where her leg met her hip. Lady Phoebe nodded and hiked up her skirt even farther, and Anke's jaw dropped. "My lady..." Her eyes traveled up Lady Phoebe's curvaceous limbs, to where she expected layers of underwear, even a single piece of cotton, to be—but there was nothing there. Merely Lady Phoebe's pudenda, soft and pink and perfect, covered in ringlets of dark blonde hair.

"Oh, apologies." Lady Phoebe covered her mouth with her petite hand, but Anke could tell there was a smile behind it. "I supposed it might simply be more efficient to come to the laboratory like this. Less clothing to work through in case one of your inventions required it."

Anke caught her breath. "Have you been coming to the laboratory like this every time?"

"Recently, yes." Lady Phoebe tossed Anke a wicked grin. "Does it shock you a bit, my dear Anke?"

Anke closed her eyes. If any time was the right time to act on her resolution, it was now. She took a deep breath and imagined that Lady Phoebe was merely one of her dolls, fabric and rubber instead of flesh and blood; that she was a stranger, some lady Anke had never met and cared nothing for; lastly, she imagined she herself was a doll, or a robot, that her hands were steel instead of flesh, and that nothing in her could feel.

Thus prepared, Anke ran her hands up Lady Phoebe's leg. She kept telling herself that the warmth of Lady Phoebe's flesh did not affect her, that the place where the silk stockings met soft skin meant nothing, her fingertip grazing the lip of Lady Phoebe's cunt meant nothing. She fastened the metal rings around Lady Phoebe's thighs, dispassionately noting the shivers that went through her friend's body when the cold metal met her skin.

She snapped a larger ring around Lady Phoebe's slim waist easily, then plucked at her friend's sleeve. Her fingers brushed over her friend's palm as she slipped the next ring around Lady Phoebe's wrist. "The next ones go around your arms," she explained, and as her hands traveled over the muscle of Lady Phoebe's graceful arms, she told herself she felt absolutely nothing. But a shiver ran through her when Lady Phoebe closed her eyes as the last metal ring clicked into place.

Lady Phoebe moved her limbs, dancing in place a little, like a waltz with no partner. "They certainly feel strange," she said, "but they're so light. I can barely feel them."

"They're a special magnetic alloy," Anke said. "The machine is made with the same stuff. It emits a magnetic field which can only attract the same metal, so you can wear it all day, if you like, and only this machine will be attracted to it. I intend to formulate an entire garment that's meshed with the material for greater accuracy, but this will do for now."

Lady Phoebe blinked. "Greater accuracy?"

"You'll see. Stand akimbo, please." Anke switched the device on as Lady Phoebe spread out her legs and arms.

The two women strained their eyes and ears, Lady Phoebe quivering with anticipation, Anke in delight. Before long, they heard a soft, rhythmic clanking, a flat sound as of metal on stone. The clanking grew louder, and the dark recesses of the workshop in front of them revealed the gleam of gaslight on shining metal, a stark outline of a man.

The machine was a head taller than Lady Phoebe, and had arms and legs and a torso, but the resemblance to anything human stopped there. Its arms and legs were flat, jointed beams of metal with rings attached to it, corresponding to the rings that were now on Lady Phoebe. Its torso the same flat beam but with flat strips of metal sticking out to resemble a ribcage, and there was a mysterious metal box at the place where its legs met the torso. It moved more like a spider or a horse than a human, something purely leggy, graceful and creeping.

Lady Phoebe gasped and flattened herself against the workbench. "My god, Anke, it's a monster!"

"It's not." Anke pushed a button, and the machine stopped. "It's completely controlled—the speed, the intensity, everything."

"Intensity?" Lady Phoebe asked.

Anke slid a lever up, and a hole in the metal box opened. A metal rod about the width of a thumb, with a rounded end, slowly began to protrude. As Anke toggled the lever, the rod moved in and out of the box, slowly. A few more adjustments, and the rod slid in and out automatically. "Here, it's going agonisingly slowly," she said, "as a sort of teasing. But if you wish..." She showed Lady Phoebe how the machine could speed up until the rod was pumping out of the box with blinding speed.

"You can control the thickness as well," Anke explained, and with another toggle, a metal shell slid out of the box and covered the rod. Three more shells of such a kind, and the metal rod was now roughly the thickness of Lady Phoebe's arm.

She glanced over at Lady Phoebe, who was biting her knuckle and looking at the machine in terror. "I could never take something that thick," she said, her voice quavering.

"You don't have to. It's merely adjustable." Anke retracted the shells and slowed down the machine. "The device takes its cues from the magnetic fields of the rings I've put around you, as well as the fields from everything around it. It knows to avoid touching anything that doesn't emit that particular field, so it will always be able to find you."

"Find me?" Lady Phoebe looked askance at the machine.

"It has two settings," Anke explained. "Manual, and random. On manual, you control every aspect of it—on random, you merely turn the machine on, walk away, and allow it to find you, then do with you as it will according to an algorithm in the box." Now was the moment of demonstration—could she ask Lady Phoebe to expose herself? Her friend had clearly come prepared to try out any invention Anke might have for her, but it did not appear that she'd anticipated Anke creating such a massive device for her. Anke began to have doubts. Perhaps she should have taken her inspiration from the "hysteria devices" they'd created during the First Victorian Empire on Earth, given Lady Phoebe something discreet and handheld.

But for all her nervousness, Lady Phoebe seemed impatient. "Anke, darling, just show me. I'm going mad wondering what it will do." She clutched at Anke's arm. "Tell me what to do!"

Anke swallowed the lump in her throat. "You'll need to turn your back to it," she said. "You don't need to bend over or hike up your skirt, but it will be a little easier if you do. It's quite capable of, er, doing what it needs to function."

Lady Phoebe whirled around and bent herself over Anke's workbench, hiking her skirt up to her waist. Her arse was suddenly exposed, and Anke gazed at the expanse of pink-white, flawless flesh. She felt the naughty urge to give those tempting buttocks a slap, and closed her eyes for a moment, trying to get the image out of her head. "Well?" Lady Phoebe demanded. "Start it up, Anke, for heaven's sake."

Anke opened her eyes and noticed that the insides of Lady Phoebe's thighs were glistening. "Did you," she asked faintly, "did you apply lubricant before you got here? There's really no need, there is a reservoir in the machine for it—"

Lady Phoebe turned her head to gaze at Anke. "Anke, darling, that isn't applied—I'm so ready. You and that awful device are driving me mad without touching me."

Anke drew in a deep breath. She reminded herself of her resolution—Lady Phoebe's desire could not touch her, must not arouse anything in her. "Very well." She manipulated the switches and toggles on the control box, and the machine began to move.

The machine did take its time, Anke drawing out the process a little more than she should have. The machine's metal arms clamped onto Lady Phoebe's wrists and arms, the rings on it closing around the rings on her, then repeated the process with her ankles and legs. At last, the metal ribs on the machine folded around her torso, effectively immobilizing her.

"Test it out," Anke whispered. "Try to get away."

Lady Phoebe wriggled obligingly. "I can't! It's terribly strong."

"Now your legs must be spread," Anke said, and she prided herself on not choking on the words as they came out of her mouth. She turned her face away so that she would not be tempted by the sight of Lady Phoebe with her legs apart, vulnerable and waiting, and sent the machine into its second stage of operation— penetration.

"Oh!" Lady Phoebe cried. "It's cold!"

"It will warm up in a moment," Anke said, and she considered outfitting the machine with some kind of warming device. But the designs she attempted to create in her head could not compete with Lady Phoebe's surprised squeaks and moans, and she turned her head, despite her resolution.

The machine was locked onto Lady Phoebe's frame, mimicking and shaping her movements. The metal box was pressed to her buttocks, and Anke could see the metal rod going in and out of her slowly, its shaft glistening with Lady Phoebe's juices. But even more attractive was Lady Phoebe's face. Her eyes were closed, her eyelids fluttering delicately with each thrust of the rod. Her cheeks were flushed, and her golden hair was already beginning to fall out of place, one ringlet straggling over her forehead. Her lips were as red as Anke had ever seen them, parted slightly like she was waiting to be kissed, and her bosom fell and rose with her increasingly quick breaths.

Anke stood in front of Lady Phoebe. She planted her hands on the workbench, forcing herself not to touch Lady Phoebe, not to caress her face or her breasts, not to touch her mouth to the delicate shell of her friend's ear or her soft, red lips. "Is that good, my lady? Do you need it harder?"

Lady Phoebe opened her wide, blue eyes and gazed at Anke. "Oh," she breathed, "oh yes, Anke, give it to me harder."

With trembling fingers, Anke slid the "speed" toggle up a notch. "Like this?" she asked, and she saw Lady Phoebe's head drop, her body adjusting to the new intensity.

"That's good, Anke, so good," Lady Phoebe moaned. Anke saw her hands flutter in the grasp of the great metal machine. "Anke, I wish this wasn't so tight, I need to move, I need to—" Her body jerked in the cage of metal that surrounded her, and she stopped speaking, her words replaced by soft little cries.

"Are you all right?" Anke asked, and she dared to touch Lady Phoebe's cheek. At her soft touch, Lady Phoebe uttered a wild cry and squeezed her eyes shut, her body rocking with orgasm. Anke stood rooted to the spot, not daring to speak, watching her friend spend her pleasure.

Lady Phoebe lifted her head, her eyes glazed, her lips glistening, the rod still pumping in and out of her. "Oh, Anke, Anke darling—" And before Anke could react, Lady Phoebe turned her head to the side and pressed a wet, soft kiss to Anke's hand, sucking on the tips of her fingers, dragging her mouth and her tongue down Anke's palm.

Anke removed her hand, feeling almost as dazed as Lady Phoebe herself, and groped for the control box. She shut the machine off, and in just a few moments it had entirely disengaged from Lady Phoebe's body and stood motionless. "Are you all right?" Anke asked.

It took a moment for Lady Phoebe to nod, and then she straightened herself up and pushed her skirts down. "That was lovely," she said, a bit stiffly. "I don't think I've ever felt anything quite like that before."

"I'm glad," Anke said. She averted her eyes from Lady Phoebe and fiddled with the control box, directing the machine to clank its way back into the recesses of the workshop. "If it suits your needs, I can make a few adjustments and deliver it today as it is."

"But it didn't," Lady Phoebe said. She stood with her hands behind her back, and Anke realized her eyes were shining with tears. "It's wonderful, Anke, but it's not what I really need. It's cold metal, but I need warm flesh—I need to be touched."

Anke forced herself to look into Lady Phoebe's eyes. "That's something I can't invent for you," she said. "I'm truly sorry, my lady, but my inventions only go so far."

"Oh, Anke, can you not give that one thing to me?" Lady Phoebe asked.

Anke told herself again to be strong, to be cold, to be made of metal, but the words still barely left her lips. "I cannot, and you know why."

Lady Phoebe nodded, then turned her head. "Then there's nothing for it," she said. "I simply can't go on like this anymore, Anke. I shall return home and send the Countess Montbaden a message announcing my acceptance of her proposal."

Anke's heart felt as though it would shatter into a million pieces. "You mustn't! So soon!"

"Are you telling me my business?" Lady Phoebe sounded haughtier than Anke had ever heard her. "Do not presume, Anke."

Anke bowed her head. "I apologize, my lady. I just..." She set the control box down on the workbench. "It is hard for me to know that you'll be gone. Please understand this. I know I will never be able to prevent it, but I had hoped we might have a little more time before you took your leave."

Lady Phoebe was a sweet, joyful woman, and ordinarily that was the only side of her Anke saw. But she had been raised with money and with power, and although she rarely had to do much to get what she wanted, she knew how to if she had the need. "I can drag out the engagement with the Countess for a year or two," Lady Phoebe said, "or I can get married next week. It all depends on whether I can get what I need, Anke, and I think you know what I need. If your ingenuity can find some way to satisfy me, then I shall be able to stay. But if you cannot, or you will not, then I must leave with the Countess."

"Give me a week," Anke said. "One week, my lady, and I'll see what I can do."

Chapter 3:
The Clockwork Doll Does her Dance

Anke knew that she could never engineer herself to be beautiful. She never even kept mirrors in her workshop, not needing them. In order to create her latest illusion, she'd chosen to polish a sheet of tin to a sheen and prop it up against a worktable rather than torture herself by purchasing a real mirror. After all, she'd only need it the once, and afterwards she could beat the tin that had once contained her reflection into something useful that would never show her face again.

Anke's skin was already as pale as a bone china dish, the telltale pallor of a woman who never left her lab. She stared at herself in the makeshift mirror, her eyes tracing the lines of her face, her hands busy mixing powder into water. Anke had managed to develop an organic glaze that, when applied to a human face, would give it the shiny, cold mien of porcelain instead of the soft warmth of flesh. She applied it now, her eyes closed tightly as she drew the brush over her skin, feeling the slickness of the solution tighten and dry. When she opened her eyes, her face shone stiff, like a doll's, and she felt not herself. It was the first time she had looked at herself in ages.

Her cheekbones were too harsh, defined and masculine, unlike Lady Phoebe's soft, welcoming, rosy cheeks. She whisked a soft layer of blush onto them and winced, feeling like a whore painting herself. Her eyes were like black coals compared to Lady Phoebe's sparkling blue eyes, clear and gorgeous like the sky. Anke drew lines around them with kohl, wincing at the final result—her eyes only stood out more against her pale skin. She looked sick, she thought, unhealthy, not like Lady Phoebe's own golden glow. Her lips were thinner than Lady Phoebe's lush red pillows, and paler too, and she slashed bright red lipstick across her mouth before sighing and rubbing it off, then reapplying it. She knew she would never possess Lady Phoebe's subtle loveliness, her feminine charms. Her best strategy would be to make herself look blatantly whorish, blatantly sexual, to make it clear that she was Lady Phoebe's plaything, a being constructed only of Lady Phoebe's desires.

With that in mind, she lifted her sleeveless shirt over her head, exposing her petite, firm breasts. Her nipples, dark and small, pebbled quickly in the cool air of the workshop. She forced herself to look at her body,at her breasts that would never be luscious and soft like Lady Phoebe's. They went in a black, lace-covered corset to push them up—she'd taken the corset from a doll that Lady Phoebe had been particularly intrigued by, a wasp-waisted dark beauty draped in spiderweb lace, so different from Lady Phoebe's own sunny demeanor. Her stomach was naturally flat and taut from a deliberately spare diet and so the corset did little to shape it, and Anke thought jealously of Lady Phoebe's round stomach, well-fed and kissable. Her legs were slim and strong, the silk stockings she pulled on over them clinging to the contours of her muscles. They looked ugly and mannish to her, not like Lady Phoebe's slightly plump, agreeable limbs. Even her buttocks were tight and muscular —flat, she thought, unlike the soft round globes that sat under Lady Phoebe's bustle—and they were still barely covered by the frilled skirt she pulled on.

But the costume had its effect. Anke no longer looked like a slim but sturdy inventor, a woman who cared only for what her body could do for her rather than how it looked to other people. She looked like something created, something devised for pleasure. Her body was shaped into an hourglass by the corset, instead of her usual flat, masculine form. Her legs looked slim and strong, her arse tight and pert. But the biggest change was her face. Even her meager artistry with makeup had changed her plain, honest face to something artful and false, smooth as china and exaggerated as the painted face of any doll. She looked like a parody of herself, absurdly winsome and seductive. She winked at herself in the mirror, and it was like a stranger winking back at her, an awkward and desperate prostitute on a street corner in some other world.

She held her head high and walked out the door of her lab for the first time in weeks. She'd spent hours during the week practicing her movements, imitating the smooth, rolling strut of doxies and dancers while throwing in the jerks and hitches that characterized the movement of a clockwork doll. This was as much to fool men she might pass on the street as it was to fool the Fitzbaine household, for even though Anke did not go out on the streets much, she was not naïve; she knew what any man might assume about a woman in a corset and stockings and little else. The telltale movement of a clockwork thing would, she hoped, fend them off. And indeed, strolling down the street, she caught quite a few stares and nearly as many murmured remarks, but nobody approached the mad clockwork doll.

Anke walked stiffly up to the door of the Fitzbaine residence. Lifting up her fist, she gave three mathematically precise raps on the door, and then let her hands fall to her side, waiting.

The door opened, and Constance the butler stood there. While many newly rich households opted to have only mechanical servitors, with a skeleton staff of one or two repairmen in case the robots broke down, the Fitzbaine family liked to retain a full staff of real human servants as a way to show off their wealth and influence. In a world where robots were cheap and mechanization had freed the workingman to switch jobs at will, having servants bound through loyalty spoke volumes about the influence of a well-established family.

Where Anke's appearance was masculine simply out of utility, Constance went to great pains to present the image of a fussy, polished butler. Her short brown hair was slicked back with not a strand out of place, and she carefully bound her breasts beneath a starched shirt, a waistcoat, and a long-tailed velvet jacket. Now, looking at Anke, she raised a plucked eyebrow.

Before Constance could speak, Anke presented her with a card she had hand-written. The card read: "By order of Anke Schopfer the inventor, I am here to see Lady Phoebe Fitzbaine. I am her new toy. I will take verbal orders from her."

Constance read the card and merely sighed. "I see," she said slowly. "Another clockwork doll, is it?" She smiled a small, private smile. "How clever. Your inventor is a very clever woman, making a doll in the image of herself." She extended her hand to lead Anke in. "Lady Phoebe has been mooning about the house all week, pining after that little engineer, and this should be the perfect elixir for her."

Anke thought that Constance would lead her to Lady Phoebe like any visitor, but instead Constance placed her gloved hands around Anke's waist and steered her towards the stairs. "I'll take this toy to Lady Phoebe," she said into Anke's ear. "She is resting upstairs, and I'm sure she would welcome a diversion."

Constance kept her hands on Anke all the way upstairs. "What an exquisite doll," she said, squeezing Anke's waist. She stroked Anke's arm. "What realistic skin. And the way you move! It's like a real human being. I shall have to order one for myself." She winked at Anke, and Anke reminded herself to move a bit stiffly, with stops and jerks like a clockwork doll would. The dolls she had actually made were better-engineered than she was pretending to be, but she knew that the illusion had to be exaggerated if she was going to keep up the barest pretense.

They made it up the stairs, Constance groping Anke until she felt as though she was being manhandled by one of the sentient cephalopods that swam amongst the aether of Mundus's satellites. She wondered if the butler was trying to get her to drop the charade, or if she was simply taking the opportunity to grope Anke at a time when she would not be told to stop.

Constance turned Anke to the left, and marched her down the second-story hall, stopping her in front of a door. She opened the door and shoved Anke in. "Delivery for you, my lady!"

Lady Phoebe sat up in her bed. She was clad only in a diaphanous nightgown, the relative darkness of her nipples and her pubic mound visible under the sheer fabric. "Constance! Do knock!"

"It's just a toy." Constance winked at Anke. "A delivery from the inventor. Enjoy." She handed the card Anke had brought with her to Lady Phoebe and sidled out of the bedroom, closing the door behind her.

Lady Phoebe stood and stared at the card, looking from it to Anke and back, her forehead creasing in confusion. Anke stood still and tried to look blank. Lady Phoebe reached out and touched her, trailing her soft fingers over Anke's face, her lips, and it was all Anke could do to keep her expression stiff and still, her very nerves screaming to soften her face and show Lady Phoebe the thrill in her heart.

"Well, well," she said, "how interesting. Anke has made me a doll that looks like her." She traced the lines of Anke's lips, then drew her fingers up the side of Anke's jaw, her cheek, and brushed her fingertips along the shell of Anke's ear. She put her own soft lips to Anke's ear, and Anke had to breathe deeply to keep from shuddering as her friend whispered, the warmth of her breath teasing, tormenting. "I wonder if you feel like her, too. Hold still so I can inspect you."

Anke felt like a soldier at attention, fighting to keep stock still, as Lady Phoebe inspected her body. The lady put her hand on Anke's shoulder and slowly walked around her. Anke could feel Lady Phoebe's guileless blue eyes moving up and down her body, taking in every detail of the scanty clothing, the way she'd shaped her body just for this encounter. She trailed her soft hand down Anke's straight back, her fingers dancing over her backbone. "How well-made you are, doll," Lady Phoebe said, and her hand went straight to Anke's buttock, slipping under the short skirt and squeezing the fleshy mound. Anke bit her lip, stifling the squeak of surprise that wanted to find its way out of her lips. Lady Phoebe simply giggled, her laugh like bright bells in the room, and ran her hand down the back of Anke's thigh.

Lady Phoebe moved around Anke and stroked the tops of her bosoms, pushed up by the corset. "You're so warm," she murmured, "and you feel so real. How inventive my Anke is!" Her blue eyes searched Anke's dark ones, and Anke let her eyes unfocus, mimicking the blank eyes of a doll. Lady Phoebe became a beautiful, warm blur for just a moment, and then she came back into view, her face becoming closer, clearer.

She smiled and pressed her own lips to Anke's. Anke opened her mouth as mechanically as she could, thinking of creaking hinges, but Lady Phoebe's lips were far too soft for her to resist, and the tip of her tongue moved over Lady Phoebe's lips. Lady Phoebe drew back from Anke, delighted. "And it kisses like her, too!"

Anke couldn't help from blushing, and Lady Phoebe giggled. She threw the card over her shoulder, then sat on the bed and crossed her legs, batting her lashes at Anke flirtatiously. "Dance for me, doll. I know you can."

This was the moment Anke had dreaded. She had spent hours each day trying to mimic the movements of her dolls, the effortless way they gyrated and stretched. But programming those movements into the dolls was somehow so much easier than doing them herself, and she'd been frustrated and disgusted with herself every time she tried.

Still, she steeled herself, reminding herself that it was all for Lady Phoebe's sake. She stood in the middle of the room and placed her hands on her waist, moving her hips as though she was in the throes of coitus (something she had no experience with, but of course there were always filmstrips... movie reels... holograms... plenty of educational material). She thought of how it would feel to be on top of Lady Phoebe, moving with her, and her movements became more fluid, her body undulating naturally like a sine wave.

Lady Phoebe gasped and clapped her hands in delight as Anke ran her own hands over her body, feeling the warm flesh that she knew was more lovely, more desirable, when it was mimicking cold metal and smooth plastic. She threw her head back and swayed, imagining herself moving to music that was not the tinny ragtime of a gramophone or the honk and screech of an orchestra; the only music a clockwork doll could truly move to was the rhythm of the clockwork world, the beat and melody of the clanging machines that powered the life of the city.

Before she knew it, she was throwing her head back in a parody of orgasm, the finale of a burlesque dance. She looked at Lady Phoebe to gauge her reaction, and was pleased to find her friend red-faced, trembling on the bed, her legs drawn up to her, one hand massaging her own thigh in an unconscious gesture of desire.

Lady Phoebe took a deep breath. "Beautiful," she murmured, and she uncrossed her legs, spreading herself out on the bed without ever taking her eyes off Anke. "And now we'll see what other tricks Anke has equipped you with," she said. "Start by removing my nightgown, please."

Stiffening her limbs, Anke stalked towards her friend. Her hands trembled, betraying her, as she reached down and stroked her fingertips over the silky fabric of Lady Phoebe's nightgown. She dug her fingers into the fabric, internally recoiling at the violence of the gesture. Anke yanked the nightgown from Lady Phoebe's body in one movement, making her squeal, and raked her eyes over the other woman's luscious body. At last, Lady Phoebe was naked, spread out on her bed, and all for Anke—all for her to touch and pleasure, to cherish and adore.

Lady Phoebe sighed and spread her legs. "Now touch me, doll, kiss me." The words were words that Anke had longed to hear, but the epithet "doll" was so cold, a reminder that she could only have this as long as she kept up the facade of a heartless, thoughtless automaton.

Anke stayed still. Lady Phoebe cocked an eyebrow. "Must you be so literal? All right, then, doll. Kiss my breasts."

Anke bent to press her lips to Lady Phoebe's breasts, first dragging her lips over the globes of her friend's bosom, then putting her mouth to Lady Phoebe's nipple, flicking the hard nub with her tongue. Lady Phoebe moaned and put her hand on the back of Anke's head. "Now the other, doll, attend the other. With your hand." And Anke placed her hand on Lady Phoebe's other breast, stroking her silky skin, rolling the hard nub of her nipple between her thumb and forefinger.

Lady Phoebe moaned and tilted her head back. "Kiss my throat." Anke obeyed, licking a trail up Lady Phoebe's chest and neck to place her lips on the hollow of her friend's throat. She kissed lightly at first, but soon began to suck, to bite gently at Lady Phoebe's skin.

"My god, that's good!" Lady Phoebe giggled. "Now, doll..." She spread her legs apart. "Finger me."

Anke's hands wandered up Lady Phoebe's thighs, stroking and touching, trailing up to the space between them where her sex lay. She slid a finger into Lady Phoebe's cunt, enjoying the sound of her friend's moans, her sighs, all the while staying quiet herself. She crooked her fingers inside Lady Phoebe's warmth, loving the way a flush spread over her friend's body, how her hips bucked and her body shook. She thought she had never seen anything so lovely, so beautiful.

Lady Phoebe's quivering quim was pink and wet, ringed with a halo of blonde curls just a little darker than the hair on her head, like bright burnished brass. Anke knew that she could not hold her passion back, that she could no longer pretend to be a crudely constructed clockwork that only took precise orders from her mistress. She bent her head to where her fingers met Lady Phoebe's flesh, running the tip of her tongue over the joining of their bodies, and ran it up Lady Phoebe's quim until she tasted the smooth nub of her clitoris.

"Oh, oh, Anke!" Lady Phoebe threw her head back and ran her fingers through Anke's hair, then gripped the hair at the nape of her neck and pulled hard as she came, her cunt convulsing. Anke jerked her head up, a flash of pleasure curling through her body as Lady Phoebe dug her own fingers into that spot, the same way that her fingers could still feel Lady Phoebe's body spasming against her fingers.

And then Anke went stiff and still at the sound of her own name. It was clear that Lady Phoebe was not fooled, but her voice might have woken anyone else in the house, who'd certainly wonder why Lady Phoebe was calling the inventor's name. Their charade would be ruined, Anke would be found out, and Lady Phoebe's marriage to the Countess Montbaden would be ruined. But perhaps... perhaps both of them might be free, then; Lady Phoebe from the expectations of marriage, and Anke from her contract to only serve.

There was no sound at all from anywhere else in the household, and both women relaxed. Lady Phoebe flopped back onto the bed and sighed. "That was wonderful," she said. "Just what I needed. I suppose I shall have to call upon Anke in the morning and thank her."

Anke bowed stiffly to her lady, disappointment weighing down her limbs, and then turned towards the door. Perhaps Lady Phoebe had not been fooled after all, would not be willing to part with her family name for a chance at love with a common engineer, and only ever wanted the facsimile of Anke to sate her desires. Anke would serve her in this guise, but no acknowledgement of love, no real emotion, could ever flow between them.

"Don't leave!" Lady Phoebe burst out. "Do come into the bed with me, doll. It's been ever so long since I've had a doll or a toy to keep me company while I sleep."

Anke turned on her heel and came to the side of the bed that Lady Phoebe was not occupying. She sat down and swung her legs into the bed, lying flat. At least she could take this comfort from Lady Phoebe, the chance to cuddle with her for a night. She wondered if she could keep still and quiet like this, keep from betraying herself by touching and caressing Lady Phoebe all though the night.

Lady Phoebe draped an arm across her and snuggled up to her. "How lovely," she said, "my very own little doll." She drew the covers over them both. "You're so cunningly made. I shall have to take you with me to the Countess Montbaden's house when I do go."

"Really?" Anke asked in a whisper, barely daring to breathe. "I can come with you?"

"Of course, darling," Lady Phoebe exclaimed, and she dropped her pretense entirely, as Anke had. "Be invention or inventor, whatever you like, but I'm not letting you leave my side. If I go to the Countess, then so must you."

Anke smiled broadly in the dark, relief and happiness filling her soul. She let her body relax, pressed herself against Lady Phoebe, her nose and lips on her lover's soft neck. "Anywhere," Anke breathed, and dropped off to sleep, secure in the knowledge that she would never be separated from Lady Phoebe.

If you enjoyed this story, you can sign up for a free membership at ForbiddenFiction and discuss it with other readers and the author at the *Clockwork Dolls* story page at http://forbiddenfiction.com/anthology/spc-1-100013.

About the Authors

Alex Douglas is the dirty-minded alter ego and pseudonym of a Tokyo-based Irish gaming geek and writer whose life ambition to date has been to pen an epic fantasy fiction trilogy, but who somehow can't stop the characters from leaping into bed together.

Laylah Hunter has been writing erotic fiction for the last decade, starting with fan fiction and branching out into original work when the draw of imagining entire worlds became irresistible. Most of Laylah's work explores speculative themes, queer relationships, power imbalances, or combinations thereof. When not writing, Laylah enjoys long walks through scenic video game landscapes, drinking froofy coffee, and being at the mercy of two very needy cats. It all comes back to the writing eventually, though.

KJ Kabza's has sold over 50 stories to venues such as F&SF, Nature, Daily Science Fiction, Beneath Ceaseless Skies, Buzzy Mag, and many more. His short fiction has made both the 2013 Locus and Tangent Recommended Reading Lists and has been reprinted in *The Year's Best Dark Fantasy and Horror 2014* (from Prime Books) and *The Best Horror of the Year, Volume Six* (from Night Shade Books). His two self-published omnibus collections, *"In Pieces"* and *"Under Stars,"* are available now as ebooks through Amazon and Smashwords.

M.E. Litman has been a member of the kink scene for many years, and a literature geek for even longer. He earned a degree in Creative Writing from Fairleigh Dickinson University, which he immediately put to use writing unspeakable volumes of erotica. His favorite form is short fiction, and his drink of choice is the Cosmopolitan. When he isn't writing smut, Litman enjoys reading, role playing, and wearing a variety of sweater vests. He lives happily with his partner of five years and their cats.

Slave Nano is an author of erotica drawing on the themes of female supremacy, BDSM, and fetish often in fantasy or historical settings. His erotic novel, Adventures in Fetishland, has been published by Xcite Books. His short stories and novellas have been published by Forbidden Fiction, Xcite Books, House of Erotica, Coming Together, and Greenwoman Publishing.

Elizabeth A. Schechter has been called one of the top erotica and alternative sexuality writers in the world. Her writing credits include the award-winning steampunk erotic romance *House of Sable Locks*, the science fiction BDSM duology *Tales from the Arena*, and the Celtic fantasy *Princes of Air*. Her shorter work has appeared in anthologies edited by D.L King (*Carnal Machines*), Laura Antoniou (*No Safewords*), and Cecilia Tan (*Jingle Balls; Like a Prince*).

Schechter was born in New York at some point in the past. She is officially old enough to know better, but refuses to grow up. She lives in Central Florida with her husband and son, and a most accepting circle of friends who are both very amused and very proud of the pervy, fetish writer in their midst.

Madeleine Swann has had several articles published by various magazines including Bizarre and The Dark Side, ranging in subject from church restorations to toe wrestling championships. She writes from her home in Essex and has erotica published on the ForbiddenFiction website and *The Darker Edge of Desire* and *Big Book of Bizarro* anthologies. She also has surreal comedy and horror in *Polluto* magazine, LegumeMan Books and *Black Petal* magazine.

R.W. Whitefield is an old-fashioned party girl who loves literature. She has a Bachelor's of Science in English, against all known probability, has her own open mic AND her own coven, and daily eats toast on Elmore Leonard's breakfast table.

About the Publisher

ForbiddenFiction.com is a publisher devoted to writing that breaks the boundaries of original erotic fiction. Our stories combine intense sexuality with quality writing. Stories at ForbiddenFiction.com not only arouse readers through sensations, but also engage them emotionally and mentally through storytelling as well-crafted as the sex is hot.

ForbiddenFiction.com is also designed to be a social reading environment. You'll have fun even if just reading the latest post each day, yet you will have the chance for so much more. Readers and authors can be part of ongoing discussions of specific works and individual authors as well as more general topics.

Sign up for a FREE Membership today at ForbiddenFiction.com